craving
dragonflies

USA TODAY BESTSELLING AUTHOR

TERRI E. LAINE

Tracy,
Thank you
for being a fabulous
Assistant!
Enjoy Ash? He will
Steal your ♥
Terri E. Laine
RARE PARIS
2019

Cover design by Michele @ Michele Catalano Creative

Photo taken by Scott Hoover

To all the survivors.

Victoria Field's poems do the job
wonderfully well of singing both
the liturgical life and the incident[s]
of being out and about. Her
writing knows vulnerability more
than certainty, the poems have th[eir]
own newly made life, and there is
something rooted and new here:
of the personal, of Cornwall, of th[e]
fierce claims of attentiveness.

David Hart, Poet in Residence,
Worcester Cathedral, 1998-9

Truro Cathedral

SUPPORTED BY

Ecclesiastical

Insuring, Investing and Protecting

University Colleg[e]
FALMOUT[H]

ARTS COUNCIL
ENGLAND

Approved Origin Scheme

MADE IN

Cornwall

fal £6

ISBN 0-9544980-7-0

9 780954 498078

"Darkness cannot drive out darkness; only light can do that. Hate cannot drive out hate; only love can do that."

— Martin Luther King, Jr.

AUTHOR NOTE

If you want to know when my next release will come out, please sign up for my newsletter.

http://eepurl.com/bDJ9kb

If you are a fan of this series or me, make sure you join my fan group. Terri's Butterflies:

https://www.facebook.com/groups/671789082985465/

And you can join my reader group to talk books. Terri E. Laine Reader Group:

https://www.facebook.com/groups/1738725283032502/

PROLOGUE

Ashton

DARKNESS COVERED me like a shroud and I was too paralyzed to end it. Gripped in memories where blackness meant pain or loneliness, I struggled for breath.

Somewhere far off I heard my name, but my eyes were glued shut. I tried to pretend I made the light disappear on my own so fear wouldn't overtake me.

But it was in the absence of light where the monsters lived.

My savior was gone, and I had nothing more to live for.

I'd been a pawn in someone's game all my life.

For the monster, I was blackmail, an exhibit in a legal document to force my father to pay.

For the devil, I was the vessel for pain in his pleasure.

For my savior, I was his disciple to rule.

For me, I was no one.

I thought again about death as an ending for my suffering.

I had nothing left to live for.

A hand on my arm jerked me out of my torment. Light filled

the room, but his touch was no longer welcomed. It didn't ease the pain it once had.

"Ash," Sawyer said.

I didn't turn to face him. If I had, I'd only be lost again. He'd made it clear, I wasn't his to find.

He was temptation, my ultimate self-destruction.

I was nothing without him and nothing to him. He'd made that all too clear.

"You don't have to stay here. Come back home," he said.

Why? I wanted to say. So I could listen to him be with someone else?

No thank you. I was good here in the frat house where I could learn to live by myself or die on my own terms.

"You're not going to talk to me now?" he asked.

No, I couldn't. I wouldn't. I would no longer blindly follow in hopes that he would see me.

"Please," he begged.

I closed my eyes, even knowing I would go back to that dark place. Locked away in my own prison of memories was better than his pity.

He reached out again, fingertips grazing my arm. I pulled free, rolling away, curling into a ball.

"Fuck, Ash, don't be this way."

Mentally, I shut him out and thought of all the ways I could end things.

A blade, a pill, a drive, a gun... all too easy.

My life had been hard. My ending should be harder.

A door closed, and I was alone again.

This was my destiny, and it was better for all if I not only honored it, but accepted it.

Fate had only ever been a bitch to me. I didn't expect anything less.

1

Ashton

THERE WERE days when I missed the townhouse I'd shared with my friends, Chance and Sawyer, like today.

The dark-stained wall carved out of someone's Gothic nightmare was a show of wealth and privilege in the Sigma frat house I didn't subscribe to. My *brothers* thought of themselves as living in a throwback to times where smoking jackets were a thing.

I hated that I missed the brick and plain painted walls of the townhouse I couldn't go back to.

Catcalls were a precursor of what I was walking into. It was a new semester and the start to my senior year here at Layton University, the Darling of the South. Pledge Week was in full swing. New recruits were brought in to be humiliated, thinking they had a chance in hell of getting into Sigma fraternity. I hated it.

The great room had tufted leather sofas and other pieces I couldn't name that blended into the walls and built-in bookcases that displayed Sigma paraphernalia and old books no one actually read.

Some of my *brothers* stood. Others lounged on the sofas where sunglasses hid their utter glee as they watched the dumb freshmen on their hands and knees wearing aprons that didn't cover their bare asses. But that wasn't what they were laughing at. The pledges were using toothbrushes to clean the rugs and floors.

The irony lost on the dozen that wanted in was that we had a maid service that cleaned daily any mess made the night before. Their labor was nothing more than entertainment.

Trent Willhouse, son of a media mogul, stood in the middle of it all. He was laughing so hard when he spoke, I almost didn't get what he said.

"We should make them wear tails and neigh and shit."

His sunglasses tipped lopsided on his face as he sprawled onto the sofa from the arm he'd been sitting on.

"What, like pin the tail on the donkey?" another idiot said who was filming the pledges with his phone.

"Like, would we use duct tape or something to keep them on?" someone else said.

Just as I was about to ignore it all and leave to hunt for food, Willhouse, doubled over in laughter and holding his middle, straightened.

"I've got an idea. Let's make them wear those tail butt plugs."

I pivoted to face them. "No."

That's when they noticed me.

"No?" Willhouse asked.

His face had more wrinkles than a Pug when he turned in my direction. "What the fuck, man? You decide to speak and we're supposed to listen?"

All was quiet. Even the pledges stopped. I glanced at a few of their faces and saw relief.

"It's not going to happen," I declared.

Willhouse popped off the sofa and stalked forward to position himself in front of me like he held some power. Problem for him, he was a few inches shorter than me. As much as he tried, he couldn't look me in the eye without angling his head up slightly.

That didn't stop him. His ego was charged and spoiling for a fight.

"You think that after three years of reaping the benefit of brotherhood and not doing a damn thing to earn it, I should listen to you?"

There were quiet murmurs and chuckles as the peanut gallery dug out their metaphorical popcorn ready to watch what would happen next.

"You're not the king here," he said.

I didn't eye the crown and scepter that belonged to Sawyer.

A muscle twitched in his eye when l said, "Neither the fuck are you."

My former best friend Sawyer was. He'd been voted in without so much as a campaign.

"I don't see Cargill here." Willhouse's hands were held up, but the crowd was reluctant to join his side in this. They kept looking at me for my response.

Thing was, Sawyer had no desire to be president of our fraternity. He had all the women he wanted and that was power he desired. Real responsibilities for the assholes in front of me he cared little for wasn't his thing.

I stepped into Willhouse's space and jabbed a finger in his chest. "It's not happening."

"We've established that Sawyer's not here for you to suck his dick, so who's going to stop me?"

I didn't think. It was a reflex. One second Willhouse stood there daring me to punch him, the next he was on the floor looking up at me through fingers that covered his bloody nose. I studied my knuckles and the spray of red. I roughly wiped them on my jeans.

"You bastard." His muffled words hung in the air after penetrating his crimson hand, which he held to stanch the flow.

But the way he glared at me, I knew there was more he wanted to say.

Secrets were a thing with the rich. They used them as leverage and bargaining chips. His choice of words to jab at me meant he might know about my father's indiscretion. My parents weren't married despite my mother's aspirations. She'd snake charmed a lonely man into bed while his wife was dealing with ovarian cancer and gave him the one thing his wife couldn't. *Me*.

"I think you broke my nose," Willhouse whined, which was louder than his bark.

I raised an eyebrow. "I guess you can get that nose job you always wanted."

He snarled as he ambled to his feet, but the *brothers* were there to hold him back ostensibly to save me.

This wasn't the Omega house filled with steroid charged sports players. This frat was filled with trust fund babies. They fought with lawyers not fists when they had an opponent they weren't sure they could physically beat.

"This isn't over," Willhouse warned.

His arm was aimed at me like a missile. Part of me wanted him to try. I had pent- up anger that needed an outlet.

I didn't respond and headed for the door.

"Let me go," he told the guys holding him.

I'd ruined his fun, and retribution would come. Hopefully, some of the freshmen heard my message and got out while they could. No amount of following orders would get them in if their parents' bank account didn't have enough zeros.

I stepped out into the light and glared up toward the sun. The clear day like this I liked. The heat that came with it, not so much. Where I grew up in the Hamptons, low eighties was the norm for the summer. Daily hundred-degree heat wasn't something I loved. Even if it got hotter in New York, we had the sound and ocean close by to cool us off.

The door opened behind me and two wide-eyed freshmen held balled up clothes to cover their front with one hand and the back with the other.

"And don't fucking come back," Willhouse yelled.

He turned his steely gaze on me. I ignored him and jumped into my Challenger. Since my Hellcat had a muffler delete, I revved my engine a few times, creating noise pollution before peeling out. The growl my car made could drown out anything, including my thoughts. That's why I'd chosen it.

By reflex, I realized I was headed for the townhouse. I made an abrupt course correction at the next corner toward campus. That was the thing about Oklahoma. There wasn't much to do in the small town that was made up mostly of our campus. Back home, I could drive to the city or to the beach to get away. Here was nothing outside of the college town for miles on end.

There was one spot where I could find some peace, but I didn't drive there either. I ended up in the parking lot, a growling stomach leading my way. The café was open. I checked the time and decided it was unlikely I'd run into Sawyer. The fact was, I didn't want to see anyone. I had shit to figure out. One year left and then what would I do?

When I parked, I spotted a tiny girl with a mass of curls framing a pixie-like face scrunched up in frustration.

There was something familiar about her. My mind filed back to a movie Sawyer and I watched when we were kids. He'd been flipping through channels and stopped when he saw a chick in her bra and panties. Barely in our teens, it was enough to get him to stop. I racked my brain for the movie and he'd been enthralled as she jumped in and started getting hot and heavy with another guy on screen. I thought it might be called *Seduce the Babysitter* or something like that. I couldn't remember.

What I did remember was the girl in the movie had hair like this girl's, big and curly.

I popped a baseball hat onto my head and pulled the brim down to cover my face. I got out with every intention of the world not to stop until I watched her kick her tire. *Fuck me.* I really didn't want to stop. The last thing I wanted to do was make conversation. If I helped her, she would expect me to talk. If I didn't, what would that make me? *Shit.*

2

Willow

OKAY, kicking it hadn't helped. The tire was still flat, and I was going to be so late. I looked at the vile thing in my hands, knowing any minute it would ring. Celeste was not going to be happy, and I cursed my phone, though it wasn't its fault.

The parking lot behind the building wasn't empty, but it was filled with silent steel traps that in no way could help me. Then the air combusted with sound. An engine that meant to be heard roared into the area like an amplified swarm of bees.

Black paint so shiny the sun reflected off in bursts of starlight had me lift my hand to stave off the brightness. That's when I noticed the double gray racing stripes down the middle of the car.

With my jaw hanging open, I could only stare, especially as a blindingly beautiful boy stepped out from behind the wheel. A cap left his face in shadows, but there was no mistaking how gorgeous he was. The newly created silence when the engine died was a gift from heaven like he was. I stood holding in my other hand a lug wrench that looked more like a cross as if I was warding him off. And maybe I should. He was most definitely one of those guys who didn't have to work hard to get any girl he wanted.

Tall with a short crop of hair that curled around the fringes of the hat he wore crowned him the prince he was. He strode forward with purpose, never once looking in my direction. I wasn't surprised. I wasn't the prize my stepsister Celeste was.

The breath that I'd been holding escaped as my own stupefaction kept me from asking for help.

As if that air that left my lungs somehow created a breeze strong enough to reach him, his eyes rolled heavenward and he switched course to head in my direction.

There was a gathering storm brewing in his blue eyes as they narrowed on me and down to the tool I held in a white-knuckled grip.

When he reached me, I sputtered words because he looked very much put out to help me.

"I know how to do this. It's just the nuts are tight."

I clamped my lips shut, sounding like a complete idiot. He towered over me, reaching me in a few powerful strides. I stared up at him like some zealous fangirl unable to speak.

He held out his hand and I glanced down at his large palm before slowly handing over the tool.

His gaze zipped away as he bent down and easily loosened the nuts one by one with powerful jerks. His biceps flexed, and I was pretty sure I drooled a little.

When his focus landed on me again, I was paralyzed. His silent communication went on deaf ears as I was lost in just how gorgeous he was in a tragic way. It was like how my scientific specimens stared at me with abject horror that their lives had ended just to be pinned to a petri dish for study.

"Spare tire."

I blinked. His gruff voice was like a command forcing my body into action. It took a second for my brain to process his words. I shuffled away, feeling more like a complete loser than I ever had. I shoved back my sun-bleached curls, muttering curses in my head.

Clearly, I'd been moving too slow for him as he wedged in behind me, something I was keenly aware of. He was so close I could smell the faint scent of soap he'd used to shower with. Even with barely millimeters between us, his skin never touched mine. I stepped out of the way when he effortlessly lifted the tire from my trunk like it was an inflatable beach tube.

Then he slid by me and worked the spare on in a matter of a few minutes.

"I've never seen anyone work as efficiently as a worker ant before."

Had I really just said that? Not that it mattered. He didn't so much turn and acknowledge that I'd spoken.

I pulled the elastic band I used to tame my hair from my arm and worked it around the mass that begged for a flat iron. I managed to wrangle the mess into a half-formed bun at the base of my neck before he stood, hefting the damaged tire into my open trunk.

Metal clanged shut when he called over to me. "Don't drive too long on that."

"Thank you," I said to his retreating form. Though he didn't run, his lengthy stride had him out of earshot in seconds. "Thank you," I muttered again, more to myself.

My phone had vibrated a few times during the short time he'd taken to sort me out.

"Celeste," I said into the phone.

"Where are you? I've called a dozen times and you haven't answered—"

"I know. I'm sorry. I'm on my way."

"On your way? *Seriously.* I'm standing out here wilting in the sun. I should have driven myself..."

The shrillness of her voice made me flinch. I got into the car, knowing it was better for me to be on my way than to listen to her give me hell for not being on time.

I set the phone in the cradle and let her continue barking into the phone. Hopefully, getting her rant off her chest would leave her in a better mood once I picked her up.

By the time I arrived in front of the beauty spa my stepsister frequented, she stood tapping her foot in time to the barrage of unflattering words directed at me. Apparently, I was an awful sister. My tardiness was a reflection of how little I cared about her.

I sighed and pulled to a stop directly in front of her. She barely had to reach to open the car door and get in.

"Where is your mind, Willow? I'm practically dripping with sweat."

"I'm sorry."

Finally, she took a breath. "What happened? It's not like you. Tell me it's a boy. I could forgive that."

My tongue loosened, but I stopped myself. If I told her about the nameless boy who had changed my tire, she would make it her mission to try to hook us up and only end up making the boy like her. She didn't mean it. She hadn't asked to be born with perfect hair, a movie star face, and a picture-perfect body that made guys weak. No, it wasn't her fault. At the same time, I couldn't lie.

"I had a flat tire and a heck of a time changing it."

She glared at me. "And you didn't get some guy to help you?"

For her, this was the obvious move. For me, I wasn't helpless and I couldn't fault her for being so. Her father doted on her like she was the princess she acted like.

"One did," I admitted.

Her frown morphed into a blazing smile. "And?"

I shrugged as I pulled out into traffic. "He helped and I told him thank you."

Though it was probable he hadn't heard me.

"What's his name? Is he cute? Did you get his number?" When I only shrugged, she frowned again. "You can't leave college a virgin. Seriously, Willow. This isn't the 1950s. No guy is going to respect you more for saving yourself for marriage."

Talk about burn. I hated that I flinched. It wasn't like I was purposefully saving myself. I dated a few guys over the years, but either they'd used me to get to Celeste or once they met her, they forgot about me.

"Guys aren't interested in me," I said half-heartedly.

She sighed. "Willow, you're so pretty. There are so many guys out there. You just have to stop hiding in that lab studying bugs to meet them."

Bugs didn't hurt you like people did. At least the dead ones, not that I killed them. Though she was trying to be kind, the nameless boy hadn't even given me a once-over.

Mom and Celeste could call me pretty all they wanted, but I'd never felt it. I was the ugly stepsister who didn't catch the beautiful gene.

I wondered again what it would have been like if my father hadn't died. I envied Celeste and my stepdad's relationship. He was nice to me to a point, but his eyes didn't light up when he saw me like they did when he looked at his precious daughter.

"Willow."

I blinked and came to a stop. My mind had wandered, and I almost ran a red light.

"Don't kill us. We are going to a party tonight, and I'm going to glam you up. Tonight's your night."

She didn't stop there, though I tuned her out. There was no

stopping her once her mind was made up. I would be going to the party whether I wanted to or not.

Would I see my savior again? If Celeste dressed me like her—a doll in clothing too short or too tight—would he see me? And if he did, would I want him to like the version of me Celeste created?

3

Ashton

BETWEEN TWO FINGERS, I held the glass neck of my choice of poison for the night. I'd been irresponsibly mesmerized by the sight in front of me, hooked on the truth of what I was seeing.

"Shit."

I glanced over at Chance, one of my former roommates. He'd muttered a curse staring at his girl, Brie. With her hands in the air, she moved to the beat with her friend, Shelly, who was in front of her. They were equally engaged in a snake charmer's dance. The two had caught the attention of every guy in the room, including Sawyer who had worked his way behind Shelly. I didn't want to notice him moving like he fucked, grinding behind her ass like she was everything he wanted and more. I looked away.

The 1952 Macallan glided over my tongue. It was like honey coating my throat, taking me back to a time when he was behind me. It had been a one-time thing that happened when he'd been too fucked up to realize what he was doing. That single moment looped hopelessly in my mind and I couldn't let it go.

The rare scotch that cost upwards of five figures didn't fill the empty spaces in me. By the time I brought the bottle down, Shelly's face was mottled with anger as Sawyer glibly walked in our direction.

"I wouldn't mind being in that sandwich," he said, eyeing Chance.

"Don't you fucking think about it!" Chance declared with menace written in the tightness of his brows.

Then Sawyer's gaze slid my way. I knew him well enough he'd realized what he said. How many times had it been the two of us the ends with some random girl between us? Those times were long over or so I told myself. Sawyer had a way of talking me into stuff.

Time to go. I turned away from that stare I knew better than my own. His hand landed on my arm to stop me. It only took one death glare over my shoulder for his hold on me to fall away. I hated the shiver that raised the hairs on my arm.

I headed to the only place I could think of that offered solitude, the backyard. My new dwelling upstairs belonged to Sawyer and me. I wouldn't allow him to trap me there to talk.

Outside, I breathed in the wood smoke coming from the fire pit and moved past the milling people to find a spot to claim.

Before I got past the deck, a small crowd gathered in a semi-circle. Just as I was about to pass, I noticed a girl dancing to the beat of her own drum. She had a captivated audience of guys counting their chances to find out the color of her underwear. She lifted her head, grazing her hands sultrily over her breasts and down the center of her body. That's when I caught sight of her face. It was tire girl from earlier today.

"Fuck, man, I wouldn't mind getting a piece of that."

That voice had my head snapping in Willhouse's direction.

Even with nothing but strung Christmas lights, I could see the drool practically running down his face.

The "*Wait. No. Stop,*" snapped my focus back to the girl. She struggled against the hold of another girl. They played tug-of-war with her arm until the one holding her let go.

"Come on. Let's go," the second girl said, like she was calming a terrified animal.

"Can't a girl lose her virginity in peace?"

You would have thought time stopped with how deathly quiet it got until a few snickers from the growing crowd seemed to break the girl out of her drunken haze.

"Did I just say that?" she slurred. Her friend nodded. "I think I'm going to be sick."

She took off like a frightened bird.

Immediately, I glanced Willhouse's way. His nose was covered in something white like he was avoiding a sunburn. The dark glasses he wore only played off the look. People probably assumed it was some kind of inside joke or a frat prank.

He knocked fists with another one of our brothers, and all I could imagine was punching that smug smile off his face. It wasn't my business or so I told myself when I managed not to. Why should I care about some girl? I had a lot of my own shit to deal with. Yet, I found myself doubling back toward the house.

It wasn't hard to find her. Her back was to me as she clung to the railing of the deck. Her voluminous hair in different shades of blonde wasn't as curly as it had been earlier, though it had begun to wave, probably because of the heat. Still, it made her distinctive and easily marked.

Only she wasn't alone and didn't need my help. Standing next to her was a guy whom I'd caught looking at me several times tonight.

His hand was on her back rubbing circles. Whatever he was saying, her head bobbed before they turned as one. My body instantly tightened.

She looked nothing like the innocent girl I'd helped in the parking lot. No longer dancing, my eyes followed the line of her throat down to a top dipped dangerously low and a skirt that wouldn't hide a thing from behind if she bent forward.

Then there was the smile the guy next to her gave me. It was very different from the one he'd aimed at her seconds ago. His eyes dropped to where my dick decided to make a stand.

Her eyes, on the other hand, softened. "You," she said sloppily.

She stumbled forward as if she planned to flee. I stiffened, prepared for the shock of pain to stab at my nerve endings when I had no choice but to catch her or let her face-plant.

It should have been lucky for me when the other guy caught her. Then he gave me a smirk I didn't want to interpret. I wasn't sure how to feel about it.

"Let me help you with that," he said as smooth as cognac.

As his eyes found my dick again, I had no idea if he was referring to catching her or how hard I'd gotten.

It was more messed up I couldn't determine if it was his heated stare or the swell of her breasts that had gotten me that way. Anger tightened my jaw. I hated that I wasn't sure. I wasn't sure of anything. The only person I'd ever desired was lost to me.

"I'm sorry," the girl said. She wiped a hand over her mouth and repeated, "I'm sorry."

Then she looped off in a half-run, half-sway.

The guy helping her didn't follow. He just stood there with his eyes on me.

I turned away, realizing I wasn't ready for answers. Even subconsciously, Sawyer was there in my head yelling at me to follow through with one of them. When would I be my own person? When would the fucking one-sided feelings fade? I drifted around the side of the house and found a spot of wall to rest my back.

I'd stood there long enough that my smart watch told me to breathe. I almost snatched the thing off and threw it. But the bottom of the bottle held more interest as I searched the sky for stars, tipping it back to swallow away my pain. The smooth way it went down had me longing for the burn of cheap alcohol so I could feel something other than the hollow spaces that made up my chest. Instead, the faint citrus taste clung to my tongue as I knocked the back of my head onto the wall as if I could gain sense from the action.

A giggle caught my attention. Hidden by shadows, a couple emerged through the back gate, making their way toward the front of the house, and hadn't spotted me.

"You think I'm pretty," the girl said, smiling up at him.

"Of course."

I heard the lie in Willhouse's voice. It wasn't that he didn't think she was pretty, more that he would have said whatever to fuck her.

As they neared, I would have appreciated remaining hidden until I saw who it was.

Tire girl. And she was barely walking on her own. Willhouse had an arm looped around her, helping her balance as they walked. The way he looked at her suggested her drunkenness was an answer to a prayer.

His rep made slim seem appealing. Likely, he'd do her passed out and take pictures to share without a second thought. When he spotted me, his smirk grew.

I stood straighter, pushed off the wall, and stepped to intercept their path.

"I've got her," Willhouse said.

I let my eyes drop to the tape on his nose as a reminder, and then leveled a hard glared at him. His smug smile didn't falter as if our early morning beef hadn't happened.

"She's willing," he said as if that was an excuse.

Knowing him, he'd probably already recorded her consent in case he needed a lawyer later.

"No."

My tone was a repeat from this morning, but it was a solitary word. So I shook my head to drive the point home before I shifted my gaze back down at her. She was staring at the ground as if she needed the reminder of how to put one foot in front of the other even though she was standing still.

His eyes narrowed. "You calling dibs?"

He'd sounded affable enough. But the heat in his gaze suggested there were other things he'd wanted to say and couldn't in her company without blowing his chances.

Like everyone in the backyard not long ago, he'd heard her confess her virgin status. That had made her his target for the night. Willhouse considered it his mission in life to conquer the virginal world. He had a game and scoreboard in his room with a cherry counter to mark each one he and others tagged and bagged.

I didn't play his stupid game, but for some reason I found myself nodding. I would tell myself later it was only the pureness of her smile that determined my fate.

One of the rules was that a player could claim one girl as his. She'd be off limits to any of the frat brothers even if she didn't know she'd been marked. Each player could only do it once. In three years, I'd never claimed anyone, though Sawyer had.

Willhouse nodded, taking his game seriously. He dropped her hand and she swayed on her feet. Before I could move, he was in my face talking low so she couldn't hear.

"Fuck it, you can have her. She's not the only cherry here tonight. You can't save them all in this crusade of yours. I'll mark her down. And maybe if you fuck her, you'll leave the rest of us alone." He sneered before stalking off.

After I made sure he was gone, I turned back to find wide eyes on me.

"Wait," she called after him, realizing he was leaving. She aimed those innocent eyes on me. "Where is he going?"

"You're better off," was all I could think to say.

Glazed eyes turned sharp. "Why..." She paused and swallowed as if she might be sick. "Why is everyone telling me—?" She heaved a little. "—Shit to do?" she blurted before turning her head and hurling on the shrubs.

It was a wonder why we paid so much for lawn care. There was probably an extra charge for barf clean up. It was a regular occurrence at our house.

If I thought she was done with her verbal vomit, I was wrong. The wounded expression she aimed at me hit home.

"He hasn't even seen Celeste yet."

I frowned, not sure what she was slurring about.

Then her kaleidoscope eyes narrowed on me at the same time her lips curled into amused lines as she switched topics.

"Do you know you have a beauty mark like Marilyn Monroe?"

Before I could stop her, her fingertip scorched on one of my many imperfections.

"It's like it was stolen from here." That same finger marked the divot in my chin. "How does it feel to be one of the beautiful people?"

I flattened my lips hearing the lie from her mouth. I was far from beautiful. More likely I was the aftermath of a wildfire on a destructive path.

Just as I lifted my hands, not sure if I was willing to grab hers, I paused. It was bad enough having the tip of her finger on my skin than to add my entire hand wrapped around her wrist. Her arms flayed as she tried to balance and not fall backward.

"Willow."

The tug-of-war girl jogged up in time to catch her friend.

"Celeste," Willow said with a wide grin.

I turned away, assuming she was safe now. It was better to leave than to analyze why I felt so protective of this girl.

"Where did he go?" I heard her ask.

Yet I found myself wondering just why the burn of her touch was nothing like the sting of a hundred hornets I usually felt when someone's skin brushed against mine like Mother's.

4

Past

"Ashton."

Mama wasn't happy.

I left the ant hill and ran with my dirty hands in the air into the open back door of the house.

"Ashton!"

She caught my wrist.

"Hurt."

She shoved me back.

"What have you been doing?"

I splayed my fingers as a few red ants crawled over me.

She caught my ear and tugged, dragging me back outside.

"I told you to stay clean."

I stumbled into the yard near where I watched the ants crawling over a hill. Then I'd stuck my hands in, curious what it would feel like.

Cold water hit me, making my eyes water. Ants and dirt washed off me until I stood all wet.

I shivered under the sun as my tears felt hot on my skin.

"Look at your hands," she yelled.

They were as red as her mad face.

"Take off those wet clothes," she said.

Why was she so mean? I didn't ask and did as told.

"Stand there."

Was I bad? Was that why she didn't like me?

"I'm sorry," I said.

That didn't turn her frown upside down. Instead, she marched inside. I didn't move. I didn't mean to be bad. Maybe if I stayed put, she'd be happy. She took a long time to come back. When she did, I was dry.

"This is an important day."

I nodded, not understanding what that meant.

"You will be on your best behavior."

I nodded again.

Then I did something bad. I leaned into her.

The sting across my face brought more tears.

"Look at what you've done."

She stood. Her shirt was wet. This mad face scared me. She spun and stomped into the house.

When she came back, she wasn't nice.

Her pinches hurt as she helped me dress and comb my hair. She held my neck hard as we went back into the house.

"Now, you will sit here and be quiet. Say nothing. Touch nothing. Do you understand."

I bobbed my head.

"Say it," she demanded.

"Yes, ma'am."

"Good boy."

The man who arrived later I'd never met before. He took my chin between his fingers and inspected my face the way Mom checked me every day for dirt.

"What's your name, son?"

I looked at Mother to make sure it was okay to speak. She nodded.

"Ashton."

His touch hadn't hurt, but then he moved away with Mom.

"Are you sure he's mine?"

Mom sounded different like he made her happy. "Of course."

"I will want a test," he said.

I didn't understand what that meant.

"Test all you want. He's yours."

"Why tell me now?"

"I thought I could take care of him myself, but he's a handful. And after I heard you and your wife can't have kids, I thought you should know you have a son."

He looked at me. I smiled, hoping he would say yes and be my dad.

"If he's mine, I will take care of him... and you—"

"Do you want your son to grow up here?" Her hands spread wide. "He deserves more, don't you think?"

"If he's mine, he will want for nothing."

Then the man was gone.

Mom came over and bent down so that her face was close to mine. She pushed at the hair that had covered my eyes.

"Soon, we will be out of here and you will be useful to me."

She smiled, but it made me feel cold inside.

5

Willow

I WATCHED his beautiful face disappear around the corner.

"Is that..." Celeste trailed off.

I whipped my head in her direction. "Who?"

Her eyes narrowed. "You're not interested in him, are you?"

"Who?" I asked again, my focus slipping as the alcohol coursing through my veins had my thoughts scattered.

"Oh, sweetie." She shook her head in disapproval. "Don't get your hopes up for that one. He doesn't play for our team."

I blinked, unsure I heard her correctly.

"What?" I heard myself asking.

She placed a hand on my shoulder. "He has something more in common with me." My brows knitted together. "You know Sawyer." Everyone did. He was the kind of guy people wanted to be around. "He watches Sawyer as much as I do, not that I blame him."

My mouth slightly parted before several thoughts connected.

My savior. He'd stopped me from hooking up with Trent. That was the other boy's name, right?

"You don't know that. Besides, if he does, so what?"

She patted me like I was a small child who didn't understand.

"This isn't just me. His exploits with Sawyer are legendary. Though not once have I heard about him and some girl without Sawyer. It's kind of sad."

For whatever reason, I didn't like her talking about him like that. Yet there was something so tragic yet beautiful about his eyes. Besides, she was making me feel stupid.

I jerked out of her grip. "I'm ready to go," I managed to say, only slurring a little.

My anger wasn't so much for her but my own idiocy. I'd thought because of the way he'd looked at me and stopped me from getting with the other guy, he liked... And when my eyes had dipped, I'd assumed all that he was packing was for me. But why should I think that? What boy had ever liked me? Maybe his reaction had been for the guy who helped me.

"Don't tell me you thought..." she said, speaking what I thought.

I backed away from the sudden burn of embarrassment. The sting at least had cleared my head some. Celeste was many things, conceited and spoiled, but she wasn't a liar.

"I'm ready to go."

"Come on. We just got here," she said to placate me.

That was an overstatement on her part. She probably hadn't gotten all the attention she craved for the night.

"What happened to the other guy I saw you talking to?" she asked.

Just a reminder of what a colossal mistake I'd made. I'd let nameless boy scare off Trent who'd actually seemed interested in me.

I wasn't judging him so much as berating myself for being

foolish. He'd left without even a backward glance. My hopes had sunk into the pit of my stomach.

"You can stay. I'll find a way back home," I said.

Her head tilted to the side. "Come on."

I shook my head and a wave of nausea rolled through me.

"You think I'm going to let you go alone," she said, locking her arms through mine. "You are looking very hot. I caught several guys checking you out. Such a waste we are leaving early."

I stroked a hand down to smooth my hair. She'd done a great job of straightening my locks, but they were starting to curl. Still, I couldn't stay. If I saw him again...

The walk home was filled with retelling her exploits of the night. She'd tried and failed to gain Sawyer's attention. Apparently, he'd been too into teasing some other girl Celeste labeled a skinny beanpole. I didn't ask any questions. My main concern had been not falling flat on my face.

My thoughts kept trailing back to the mysterious boy with the haunted eyes. Stupid me, I still wanted to know him. More than that, I wanted to know his soul.

Somehow we'd made it back to the apartment we shared and I crashed. A blinding headache was my morning wake-up call. That didn't stop me from leaving after I'd taken two aspirin. I had a mission at the lab and grabbed a banana and a bottle of water for breakfast.

It was early for campus life on a Sunday. Everything was quiet. Nothing stirred outside of the musical chirping sounds of insects. If it wasn't for the radiating heat, my morning hangover wouldn't be half as bad.

I pushed through the double doors of the biology building and walked toward the back and to the right down a long hall to the very end. I keyed in the code on the pad on the door. There was a click that gained me entrance into the classroom dedicated to entomology students.

"Willow."

My heart stopped and raced at the same time as I glanced around to find Derek at a table in a far corner.

"Sorry, I didn't mean to scare you."

I clutched the dragonfly pendant that hung right about where my heart was beating like it wanted out of my chest.

The second I took to catch my breath, I'd closed my eyes. I opened them and said, "No problem. I didn't expect anyone here this early."

"It's ten," he said.

That was true. But most everyone was sleeping off the aftereffects of partying. I stopped myself from saying that. Derek was like me. We weren't social butterflies. I would avoid parties altogether if not for Celeste occasionally coaxing me out.

I forced a smile, grateful for the aspirin I'd taken. That coupled with eating potassium-filled fruit and chugging down a bottle of water had cleared my head some.

"Campus is quiet. That's all." He blinked at me. Had he said something I missed? "Sorry."

"No problem."

I shuffled over to my station, staring at all the tiny faces paralyzed in death. I hated their demise could solve many problems our planet would face in the future. I hadn't killed them and only worked on ones that were already dead. I'd taken many a walk in our campus man-made forest searching for the fallen to study instead of those slain in the name of science.

"We have a live one," Derek said, breaking into my thoughts.

My head snapped up, and with wide eyes I watched as he pointed toward the back closet where specimens were kept.

Not everyone thought like I did. Many had no compassion for the creatures we studied. On unsteady feet I trudged in that direction. Beyond the solid wood door, racks held insects of all kinds. I passed a tank that held a venomous spider. I couldn't free it.

There in the back was a plastic case not much larger than the creature jailed inside. Its wings flapped as the poor thing tried to leave captivity. *A dragonfly.*

Another voice pierced the silence from the main room. I silently promised I'd free the beautiful insect and left the closet before the person who'd shown up figured out I'd been the rescuer of many insects left to die in this room. What kind of researcher was I when my bleeding heart couldn't watch the death of any living thing?

I joined the growing group in the lab and tried not to look guilty as a newcomer eyed the specimen closet door suspiciously as I exited. Apparently, I wasn't the only one who had to finish the lab assignment due tomorrow.

At my station, I took measurements and wrote in my notebook as I waited patiently. It might have been a few hours later, but someone mentioned lunch. Derek eyed me, but quickly agreed to go grab some with our classmates.

As soon as the door closed, I made haste to make my rescue. I hadn't brought my backpack, so I was forced to grab some books and cover the plastic habitat as I made a run for it.

It wasn't exactly a jailbreak. But I walked as swiftly as I could, hoping the books would legitimize my removal of the holding cell for one of the most beautiful insects in the world.

Outside, campus had woken up. I kept my head down and walked the path, heading toward the man-made pond near the forest. It was more of a swamp if you asked me. A class of biology students had created the ecosystem years ago. In fact, the entire area had evolved over the years from experiments created by students, including the woody area that flanked it.

In my haste, my foot connected with a break in the concrete. I watched in horror as my arms extended on instinct. The books and the dragonfly flew from my hands as I went sprawling like I was diving for a flat-water slide.

An arm snagged me in mid-air and steadied me as my books

skittered across the pathway. The caged dragonfly slid even farther away.

"Are you okay?"

I looked into the eyes of the guy last night who'd held my head for me as I hurled and my cheeks burst into flames.

"I'm fine."

He hadn't let go of my hand.

"I'm Kent, by the way. I didn't get a chance to tell you that last night."

Embarrassment mottled my response.

"I—I'm Willow."

His disarming smile relaxed me some until he asked, "How are you feeling?"

The five-alarm fire in my face returned. Before I could answer him, a long arm attached to another good-looking boy slung around Kent's neck.

"Brother. Who do we have here?"

The guy's gaze traced down me the way most boys check out my sister.

"She's cute," he added. Then, he held out his free hand to me. "I'm Lance, his brother."

I shook it. When neither Kent nor I added anything, Lance jumped in. "So, my brother here is a bit shy. He probably wants to ask you out, right?"

He eyed Kent, who for a second looked stupefied. When he spoke, it sounded hollow.

"Uh... yeah. There's a concert Friday. Do you want to go with me?"

Once a month or so, indie bands would play on campus.

Lance panted his brother's back and saluted us both. "You got this," he said before leaving.

We both watched as he walked away as quickly as he arrived. Our words tangled as we tried to speak at the same time.

Kent proved to be a gentleman deferring to me. "You first."

His disarming smile seemed trustworthy, not holding any malice in it. I took him for a nice guy. He had been there for me when I'd gotten sick.

"It's okay. I won't hold you to asking me out," I said.

My plastic smile was brittle around the edges as his softened on me.

"Honestly, I would have asked you even if my brother hadn't intervened. Do you want to go?"

Maybe going out with him could help me not think about a certain boy. Though I was probably being stupid, I nodded.

Looking back, I really couldn't tell you what made the two of us turn at the same time. The very boy in question scooped up the plastic case that had survived the fall. He stared at the two of us with the same surprise I had in seeing him.

When I glanced over at Kent, he was already in motion, bending over to gather my scattered books. I'd seriously forgotten about them.

Despite my momentarily loss of the English language, I robotically said, "Thanks," to the beautiful boy who had friend-zoned me. He walked forward, my breath hitching. A quick glance at Kent and he seemed just as frazzled.

Kent stood and held out my books to me just as nameless boy reached us, a scowl marring his gorgeous features.

I reached for Kent's offering, but kept my eyes on the other boy. Once I had the books, I extended a hand to take a disoriented dragonfly fluttering around in his plastic cage.

One arch of his brow was all my savior offered us as he let go of the clear box.

"Thanks," I muttered again.

He granted me a tip of his head before disappearing down the path.

"Do you know him?" I asked Kent, not taking my eyes off the retreating boy.

Out of my periphery, I caught him shaking his head. I gave

him back my attention and we exchanged numbers before saying our goodbyes.

I clutched my books to my chest with one hand and the case hung by the handle from my other. I took a turn off the concrete onto a well-worn path into the woods that led to the pond.

It was a bit of a hike as I drifted on invisible clouds. Once again, my thoughts had turned to the guy who wore a frown easier than a smile.

Just as I was about to reach the edge of the trees into the park area around the pond, a truck pulled up into the small parking area. Two figures got out. I recognized the guy as one of Sawyer's friends or so it had seemed at the party. The girl held a jar, which confused me for a second.

Were they here to catch something? Anger built inside of me until the girl began to unscrew the top. Though I was too far to see as she held it up, I guessed they were there to let something go.

I moved back behind the tree, feeling like I was intruding on something private. With my back to them, I bent to set down my books. Then I crouched and freed my own prisoner. It took only a second for my disoriented dragonfly to realize he could rise higher than before. When he did, he zipped away faster than my eyes could track.

I pulled my notebook free and jotted down my observations. Though I hadn't been as close to the marshy area as I'd wanted to be, my dragonfly headed straight in that direction. His keen senses led him to his new home.

It made me think of Mom. A reasonable time after my father died, Mom married Dan and we moved in with him and Celeste. I'd never truly felt settled. The big house with all its rooms and fine furnishings had never felt like home to me.

I wished that something inside me would point home like it had for the dragonfly. There was nothing wrong with Dan or Celeste, but I missed my dad and frankly my mom too.

Giggles brought me back to the present. I caught sight of the couple clinging to each other in that *in love* sort of way. Their mouths were fused in an *old as time mating ritual*. Unfortunate for me, my apartment was in their direction. I'd feel like an intruder if I walked that way.

Just as I contemplated taking the long way around, their laughter sounded closer. I quickly scrambled to my feet and stupidly did a quick walk-run thing in the opposite direction, unsure why. Instinct? It wasn't as if I'd done anything wrong, until I tripped for the second time that day.

6

Ashton

IT WAS hard for me to believe in anything these days. I couldn't trust my instincts. I'd thought for sure that guy had been checking me out on more than one occasion. If that were true, why had he asked tire girl out? I couldn't puzzle out if my anger and disappointment were aimed at him for asking her out or at her for accepting?

The voice from the past would have me believe I was gay. Yet Sawyer insisted I was straight. I wasn't sure of anything. My reality held no meaning.

The hand that stopped me in my tracks didn't scare away the loneliness; he inspired it.

"Ash."

My name left his lips like glowing embers that die quickly and brightly.

I had no words left to give him. I'd given him all that and they were met at an impenetrable gate to his heart.

"This is bullshit," Sawyer said.

I glanced away, not mentally strong enough to break out of his hold. Once he'd inspired me to endure the chains Mother had kept me in, forging a bond between us that had been unbreakable. Now we were little better than strangers.

People had to walk around us, but Sawyer didn't care.

"You don't have to stay at the frat house just to get away from me. Come home. I'll leave," he said.

I glued my eyes shut, afraid my words would silently spill from them.

"Please," he begged.

There was a time I would have done anything he asked. I longed for the past when we had Neverland, a place where we'd been free from everything. Where love had no gender. Now he'd found his Wendy and I was more than ever a lost boy.

He sighed at my total non-response. There was no point to speak, so I didn't.

"You should know Shelly needed a place to stay, and I told her she could move in," he said.

Of course, he had. I gave him a stiff nod. When he finally let go, I moved away before I gave in to his charismatic smile. I darted off the main path onto a rocky one. Like life had been before him, my shadow was the only one to follow me. It wasn't until I was camouflaged by the trees did my urgent steps turn into a slow jog.

My arm still burned where his touch branded my soul and I collapsed into the reeds. The tall plants near the water swallowed my prone form. Then I was swimming in the endless blue sky, reminded of the first time Sawyer and I met.

I'd been lying in the short grass, hoping to feel something other than pain. The sky had opened up, letting cool drops to rain over my welcomed skin. He'd stood over me with a hand out like my personal Peter Pan.

Eventually, he'd fought my mother, who'd only needed the pirate hat to play the part of Captain Hook. His promise to always slay my dragons paved a way to a new reality, one without monsters and devils.

I faintly heard the footsteps before a shadow grew over me. In the blink of an eye a body landed on me, shrouding me in darkness. A mass of curls had blotted out the sun.

Before I could roll the invader off of me, she pushed up to her hands and knees just as the sound of giggles neared. She dropped back heavily on my chest, pushing air out of my lungs. Was she hiding from someone?

Before I could ask that question, another came from above us.

"What do we have here?"

I'd just brushed her hair from my eyes to see Chance above me. His twinkled with mirth as Brie also struggled not to laugh.

I'd caught my breath and was about to explain that it wasn't what it looked like when Chance winked. He steered Brie away, saying he'd call me later.

The girl who had fallen on me rolled off and I saw who it was as if there was any doubt. Her hair had given her away, fanning out all around her as she lay next to me. *Tire girl.*

"You again," I muttered.

What was up with me running into her?

"Sorry."

Her face was splotched in red, a familiar sight.

"What were you running from?" I asked.

She bit her lip as a sheepish smile grew on her face, blinding my thoughts.

"I didn't want them to think I was some creeper," she said, muttering another apology. I struggled with what to say. She didn't have the same problem. "What are you doing here?"

Hiding... longing to be comfortable in my own skin.

She sat up, the sun spotlighting her like she was on stage.

"Never mind. You don't have to answer that. It was rude of me to pry," she said.

My thoughts tripped over each other in my head, leaving me speechless.

"I should go." She suddenly sounded shy.

She got to her hands and knees as I lay there coming off like an asshole.

As her things were safely cradled in her arms, she tilted her head quizzically.

"Most days I feel invisible in a crowd. But when I want to be alone, suddenly I'm surrounded." She pointed to the ground. "I hope you don't mind if I steal your idea and come back here sometime. I have a feeling this is ground zero for true solitude." Then she was gone.

Everything she said rang true for me in its opposite form. I felt too visible, longing all my life not to be seen at the same time, hating to be alone in my own skin. What I realized that moment was I'd wanted someone to see and hear me without words.

The hurricane of a girl stirred in my thoughts. Her body had tumbled onto mine and had zipped all the breath out of me. Yet a thousand needlepoints hadn't lit up my skin. Then again, had her bare skin touched mine?

It was too hard to think. I was overwhelmed with the whys and hows. I was taken back to a six-year-old me, and Sawyer hovered there asking me why I was lying in the rain. Funny thing was, his and tire girl's expression when they looked at me on the ground had been similar. No matter what my answer was to their questions, it would be accepted.

7

Past

"Ashton, I expect you to stay quiet in your room. I have company coming over."

I nodded.

It was against the rules to ask questions.

As Mother would say, my mouth had a life of its own. Something that would eventually be beaten out of me.

"Why can those men hug you and I can't?"

I barely noticed the painful slap, I was so used to it.

Then she pointed. "Your room, now. And don't come out."

Life wasn't fair, I'd been told many times. Still, my tears littered the floor, marking my path.

I crawled onto my bed, putting my back to the wall. I faced the door, afraid she was coming with more punishment.

When the doorbell chimed with the first visitor, I looked around for something to do. Toys weren't allowed in my room. The few I had were locked in a downstairs closet.

With words locked in my head, I played with the friends she

couldn't take away from me. They were nicer than the kids at school. They didn't make fun of the way I spoke.

"Ashton," Mom called out in her warrior's voice. "Are you running around up there?"

I stopped, realizing I had pretended I was a plane flying away. I took slow steps and crawled onto my bed. I lay looking at the ceiling. I closed my eyes and took to the skies in my head.

When I woke up, my room was dark. The gray walls appeared black. I lay still, listening. I heard no sounds of Mother's company around. I had to pee and got to my feet.

Just in case, I made it to the door without making a sound.

I reached for the knob and turned it slowly.

The door opened, and I popped my head out, looking and listening.

When I heard and saw nothing, I tiptoed to the bathroom.

I waited for the door to close before I turned the light on. So far so good. Mother hadn't heard me.

I used the bathroom and washed my hands like Mother always said.

Then I turned off the light, trying not to be afraid of the dark.

I opened the door and took a step.

"Well, hello."

I turned around and a man stood in the hallway. Was he my father? It was too dark to tell.

"Aren't you going to say hi?" he asked.

"Hi," I said.

"It's late. You should be in bed."

I nodded, afraid he would send me to the basement for disobeying like Mother did.

"Let me tuck you in."

He came over and took my hand in his and smiled.

He was nice.

He closed the door behind us when we walked in.

"You're a big boy, aren't you?"

I nodded as I climbed up onto my big boy bed.

He sat down. "Let me help you get tucked in."

But his hand reached under the covers instead. "I think you can thank me for walking you to your room."

He wasn't a nice man after all.

My screams went unheard by Mother. He'd covered my mouth with his hand. I'd been bad by leaving my room. He was punishing me. His touch hurt me everywhere, and though I begged, he didn't stop.

8

Ashton

As if electrified, I jolted out of sleep and sat straight up. I swung my arms as if I could fight the ghosts of my past. Instead, my blows only broke through air. Orienting myself, I wiped moisture from my face as I searched all around me trying to remember where I was. In the dark, it took more than a second to figure out I'd fallen asleep outside cradled by reeds.

I thought about the girl, the one who had found me here days ago. Had I come back hoping she'd keep her word and find me here? I got to my feet, my body stiff. Football practice the last few days had been grueling.

If only a sledgehammer could knock away all the memories from the past. With purpose, I hiked it back to the frat house, needing out of my head.

No matter what day of the week, the place was far from empty. It wasn't quite a party, but there was more booze sitting around than a liquor store. I grabbed the closest bottle, which happened to be Grey Goose, and took the stairs two at a time.

What greeted me in my bedroom wasn't shocking. A tiny girl had Sawyer's hard dick in her hand. She was moving to climb on top of him. Only Sawyer was far from participating. He lay there like a corpse. If not for the rise and fall of his chest, I would have mistaken him for dead.

"Get the fuck out," I said, shocking the shit out of the girl.

"What? Can't you see we're busy?"

She tried and failed at a sexy smile.

"It's my room and I say go, now."

Apparently, she caught the deadly intent in my voice because she let go of him. He didn't react when she huffed and puffed her way to the door. As she opened her mouth to give me her parting words, I shut and locked it in her face.

I sighed loudly, but Sawyer still hadn't moved. I found myself checking his pulse before reaching for the sheets and covering him with them. Then I sat on the floor with my back to the bed and opened the bottle of Goose. I drained it, waiting for oblivion to take me.

Though I got what I asked for, the devil returned in my dreams like he had in life. When I'd told Mother what happened to me that first time, I'd never forget what she said.

"You got what you deserved. I told you to stay quiet and in your room."

Hadn't her words come back to haunt me?

I should have never told Sawyer the truth of my feelings. It hadn't been so bad sharing him with someone else. It was the closest thing to having him.

My thoughts mixed with the nightmare of being forced facedown and used. It held me in its bitter embrace as I clawed my way free. Distantly, I heard Sawyer's voice and felt his touch as it soothed the pain.

"It's okay. No one can hurt you now. I won't let them," he crooned.

Before my violent shaking stilled, I freed words in reply.

"But you're the one hurting me now."

The next morning I woke up curled in a ball, the hard floor on my side. I noticed two things that hadn't been there before: a pillow under my head and a blanket around me. I turned to glance up at the bed, but it was empty. Sawyer was gone and my chest involuntary tightened.

My palms pressed to my forehead couldn't will away leftover pain that always hit like a wrecking ball. With every fiber of my being I wanted to be free of it.

With all the excess thoughts crowding my head space, I needed to channel it. I crawled to my feet and plopped in my chair. I went for my notebook, turned to a fresh page, and began to write, though putting my thoughts on paper wouldn't change anything.

Some would call my story fanfiction. It was about the leader of the lost. My character would tell Peter just what he thought about Wendy intruding into their world. That was the first step to freedom. If I could only find a fitting way to write the ending.

I put my pen down, remembering what day it was. As much as I wanted to hate Sawyer, I couldn't. Today was his birthday.

Finding him passed out at the frat house worried me. Sawyer preferred his room at the townhouse. Something was going on with him and I didn't know what. It just showed how degraded our friendship had become. Still, I couldn't let his birthday go by without celebration.

Before I got up, I noticed a black envelope on top of my laptop. I picked it up and studied my name written in perfect script. Turning it over, the seal of a sword through a V on a shield was answer enough if I hadn't already guessed. I pulled it out and read the words. I'd been *cordially invited* to join the brotherhood of the Vanderbilt Club and further instructions would come. It was Layton's version of Yale's Skulls and Bones, a secret society that inducted its members in the final year of school.

Joining the exclusive group with members all over the world

had its privileges. Doors would open. Success in your chosen field was virtually guaranteed. They traded in secrets and survived in shadows. Their charters were at all the major universities with selective recruiting. It was meant as an honor to receive the invitation.

I put the card back into the envelope and set it aside, unsurprised that I'd gotten one. My father hinted that he was a member. He'd probably nominated me to be inducted. I wondered if they knew I was his son.

Based on everything I'd heard, I would guess yes. They probably had results of DNA testing to prove that fact. I pushed that aside and got back on task.

As much as I hated to talk, I walked out of my room prepared to do what I must.

"Ashton." I glanced up. Bryant, one of my frat brothers, had stepped out of his room the same time I had. "Are you in?"

Given the envelope I'd gotten, I'd guessed he received one too. Not everyone in Sigma would be invited to join.

There had been a note at the bottom of the card to keep your prospective membership a secret. He would have received the same warning. His invitation could be rescinded if the wrong person overhead him talking about it. I lifted a finger to my lips to stop him.

"Don't," I said.

Not waiting for a response, I headed for the stairs. Bryant caught up and used two fingers to push his square glasses up to the bridge of his nose.

"Sawyer got an invitation," Bryant went on, angling his head to make sure he was in my line of sight. "I assumed you did too."

One of the reasons I moved away from Sawyer was because everyone, including myself, assumed we were inseparable. Truthfully, we had been. I stopped on the stairs.

"If you keep asking, you'll be cut."

Bryant went wide-eyed. He wasn't your average Sigma. He

looked more like he should join the Physics Club than be in a frat. But his dad was a tech god and sat higher on the Forbes Fortune 500 than either my dad or Sawyer's.

He ran a hand through hair that had a mind of its own.

"They would." I nodded. His voice went up an octave as panic set in. "You won't tell, will you? It's my only chance to ever get laid."

Though he played lacrosse and not football, we had more in common than he knew.

"No. Just don't go asking anyone else."

He bobbed his head and I came down to find most of my frat brothers lounging around in the living area.

"Announcement."

All heads whipped in my direction. I didn't speak often, so I wasn't at all surprised by their response.

"It's Sawyer's birthday. Party tonight. Drinks on me."

There were cheers and not just for Sawyer. These assholes had just been given an excuse to drink in excess in the middle of the week. One of the pledges dutifully came over.

"Anything I can do?"

I pulled out cash from my back pocket and dropped it in his open palm. His wide eyes meant he would probably be cut. No member of the Sigma house would be stunned to have a grand or more put in his hand.

"Buy liquor and top shelf."

His head bobbed, and I eyed Trent, our wannabe president in Sawyer's absence. He already had a highball in his hand and looked amused. He was using the pledges like lap dogs. I'd effectively done the same, though hardly the way my brothers were. Though I hadn't made him do it.

There was one more thing I had to do: get Sawyer here. I dialed Chance, but he didn't answer. I didn't leave a message, knowing he was most likely balls deep in Brie. Otherwise he'd pick up. That left doing it myself.

When I parked in front of the townhouse, I caught sight of Shelly, Sawyer's Wendy, pulling in. He played like he didn't like her, but he did and had for a very long time. The messed-up thing was, I very much liked her as a friend.

"Can I talk to you?"

She looked shocked and stopped in her tracks, but not more than her boyfriend, David. Everyone was always so surprised that I could speak. Didn't anyone think that maybe I didn't talk because there wasn't anything worth being said?

"David, can you give me a minute?" she asked.

She walked over and I moved farther, putting more distance between us and him. She folded her arms.

"What's going on?" she asked.

"I need a favor."

"Okay, cryptic much?"

"Today is Sawyer's birthday," I announced, watching for her reaction.

I was sure she liked him as much as he liked her.

Her eyes popped. "He didn't say anything."

"He wouldn't and he shouldn't be alone."

By the time I finished explaining my plans, she was on board. I glanced up at the place that had been my home for the last three years. It was weird not living there, but for the best.

I left to get the word out on the midweek party. If I got enough drinks in me, maybe I could make it through the night.

9
___

Willow

CELESTE BOUNCED ON HER TOES, wearing a pleading expression.

"Please go," she begged and not for the first time.

The last thing I wanted to do was go to another party.

"It's Sawyer's birthday party," she said like that explained everything.

I really didn't want to see his friend again. I'd already made a fool of myself in front of him several times.

"You go and have fun."

Crestfallen, she gave me puppy dog eyes before turning and flopping onto the couch. "No, it's fine. I won't go."

I understood that look all too well. She wore it a lot when vying for attention. Add to that, as beautiful and social as Celeste was, she didn't have a lot of people she called friends, making me feel guilty.

"Fine. But I'm not dressing up," I said.

Her face brightened with a grin from ear to ear.

"You won't regret it. You can borrow…"

Everything she said after that was a blur. We didn't dress up exactly, but I did end up in an outfit from her closet. The shorts weren't too short, and the halter top only exposed my back. An extra-strength ponytail holder tamed my hair, and not by a flat iron this time.

Muted music wafted from the rafters of the Sigma house. Patriotic plastic cups of blue and red were in the hands of everyone on the premises. It was as if they were doing their civic duty getting drunk after a grueling few days of school.

"I'll get us a drink," Celeste said, scanning the area for the birthday boy.

I nodded and moved to a shaded corner, glad I hadn't yet spotted Sawyer or his merry band of friends.

"Hey."

The voice had come from above. I tilted my head back in order to see the face of the speaker.

Deep brown eyes matched the color of flawless skin that covered sculpted cheekbones chiseled into a handsome face. In short, the guy was hot.

"Hi," I said and quickly glanced away, afraid he would see color flooding into my heated cheeks.

Celeste was the flirting expert. I had no clue what to say next.

He introduced himself as Jason and waited for me to do the same.

His hand appeared, and I took it. Not wanting to be rude, I met his eyes. "I'm Willow."

"Beautiful name for a beautiful girl."

Total line, but when he said it, it felt real.

"Thanks."

I pushed at a stray curl that had broken free and split my focus between him and the floor.

"Parties not your thing."

He certainly knew what to say to disarm me.

That time when I met his gaze I held it. "Not especially."

His head bobbed once. "I get it. I don't drink much, which seems weird considering."

I narrowed my eyes on his cup.

He lifted it. "This?" It was my time to silently agree. "It's apple juice. Do you want some? I have a stash."

I felt the smile build slowly as I said, "Yeah, that would be great, actually."

The idea of getting sloppy drunk again held no appeal.

"Wait here."

He was tall with well-defined arms and calves suggesting he was an athlete. I couldn't decide which sport he played and would probably ask when he returned.

Celeste found me first and handed me a blue cup.

"We can't stay here," she pronounced.

Her eyes were on the move. The more hidden spot I'd chosen didn't work with her plans to be noticed.

"I'm kind of waiting on someone."

Her eyes grew. "Really?" I nodded. "I can't wait to meet him."

Dread filled me. What would happen next was predicable. He would show up, hand me apple juice, and proceed to talk to Celeste like I wasn't there. Part of me wanted to ask her to leave. The other part knew it was better to have this happen now before I got my heart invested in someone who would see me as a consolation prize.

It didn't take long. Jason stumbled to a stop in front of us, his gaze bouncing between us.

"Hey," he said to either of us.

I was already looking away, not wanting to see his expression change when he looked at me.

"Hi," Celeste said.

The natural flirt she was, her one word came out sort of breathy.

"Jason, this is my sister, Celeste."

I watched the two of them and knew instantly they'd met before.

"Yeah, we've met. He's in a couple of my classes," she said.

"We share the same major," he responded on the heels of her reply.

I wasn't sure what was going on, but all of a sudden it was very awkward.

Just as I opened my mouth to excuse myself, Celeste did it for me.

"Well, I'll leave you two."

She walked away and he watched her ass. I rolled my eyes while looking at the two cups I held. Both held amber liquid. Which was the apple juice? I couldn't remember. I took a chance and downed one of them.

"I should explain," he began.

"You dated my sister," I tossed in proactively.

"No. I did ask her out. She turned me down."

I wasn't exactly shocked. "Oh."

"If this is weird—"

"It is actually."

"I would like to get to know you."

I shook my head. "Sorry. It's just—"

"Weird for you." I nodded. "It's too bad, Willow," he said sadly and looped off.

Celeste hadn't gone too far because she was at my side in seconds.

"You let him go?" she asked.

Duh, I wanted to say. Like I wouldn't always wonder if he thought he'd gotten the wrong sister.

"He seemed into you." She had that wrong. He was totally into her. "He's really quite nice."

"Then why didn't you go out with him?"

She shrugged. "He's no Sawyer."

More than likely, she wanted to conquer Sawyer. He was the unattainable guy who every girl wanted to tame.

"Speaking of..."

Her words trailed off as Sawyer walked through the front doors. The crowd immediately started singing "Happy Birthday." That's when I noticed his friend. This time I watched him for signs of truth in what Celeste had said the other night.

Sure enough, he stared at Sawyer who was immediately engulfed by well-wishing girls, including Celeste who was already heading that way. I thought I heard her say something to me, but I'd been too caught up in the mysterious, beautiful boy.

His eyes never left his friend and I could see something like longing there, or was I just reading more into his expression? All eyes were on Sawyer, except mine.

When the birthday song ended, my savior turned and swiftly left the room. I glanced over at Sawyer, who now watched him walk away. Maybe there was something between the two of them. Sawyer could totally be bi. It wasn't out of the realm of possibilities.

What I did know was that any fantasies I had about the boy who had a penchant for rescuing me had died a sudden death. And maybe that was a good thing.

On the positive side, I did have a date with Kent tomorrow. He was really cute and sweet too. Hopefully, he wouldn't prefer Celeste or I would give up dating until I moved far away from her.

10

Past

"WHAT IS THAT RACKET?"

Mother's shrieking voice woke me from the dream. I blinked the sleepies from my eyes and she stood over me wearing her mad face.

"Get up. I let you sleep the day away because frankly it kept you out of my hair. But your father will be here soon."

She whisked the blanket off me and the cool air made me shiver. Though I liked this room better than the one I used to have.

"What in the world? Did you piss yourself? How old are you? And think about how you answer me."

There was no right answer, so I kept my mouth shut. Her nails dug into my arm as she yanked me off the bed. I struggled to keep standing, knowing I'd be punished if I fell. Every inch of my body hurt.

She stabbed her finger at the bed. "Strip off the sheets and those wet clothes. We don't have a lot of time."

I did as told even if the pile was almost as big as me.

She pinched my ear as she marched me to the bathroom. She turned on the shower and ordered me inside. The water was cold, but I knew better than to complain. She scrubbed me hard. The bristles on the brush left me red all over. After, she yanked on my arms, getting me dressed and combing my hair.

"Be on your best behavior," she said when the doorbell rang.

I nodded once and sat perfectly still.

The man with the kind eyes walked in and over to me. He got down on his knees to talk to me.

"Ashton, how are you doing?"

He gave me the biggest smile I'd ever seen.

Mother hadn't followed him in and I took a chance. I moved forward and wrapped my arms around his neck. He held on and his touch didn't hurt like Mother's. His pats stayed on my back and his hand never moved to the secret places. I could trust him.

"Please take me away."

His face turned sad.

"Son, I wish I could."

"Ashton."

I pulled back, hearing Mother's mean voice. She wasn't pleased I'd touched him. He wasn't angry.

He stood and patted my head. He took the glass Mother offered him.

"You can see, he's doing fine, well-behaved, though he's a little clingy. He'd be better served at a boarding school," Mother said.

"Maybe. But then I couldn't see him."

"If you told your wife the truth—"

Father talked and Mother shut up. "And you wouldn't need such a big house. Not to mention the monthly stipend for his care."

Mother's eyes landed on me. "Must we talk in front of the child?"

He spoke and I looked at him again.

"I'll be back, son."

I liked the way he sounded. His voice was nice. I sat quietly and moved my legs like I was kicking a ball. I stared at the basket full of toys she'd put out. They were for looking at and not touching. I would get a spanking if I played with them.

I waited, making up stories in my head until Father came back alone.

"I have to go."

I hopped off the sofa and wrapped myself around his leg. "Please don't leave me here."

"Is there something wrong?" he asked.

I thought he was talking to me until I heard Mother's voice.

"Of course, there isn't. Ashton, let go of him this minute."

I let go of him and my tears. It didn't matter now. If he didn't take me, I would be in trouble.

"What's wrong with him?" Father asked in a voice that would have scared me. But he was talking to Mother.

Her mad face was back. When he left, I wouldn't sit for a week.

"What do you think is wrong with him? You barely come around," she said.

He knelt down to face me. "I'll be back. I promise."

But it would be a very long time until I saw him again. Mother walked him to the door and marched back once he was gone.

"What the hell was that? You embarrassed me."

My face stung where the back of her hand slapped me, sending me to the floor.

"After all I do for you." She hated me and I still didn't understand why. "That man you let into your room offered me money to keep 'tucking' you in when I stopped him from visiting you last night."

She hadn't stopped him. He'd already hurt me bad when she showed up. She hadn't asked why I was crying, only told me to shut up.

"If you ruin this for me, you'll have to earn your keep. Besides, you'll get used to it. I did."

She said more things. I didn't understand all her words, but they frightened me all the same.

"Daddy's business partner thought me pretty and I didn't turn out so bad. You aren't worth much more."

She aimed her finger to the door.

"Off to the basement with you. It will give you a chance to think about what you've done."

"Mother, please," I begged as she dragged me by the arm. "Please don't make me go down there."

It was dark. I didn't like the dark and the scary sounds.

She didn't look back as I slid across the floor behind her. She opened the door and pointed.

"Don't make this any harder on yourself. You did this, not me."

"Please turn on the light. I don't like the dark."

"Ashton, I've told you so many times to be careful of your words. This is a punishment. The darkness will teach you a better lesson."

She aimed a pointy claw into darkness. I didn't beg anymore. I knew better. If I did, she wouldn't feed me. I stepped into a nightmare.

11

Ashton

I JERKED, my eyes opening and finding a sliver of light. *Breathe*, I told myself. I wasn't five or six anymore. I'd survived.

Warm arms circled me. The blanket I'd used to cover Sawyer now covered us on the floor. For a second, I stayed there remembering this safe place before I pulled free. The nightmare I had last night brought out his inner slayer of dragons. Too bad, I was far from saving.

He was still knocked out, looking innocent in sleep. Did I?

Then I remembered why he was here. It wasn't for me. He'd drunk himself into oblivion after getting into a fight with Shelly's boyfriend. He'd won and passed out not long after. I'd left him on the bed. He'd joined me on the floor.

Shattered glass from the bottle I'd taken from him littered the area near the door. I grabbed a towel to pick up the pieces of the Absolut.

Once that was done, I left him, vowing to myself that I'd leave the house until I was sure he was gone. Staying would accomplish nothing. Our friendship had died a sudden death, not that it should surprise me. The few good people in my life had always left me. It was like some kind of rule.

Outside in the hall, I heard my name. Bryant asked, "I can call you Ash, right?"

Inwardly, I groaned. There was nothing wrong with the kid other than him appearing every time I left my room. He needed a friend, and maybe I did too, but we barely knew each other.

"What do you have there?"

I didn't know why I did it, but I opened a corner of the towel I held, giving him a peek inside.

"Oh—rough night?"

I gave a half-shrug and took the stairs two at a time, wanting to get rid of the evidence that something was up with Sawyer. Bryant didn't seem to mind that I didn't answer. He followed, saddling up to my side at the bottom, and began peppering me with questions.

"Do you think they'll have girls there at our first meeting?"

I glared at him and he held up his hands. I resumed making my way to the kitchen where I dumped the glass shards, towel included, into the industrial trash can.

Though I hadn't spoken a word, he continued.

"It's just I'm a virgin."

If he thought that was news, I had something that trumped that. I'd never been with a girl unless Sawyer was there. That technically made me a virgin of sorts too.

"So."

It was the first word I'd spoken. I wasn't sure why I was encouraging this conversation.

"It's just girls look past me like I don't exist. Dad says it's good. He says that I should wait for a girl who wants me and not my money."

Years of child labor under Mother's reign, I gathered empty bottles while he spoke and tossed them into the trash. Considering our dues covered the large monthly cleaning bill to have a crew show up every morning and clean up after our sorry asses, I should leave it be. But I needed to do something while Bryant poured his heart out to me.

"I used to agree with him. Hell, Dad paid for my prom date, some supermodel. She'd been willing. Dumbly, I'd wanted my first time to be real, you know."

He paused and I glanced over at him. If he thought his tales were sad, he had no idea. At least it sounded like his dad gave a shit. He continued with his monologue.

"I thought for sure things would be different in college. And when I got in Sigma..." He let that hang in the air. Everyone knew Sigmas were rich. "Now I just want to get laid before I graduate. You wouldn't understand. Girls flock to you like they do Cargill. You can have any girl you want..."

He trailed off as if something occurred to him.

"You don't like girls, do you? I mean, it's cool. Though I've heard things. Maybe you're a floater." He shook his head, but that didn't stop his babbling. "What I mean, it doesn't matter to me who you're into. To each his own, right?"

I ceased all action and faced him. I ignored rumors. People could think what they wanted. The truth was, I didn't know what I was. I'd only ever cared about one person. Though that wasn't exactly true. There had been Julie. But Sawyer had loved her too. I'd chosen him when she'd chosen me.

"If that's a touchy subject, forget I mentioned it," he said, cutting into my thoughts.

I was a sorry excuse for an advice giver. What did I know about women? Sawyer had the moves. I'd just followed his lead. But something about this kid made me speak.

"There's no girl you're interested in?"

My question, which was more than my normal look or a one-word answer, paralyzed him for a second.

"Um—well—there is one girl."

I cut to the chase.

"Who is she?"

"It's dumb. Every year I've used my elective to take a class I don't need to get close to her," he admitted.

The front door opened. The cleaning crew had arrived, wearing red shirts and armed with gloved-covered hands. I tilted my head toward the sliding glass doors in back and exited that way.

Outside, once he closed the door, I asked, "Have you talked to her?"

His shoulders slumped. "I keep meaning to. But I'm afraid of what she'll say."

I'd had that fear for a long time.

"It's better to find out now. Otherwise you'll waste time or be too late."

Maybe if I'd told Sawyer sooner... maybe.

"Should I talk to her before the Vanderbilt thing?" I pursed my lips at the mention of the club's name. He caught himself, covering his mouth. "Sorry. I won't mention it again. Their name at least."

I shook my head. "Even if you talk to her, if you don't follow their rules, you won't get in." Or so I'd heard.

How would I handle it if there were girls I was expected to touch without Sawyer there as backup?

Pain erupted when Bryant reached out to get my attention. I jumped back, rubbing at my arm, giving myself away.

"Sorry. I—I—"

His rambling was interrupted when my phone went off in my pocket. I pulled it out and recognized the number, though I didn't have it programmed in.

I swiped to send the call to voicemail.

Bryant was watching me like I was a science project gone wrong.

My phone went off again. My father usually gave up after one try and would leave me a sappy voice message. He never called two times in a row.

"You need to take that?" he asked.

I nodded and he went back into the house. I accepted the call.

Sounds of a vacuum drifted through the glass doors before they were swallowed up again as it closed.

"Son."

I didn't reply.

"Don't hang up," he pleaded.

I stood there, teeth grinding, waiting for him to spew his urgent news.

"Ashton, I know you're there and you don't have to say anything."

You don't have the right to grant me permission, I almost said.

"I'm so goddamn sorry." His voice cracked.

There were so many things for him to be sorry for, I wasn't sure what he was referring to.

"If I'd known, I would have taken you from her."

So he knew. Had the Vanderbilt Club found out somehow? Not surprising. The head of the FBI or CIA could be members, even the president. I wouldn't find out until after I was inducted.

Too bad for them, the secret they thought they could hold over me to keep me in line wasn't much of a secret. I had written down my sorry story in those notebooks Mother gave me to draw in. Without toys to play with, keeping quiet meant paper, pencils, and crayons were the only things I had in my bedroom.

"You're not dying?" I asked, devoid of emotion.

I'd been well taught to keep them to myself.

He sputtered an answer. "No—of course not." As I was about to end the call, he tried to stop me, speaking loud enough I heard. "Wait, Ashton, please."

My finger hovered over the end call button, but I put the phone back to my ear.

"I meant to come back. I planned to tell my wife that night.

But when I came home, she was on to me. Like a coward, I lied when she asked if I was having an affair. Her response was swift and a clear warning. She told me that if she found out I'd cheated on her, she would go to the press and ruin me."

IIis story didn't sway me. I felt bad for his wife. She'd been lied to. Like me, she was incidental in the game my father and mother played.

"I take full responsibility. In my defense, when I came back later, you seemed fine," he added.

Later, that was a joke. It had been months before he showed up again. If he wanted absolution, he would get none of that from me. Besides, by then, the idea of freeing myself from Mother's torment had been beaten out of me.

"Is that all?" I asked.

My monotone disguised how heavily my heart beat in my chest. It was like all the oxygen in my lungs had been choked out of me. I was done with memory road.

"After reading your journals, I told her." He meant his wife. "I'm not sure she'll ever forgive me, but she wants to meet you."

That had been his true reason for his call. I was just another pawn. This time in his game.

"How did you get them?"

There was a pause.

"I was at the house."

I let out a sour laugh. "What? Cheating on your wife again."

"No. It's not like that. Victoria wanted money, of course. We argued. I went upstairs to cool off."

Frost covered my vision. "You snooped."

It wasn't like my uncluttered room had a million hiding places. There were three pieces of furniture in my room: a bed, chest, and nightstand. I had enough clothes to get me through one week and I was expected to keep my room tidy at all times. My journals were hidden in the sole shoebox on a shelf in my closet. They wouldn't have been hard to find. I'd counted on

Mother's disinterest in my life and company banned from upstairs to keep them safe.

"No. Yes. I just wanted to—"

I cut him off. "I have to go."

Knowing more wouldn't change anything.

"Ashton, I never meant to invade your privacy. I found myself wanting to know you better. Your likes and dislikes. And there they were hidden in a shoebox. Just a quick look, I told myself."

"Now you know." I didn't try to hide the brusqueness in my tone.

"Tell me what I can do to make this right."

Nothing was on the tip of my tongue. Every opportunity for happiness had been stolen from me. My continued existence remained a huge question mark. Then a thought occurred to me.

"Take it all away from her."

Why should she profit from my pain? She'd never cared about me.

"Who? Your mother."

"Yes." The whispered word hissed between my clenched teeth.

"There's nothing to take away. I've never given her a dime. Everything is in a trust in your name, the house, the car, but you should know that."

Her repeated threats of kicking me out with nowhere to go looped in my head.

"I know nothing," I said.

"What?" His bafflement almost seemed real. "I sent a lawyer to explain things on your sixteenth birthday along with a car. You signed the document saying you understood, not that it was legally binding. I wanted proof that you'd been told."

That hadn't happened.

"Was the lawyer a man?"

He cursed as a memory surfaced of Mother getting a new car on my birthday.

"How would you know my signature?" I asked.

Silence. He had no good answer, seeing as he'd stop coming around years before.

"Ashton." It was a plea in the form of my name. "I couldn't come. Being a senator meant I was constantly watched by the press. Any interaction with you could have been caught. I warned her to take good care of you and sent others to check on you."

If anyone came, I didn't know them from the other men Mother entertained.

"It doesn't matter." I felt numb.

"It does," he yelled. "I could fucking kill her for what she let happen to you."

Why do you care now? But I didn't say it. I'd said far too much and my stomach rebelled as I was forced to face my demons.

"I'll have a lawyer contact you to sign the papers to evict her. She won't leave with more than the clothes on her back," he declared.

Mother wouldn't be pleased. The thought of her kicking and screaming as they forced her from the premises almost made me smile.

"Sell it," I said.

"What?"

With more vehemence, I repeated myself.

"Sell it all. I don't want any of it."

Keeping the house of horrors and all the memories, including living across from Sawyer and his family, wasn't something I wanted. I had to sever all ties to the past if I had any chance of surviving the future.

"I have to go," I said and hung up, not giving him a chance to say more.

I felt cold when I realized it had started raining. I closed my eyes, hanging on to the feeling. Rain was one thing that didn't burn when it touched my skin.

As I stood there, the sliding glass door opened as did my eyes.

Before me, she held there, bright like the sun peeking from the clouds. A shy smile graced her delicate face.

"Sorry to interrupt." She glanced around. "I'm searching for my phone."

I would wonder later how easily words tumbled from my lips. "When did you last see it?"

She shrugged as pink flooded her cheeks. I thought I'd been the only one who didn't value their phone like it would mean sudden death without it.

"You know it's raining, right?" she asked.

I pushed off the railing and closed the distance.

"I do. And?" I asked as water ran rivets down my face.

Something about challenging her breathed life into me.

"Do you think you could check out there? I might have put it down last night."

I scanned the area and saw nothing. I shook my head slowly, sending water flying to either side of me.

"Let me get you a towel," she said and disappeared around a corner.

She hadn't gone far. I heard her talking to one of the cleaning personnel. She came back with a fluffy yellow towel, its color too cheery to belong to any of the guys in residence.

I stepped inside and made sure our hands didn't brush when I took it from her.

"Thanks for looking," she said before I could thank her.

The corners of her mouth curled up halfway in an attempt at nonchalance before her eyes dropped back to the ground.

"I guess that means my date can't call and cancel."

The shy lift of her shoulder could have been called cute. Then I uncomfortably remembered the guy I was sure had been into me had ultimately asked her out.

"Did I say something wrong?" she asked.

I glanced up into those soft brown eyes of hers and was speechless for a different reason.

12

Past

MOTHER HADN'T COME.

My stomach hurt.

I was so hungry. I crawled over to the plate she tossed down the stairs before I'd been ordered down them.

Barely any moonlight came through the windows, but I could see things crawling over the spilled food.

I wiped away what bugs I saw and shoved the rest into my mouth, too hungry to care.

The door opened, and a shaft of light spilled over me.

"You're disgusting," Mother said.

I sat up straight, so grateful to see her, and spat out the nasty food back onto the plate.

"Get that mess and then go get cleaned up. I'll be in my room, and I don't want to be disturbed."

I picked up all the food I could see now and walked slowly upstairs.

If I dropped the plate, I would be punished, and freedom was only steps away.

"Can I go outside?" I asked before I reached the top.

She narrowed her eyes and I feared I made a mistake.

"Fine. But once you come back in, take a bath."

I nodded and dumped the food into the trash and cleaned the plate before putting it into the dishwasher as I'd been taught.

She left after ensuring I'd done as told.

Then I walked out the front door and into the rain.

The water didn't hurt when it touched me.

I lay in the grass, enjoying every drop until a voice broke into my thoughts.

"Hey. Are you okay?"

I had no idea I looked into the face of my savior.

13

Willow

UNREADABLE STORMY EYES HELD MINE. As if the ghost that haunted him floated through me, I shivered, wrapping an arm around myself. I rubbed at my chilled skin as the summer storm poured down behind him.

"I should—uh—go."

Lifting a finger, I pointed toward the front, belatedly unsure why I'd been waiting there. His looming presence with the ends of the towel hooked around his neck in his two hands rattled me.

Our continued silence became awkward. Slowly, I turned and made my way to the door. I didn't understand him. If it wasn't a stupid idea, I would almost say he stared at me the way he had Sawyer.

I shook my head because that was dumb. Besides, if I was right, it didn't mean he was remotely into me.

The rain poured down in sheets and I made a mad dash for my car. My hair already swollen from the humidity would be a sopping tangled mess by the time I got back to the apartment.

Once inside the car, I didn't immediately turn it on. I found myself looking back. The door was closed, but I swore I still felt his penetrating gaze on me.

Don't be foolish, I said to no one. I started the car and drove the half a mile to the other side of campus where student apartments were.

"Did you find it?" Celeste asked when I walked in.

I blew out a breath and shook my head, which turned out to be a total mistake. The frosty air-conditioned air chilled the water that dripped from me onto my skin.

"Dad's going to be pissed. How do you keep losing your phone?"

The only reason I had a phone was for her. It wasn't like Mom called me every day.

"Don't tell him. It's not like I really need one," I admitted.

She gave me a disapproving shake of her head and switched topics.

"Do you think they'll cancel the concert?"

Her question had crossed my mind. I shrugged and headed toward the bathroom.

"I should get ready because I don't know if he's still coming tonight," I said, considering he couldn't call me.

How did I feel about that?

"I hope so for your sake. You need this," she said with sisterly concern.

She had no clue how patronizing that sounded.

In the bathroom, I faced the mirror. The idea of detangling my hair only to step outside and have all my hard work explode into a puffball of frizz didn't appeal to me.

"Maybe it's for the best."

Though I'd spoken out loud, it had been aimed at no one.

Celeste came and leaned against the doorframe.

"My fingers are crossed for you. You deserve this."

I reached for my wide tooth comb. "Sometimes I wonder if I

should just give up and accept that I'm a spinster or an old maid depending what era you consider."

She rolled her eyes. "Don't be dramatic."

"Dramatic. I'm a twenty-one nearly twenty-two year old virgin. I'll never be you." Her nose wrinkled. "Sorry, I didn't mean it that way. It's just you can have your choice of guys."

She huffed, "Sawyer doesn't even see me."

A flash of nameless guy crossed my mind and why hadn't I introduced myself or asked his name when I'd spoken to him a little bit ago. I decided against asking Celeste if she knew it. She'd made it pretty clear that I was wasting my time thinking about him.

"Well, guys are stupid," I said in sister solidarity.

She smiled. "Exactly."

"Maybe I should auction my hymen off for charity." The curve of her mouth turned upside down. "Don't judge. I've heard of girls doing that."

"Let me put it this way. When some creepy old guy with a beer gut wins the bid, because let's face it, most guys our age won't have the cash to outbid some old dude, what will you do then?"

My grimace must have shown on my face because she nodded.

"Okay, so that's out," I said.

The comb caught on a snarl and I nearly doubled over in an effort to pull the tangle free.

"That should totally be a yoga pose," she said with amusement.

I half-laughed and winced at the same time. "Yeah. And it should be called tangled snarled."

We cracked up or she did more than me. When my comb came free, my head snapped up and my momentum sent me bending the other direction.

Celeste held out a hand to stop me and sighed. My self-serving stepsister had her moments of selflessness.

"Let me help." She pointed to the closed toilet lid. "Sit. Don't give up yet. Auctioning off your virginity is just as bad as volunteering for virgin night."

"What's that?"

I'd never heard of it.

"It's a total frat thing. Though I'm not sure which one. It isn't like it's blasted on social media. But from what I've heard, girls are chosen."

I held up a hand. "How do they know if a girl is a virgin or not?"

She shrugged. "All I know is that you're given the opportunity to lose your V-card to one of the guys in the frat. It's all hush-hush."

"Then how do you know about it?"

It should have been a bad thing. But she'd made it seem like you're given a choice in doing it or not. She didn't say the girls were tricked.

"Don't even think about it. Besides, you've never been—"

She stopped herself, but her unspoken words had been received loud and clear. I'd been to frat parties with her over the years and I'd never been chosen.

"It's stupid," she finished.

When I shook my head, I cried out in pain. She'd been combing through a particularly nasty tangle and I turned my head in the opposite direction.

"Sorry," she muttered.

I broached the question that came to my mind about how she knew all of this.

"Were you chosen?"

She wouldn't meet my eyes as she continued to comb through my hair.

"Celeste, it's okay. You know I would never judge you."

Her confession was slow. "I thought he really liked me. Stupid me." She parted another section and I remained quiet, letting her take her time. "Anyway, it was just a game to him."

"Who is he?"

Her head darted side to side in a definitive no. "It doesn't matter."

"Sawyer?"

He had quite the reputation.

"No. Just let it go."

"This guy tricked you."

That blew away my theory not to judge the so-called virgin night."

"No. I was given a clear choice. I just thought—"

She'd thought there would be more to it with the guy that way.

"Just don't do it, at least not with expectations." She seemed to shake herself. "Really, though, it's not worth it. They'll brag to their friends, and even if no one slut shames you for it, you'll feel skanky after."

Neither of us spoke for a long time while deep in reflection.

When she finished with my hair and makeup, again I was sure she was my fairy godmother. *I almost looked pretty.*

"You are pretty."

I'd said that out loud. I really needed to get a rein on my tongue. Her smile was tight. I didn't think it had anything to do with me. She still looked haunted by the past.

"Thank you. You really have a gift," I said.

"Too bad I can't use it," she said, gathering her things in the giant makeup case she kept.

Her father hadn't approved of her going to cosmetology school like she wanted. He felt her choices were a reflection on him and his business. Being daddy's little girl, she hadn't fought him on it.

"Maybe after?" I asked.

She shrugged. "I didn't major in chemistry for nothing. Maybe one day I'll make my own products."

The doorbell rang. How long had we been at it?

As she shooed me away with her hand, she said, "Go get dressed. I'll entertain him until you come out."

That old and dreadful fear of being the ugly stepsister crept in. I managed a smile and a nod of my head before disappearing into my room.

I'd showered before she decided to flat iron my hair. I glanced over at the dress on my bed she'd picked out of her closet for me. Though I longed for jeans and a tee, she'd argued against it. Since she had guys eating out of her palm, who was I to argue with her advice?

When I stepped out, I braced myself to find Kent drooling over her. Though I hadn't said a word, he turned. My stomach flipped as his entire face lit up when he saw me. He strode over and caught my hand, kissed my cheek, and said, "You look beautiful."

"My work here is done," Celeste announced, waving at us from the door.

I glanced at Kent, but his eyes didn't seem to hold that interest any when looking at Celeste. When they landed on me, I glanced downward, unused to the attention.

"They canceled the concert for tonight."

Like a ball bouncing, my gaze found his again.

"I figured with the rain and all..." I said.

"I tried to call, but you didn't respond."

My phone. "Sorry, I lost my phone."

He only nodded and didn't give me the third degree about it.

"We can do something else if you want. But first, I need to tell you something."

The pit that had been in my stomach grew into a watermelon. He was going to say that he liked Celeste more, despite doing a good job at hiding that. I swallowed another lump and tried not to hate him for it. If he was being honest and not sneaky like other guys, I'd respect him for it.

"I'm gay."

I angled my head as if that would clear up my confusion. Then I took two steps back and flopped onto the couch.

"I wouldn't blame you if you wanted to cancel tonight," he said.

There was no way I could meet his eyes with the rising anger building inside me.

"This was all a game." I thought back to how it had been his brother who'd done the asking. "You used me to hide that from your brother."

"No... Yes... Not exactly."

My gaze lifted and narrowed laser points at him.

"Which one is it?" I snapped, feeling incredibly stupid for thinking he could possibly be interested in me.

He sat next to me, leaving sufficient distance between us, sensing my boiling rage.

"The truth is, I would have asked you out—" When my glare pinned him like one of my specimens, he adjusted his statement. "To hang out—after telling you the truth about myself. But yes, I didn't tell you I was gay then because I didn't want my brother to know."

I exhaled a modicum of my anger. But it was the regret on his face that cooled more of my fury.

"Why are you keeping it from him?"

These days people were so more accepting of other's choices. But what did I know? I wasn't gay and wouldn't understand the pressure he could face at home.

"It's not just him. I come from an old Southern family with roots so deep in tradition, their God could never accept someone not rigidly straight."

"I'm sorry." I found myself saying.

It wasn't that I forgave him. At the same time, I understood it must be hard for him.

"I shouldn't be surprised. Even if you were straight, you wouldn't have ever asked me out," I said, my shoulders slumping.

I got to my feet and headed for the door.

"I may be gay, but that doesn't mean I can't appreciate the beauty in others regardless of who they are. You're gorgeous. Hell, my brother has done nothing but talk about you since that day. If he wasn't dating Mia, he'd probably ask you out himself."

The bitter laugh that escaped me almost brought tears to my eyes. I didn't know who Mia was, but there was a reasonable conclusion for his brother's actions.

"On some level it's possible he knows the truth. His flattery of me is probably just a way to convince you to his side."

I opened the door and he stood.

"You're wrong. You don't know my brother like I do."

He was right about that.

"Apparently, I don't know you either."

He sighed and stopped in front of me.

"It was a shitty move and I should have explained when my brother left." I said nothing. "I'm really sorry. And I hope you'll forgive me. Maybe we could be friends."

I didn't have a lot of those, but I wanted to be alone.

"Maybe," I said.

He gave a stiff nod and left. I closed the door and leaned back on it as a tear trickled down my face. What was wrong with me? I'd never done anything bad to anyone. Yet, every boy I'd ever dated had disappointed me. The only thing worse than what happened was sitting though Celeste grilling me about my night and being forced to tell her the truth. Her pity would be the icing on the cake.

As I closed my eyes, why did the image of the perfect guy standing drenched in the rain with lost eyes cross my mind? He was the last boy on Earth I should crush on.

14

Ashton

IF I DIDN'T HAVE to eat, I wouldn't go to the café. Seeing my friends only made me feel like an outsider looking in. But eating was imperative if I wanted to survive afternoon practice. Not that I cared much. The only reason I played was for Sawyer.

I looked up to see a big dude pointing a meaty finger at someone hidden from view by his bulk.

"You little shit," he said with a girl hanging onto one of his beefy arms urging him to go.

I almost didn't stop until I caught sight of the guy about to be pummeled with his glasses lying at his feet.

"I'm going to kick your ass," the guy declared.

"For just talking to her."

Bryant looked like he was going to shit himself. I cursed and sighed with resignation before moving to intercept what would be a killing blow.

"Westborough." I faced one of the linebackers on the team as he said, "Get the fuck out of the way so I can flatten the little douche bag."

The guy was juiced up on something more than rage. His red glazed eyes may have resembled a bull, but he was hopping on something.

"Let it go," I warned.

"The fuck I will."

Dude had a hundred pounds on me or more. He was built to stop tanks heading into war. Most would be afraid, but I'd faced far worse demons in my life.

"Walk away." It was my second warning. He had one more before I took action.

His Hulk-like expression curled in a half-smile.

"Please don't do this," the girl said in heavily accented English.

He ignored her, his focus solely on me. "What are you going to do about it?"

"Try me."

I didn't have to say last chance or anything like that. If he made a move, he would go down. That much I was sure of.

He dropped his arm from its former aim at Bryant.

"You know what, he's not worth it. Lucky you, I like Cargill or I would rearrange that pretty face of yours. But we all know he likes it." I got what he was implying but didn't take the bait. "He's captain, so you'll live another day." He faced his girl. "Come on."

After I was sure he wouldn't take a cheap shot, I turned and faced Bryant. He was still frozen in his spot. With the fear paralyzed on his face, I half-expected piss to be pooling at his feet. I scooped up his glasses and held them out to him.

When he didn't take them, I said, "He's gone."

He sort of blinked like he'd been caught in a waking nightmare. Finally, he reached for them and I dropped them in his palm.

A normal person might have patted him on the shoulder. Instead, I said before leaving, "Be careful next time."

That seemed to snap him out of it. He caught up to me spitting mad.

"Seriously. She asked me for directions." My brow rose. "She's an exchange student from Sweden." He kept going. "He wasn't around. Then he like materialized out of nowhere like Scotty beamed him there."

I didn't know who Scotty was. Probably one of those pop culture references lost on me because I didn't watch a lot of TV growing up.

"Ash." Chance, a former roommate of mine, stood three feet away. He glanced over at Bryant before asking, "Can I talk to you for a second?"

Bryant practically rolled his eyes. "It's cool. And you don't have to warn me." Then he mimicked a voice that wasn't mine but annoying nonetheless. "Stay away from bullies," he spat. As he looped off, he muttered, "I thought this was college, not high school."

"What's wrong with him?" Chance asked, hooking a thumb in Bryant's direction.

I shrugged. "Look, if you're here to talk to me about Sawyer, cap it."

"That's not why I want to talk to you. But since you mentioned it, something's going on with him. He hasn't been right since you left."

He'd said that to me before, many times. That didn't change what needed to happen. Sometimes friendships weren't meant to last forever.

"I don't think it's me. You saw what happened the other night."

Chance and I had to peel Sawyer off Shelly's boyfriend before he killed the guy.

"That's because the guy's a douche. And we both know Sawyer likes to save people."

That was true. He'd saved me, Chance, and countless others in lots of ways. His savior complex came from guilt for something that happened long ago that wasn't his fault. But the truth was, I could see how much Sawyer liked Shelly. More than anyone before.

"It's more than that."

Chance pondered that. "You think he's into her."

I nodded. "Now what did you want to talk about?"

More than anything I wanted the subject to change. We were nearing the café, and more than likely Sawyer would be there.

He stopped and shifted just off the walkway. I moved out of traffic near him. "So check it. Brie's birthday is coming up." He pulled a square velvet box from his back pocket. "It isn't exactly what I wanted to get her..." He shrugged.

Chance didn't have much. His mom had left and his father had reacted badly. The man barely held a job and spent most of his paycheck on booze trying to make peace with the past. That didn't leave much for anything. With Chance having a full foot-ball scholarship, he wasn't allowed to work.

"I just want her to know she means the world to me." He took a breath. "Anyway, I don't want her to find it in our room. Can you keep it for me?"

Brie had basically moved in. I nodded and took the box by the corner before palming it.

"Thanks, brother," he said.

I shoved it into my pocket in case we ran into Brie. We didn't, but Sawyer was there holding court with some tale.

The food was actually decent. After my tray was full, I said, "Later," to Chance.

"Come on," he said, hating the divide.

I gave him a two-finger salute and sat elsewhere. Sawyer was like a drug. Distance was the only way for me not to get sucked back in. I would always love the guy. He'd made the monsters go away. But it was like that saying, *when you love someone, sometimes it's best to let them go.*

That's what I intended to do.

After, I skipped class and made a run. I had no idea when Chance would be back for his box and there was something I needed to do. I drove outside of the small college town to a bigger one after running a search for a jewelry store.

I stood in the back with a man who wore a small magnifying glass over one eye.

"The quality of the stone, no good," he said with a slight accent.

The necklace Chance had gotten for his girl wasn't exactly cheap, but the tiny diamond pendant was little more than a speck of dust.

"I know, but I want to use it."

With money to burn, it would make good use to help a friend. Still, I didn't want to make him feel bad about his choice.

"Can you make it appear as if it's orbiting the gold center?"

Chance had said he wanted her to know she meant the world to him. I used that as an idea. I asked the jeweler to add a small gold disk about the size of a pencil eraser head.

He nodded. "I can add a tiny ring around with the diamond on it, like Saturn."

"Not exactly. More like the moon orbiting the Earth."

"I get it," he said, sounding enthusiastic.

"And can you add another diamond the same size of the other and embed into the gold."

"Better quality—yes."

"As long as it shines bright."

Chance looked at Brie with moon eyes all the time. Having the diamond Chance bought a little rough around the edges orbiting her brightness fit their story.

"I can do it and have to you tomorrow."

He quoted a price that made me blink. The diamond he was putting in had to be bigger than I requested. Ultimately, it didn't matter. Chance was one of the good ones. He hadn't deserved the life handed to him.

I nodded. "Fine. Call me when it's done."

I left and dreaded that I had to go to practice. When I got there, I didn't expect to run into the tiny girl who made me think of sunshine and angels. She was near the entrance to the athletic building and wasn't alone. Next to her stood her friend from the party who giggled every time she saw me. For a brief second, I thought Sunshine would smile. Instead, she frowned.

Why would I expect more? And why was I thinking about her in terms of more? The only person who'd smiled at me these days was that guy she was dating. I shook my head and entered the locker room door. I had to clear the craziness and get tire girl out of my thoughts.

15

Willow

LASHES LIKE BUTTERFLY wings fluttered before I realized I was staring. Could one person be that beautiful? Then I remembered Kent's admission and Celeste's warning and I frowned. Was Ashton also pretending to be something he wasn't?

His penetrating gaze lifted and met mine. My belly flopped like a fish out of water, flattening my smile and morphing it into a glower. Only he turned, his glacial gaze no longer leaving me frozen in place.

"Let's go," I begged.

Why had I let her talk me into coming? Of course, I'd run into him. No, that hadn't been a secret goal. That was a nose growing lie. There was something about him that drew me in like a blue flame. I was as helpless as a fly captured by the black light that surrounded him. He was a mystery I wanted to solve.

"Come on. He should be here soon."

It wasn't long when the object of Celeste's stalking showed his pretty face. Sawyer Cargill, shameless man-whore, had arrived.

His well-gotten reputation lived in infamy, which was saying something in a school this big. One could attend school here all four years and not know half the people you would graduate with.

Celeste was like the rest of the girls hanging around yelling his name at him like he was some movie star walking the red carpet.

"Sawyer," she called, waving her goodies at him.

That being a bag of freshly made cookies she'd baked for him.

"Hey, sweetheart. What'd you have for me?"

She froze in gawking mode. Saving her, I plucked the bag from her hand and gave it to him.

"Cookies," I said, masking my annoyance with a smile.

"Nice." He winked and said, "Thank you," before disappearing inside.

She still hadn't moved, staring at the closing door.

"Can we go now?" I complained. "I have class."

Her eyes blinked once and then twice before she snapped out of it, turning the tables on me.

"We can if you tell me what happened on your date."

I'd managed to deflect her every question yesterday, claiming I had to study.

"Can we talk about this later? I'm going to be late. Besides, you got what you wanted. He has your cookies."

I wasn't able to stop a bubble of laughter escaping me when I said that last part.

"And my number," she said, looping her arm in mine as we headed toward the main quad of campus.

"You didn't?" I asked, knowing her answer.

"I did."

She didn't sound the least bit ashamed.

"Really, you could have any guy you wanted. Why him?"

Her hand lifted, and she began to count off his many virtues.

"He's more than a snack for one."

Cue the heavy eye roll. "Don't give me that five course meal business."

She shrugged. "He is gorgeous, and there are rumors..."

She didn't go there. The last thing I wanted to think about was Sawyer's man parts.

I coughed in my hand. "Rumors he's a man-whore."

She only gave me an evil side-eye before her smile returned.

"He's never had a girlfriend," she countered.

"And you think you'll be the one?"

I got the *duh* glare next.

"He's utterly rich," she added.

"Like you've ever wanted for anything in your life."

"Him," she said unrepentantly.

"You're better than him."

She stopped mid-stride, pulling me with her.

"Like you're better than his friend." I looked like someone who should have hooted for the size my eyes got. She'd caught me looking at him? She answered like she read my mind. "Yeah, I saw you staring. But trust me when I say don't go there."

Really, I wanted to say. Like she wasn't delusional over Sawyer? But I didn't want to fight. I had to get to class. At least I knew I had no shot with him, gay or not. That didn't mean I couldn't look.

"You're right." I backed down so she'd release her death hold on me. I was already seeing half-moons her claws had dug into my skin.

"Celeste," I begged.

Only her attention had already shifted to a guy who stood several feet away. He didn't wave or smile. Then again, he didn't have to. He was more than a snack. The guy was a smoke show. I had to admit, scenery around campus was amazing.

"Look, I have to go," she said, her eyes never leaving the blond hottie.

Seriously, she was ditching me. Then again, another classic

Celeste move. It didn't matter that she'd dragged me across campus.

"Who's that?" I asked.

She gave me that look like *now's not the time.* "Taylor, if you must know. I'll talk to you later."

Selfish Celeste was back. She strode off and walked past the guy as if she didn't see him. He smirked at me before following her.

Who was Taylor?

I shook it off and doubled-timed it the half mile to class. I was so going to be late. I pushed through my classroom door, only to have everyone turn to stare in my direction.

Talk about moth to a flame. I felt the heat from embarrassment burn a path all over my body. I dropped my head, but not before I caught Derek giving me an apologetic glance.

I dropped in my seat and tried to make myself as small as possible, slouching way down. I didn't relish attention and prayed my professor wouldn't call me out.

"As I was saying. We've had another theft. I'm not sure what value there is for a live dragonfly. It's most likely some sort of prank. Since I have a large shipment of donated butterflies from the Smithsonian Museum coming on Friday, I've had a camera installed in the storeroom. In addition, the lab will now be locked sooner. After my last class in fact. For those that have ongoing projects, you will be given an additional access code to the specimen room."

That was when I noticed the new keypad lock on the storeroom door.

She continued to drone on as I thought about my next move. She was wrong about a dragonfly's worth. All life was precious. Who were we to play God with another creature's life? I get studying the dead. That had been a practice for centuries and how we learned about humanity. But studying the living, that was another story.

If a shipment of live butterflies arrived, I wouldn't be able to sit back and do nothing. They had such a short life. Was it fair for them to live the rest of it in captivity?

I wasn't a zealot. The Smithsonian had a habitat made for butterflies that allowed them a semblance of living free. Here they would be kept in glass enclosures that were nothing like living in the real world.

"I'm sorry, Willow."

At some point class had ended as I sat formulating a plan. Derek stood there with a bucket load of sympathy in his gray stare.

I shrugged. "You can't save them all."

"Maybe—"

I shook my head. No way would I drag him into the trouble I'd be in if I did anything to save the world or the little bit I could.

"It's okay. You've got to know when you're beat, right?" I said.

His lips pursed. "Do you want to grab a coffee?"

Was he asking me out?

"I—" What should I say? He wasn't a bad guy, cute even. We had a lot in common. "Sure. But can we do it tomorrow?"

His face beamed, and I smiled back. Too bad for me I didn't get the kind of flutters I got when I looked at the nameless boy.

"Okay. Tomorrow," he agreed.

I nodded at him and he nodded back. We stood there for another awkward moment before we laughed and then he left. I sat there for another minute or two. Was I really going to put myself out there again? Why the hell not? It would be easy to sit at home with a tub of ice cream and complain.

I tucked my bag to my chest and let my smile grow. Derek was cute. I even got a little excited as I grabbed a snack from The Coffee Shack on my way home.

It was quicker to cut through the parking lot than to walk the path. So why did a roar of an engine and the driver behind the wheel scare the ever-living skin off my body?

16

Ashton

PRACTICE HAD ENDED EARLY. And dammit, everything Chance had said to me made me feel guilty. I fisted my hand and punched the steering wheel, not believing what I was about to do. But I turned the key anyway.

My knuckles throbbed, and the pain cleared my thoughts. What was I really angry about? I owed Sawyer everything. I could suck it up and deal to help him out. I wasn't going to end up as selfish as my mother.

I hit the gas and immediately slammed on the brake. The car rocked forward, but stopped before hitting the girl who stood wide-eyed.

Shifting into park, I jumped out the driver's side door.

"Shit, are you okay?"

Her shell-shocked expression only doubled when she saw me. She kept a white-knuckle grip on the books clutched to her chest like she was cold. Her lashes fluttered a second before her focus crystalized on me.

"I'm fine."

I shouldn't have said it, but it popped out of my mouth as soon as the thought formed. "Are you following me?"

She seemed to be everywhere I was. And for some strange reason, I couldn't shut up around her.

Her momentary confusion solidified and flatlined her lips.

"Following you? Ego much?"

I opened my mouth, but caught the stray words before I made a bigger fool of myself. She read something else in my silence and snorted.

"Of course, you do. You're used to girls throwing themselves at you, I suppose." She unfolded her hand to reveal a key fob. Then she used her thumb to press a button. A car across the way and a few down chirped.

Stop being an asshole and say something. Normally, I didn't speak because there was nothing worth saying. That wasn't the case around her. This girl just confused me.

Her chest rose before she blew out a long breath. "Look, I've been meaning to tell you thank you for helping me. But a little advice. Even if I liked you—which I don't—I wouldn't bother. It's obvious to everyone you have a thing for Sawyer. You should just tell him."

She sauntered away as I held in growing rage. My friends had thrown similar words in my face and now they'd been used against me by a virtual stranger. *Damn you, Sawyer.*

Just as I got into my car, my phone rang.

Julie.

She was the quintessential girl next door and the first girl Sawyer loved. By the time Sawyer made his move, she'd admitted to me that I was her choice.

For a space of time, I thought I loved her too. But when I chose Sawyer's friendship over a shot with her, I realized that my feelings were just a mirror of his. After she was gone, I hadn't missed her at all.

I answered the call.

"Hey."

"Ash, how is everything?"

She called every so often. Her timing sucked today.

"I'm in the car."

It was a lame attempt at avoiding the question and would hopefully cut the conversation short.

"Going to see him."

Though she hadn't snapped out the words, I could hear the disappointment loud and clear. I wanted to hang up the phone, but I'd known her almost as long as I'd known Sawyer. She was the next best thing to family I had.

"Does it matter?"

My statement was little more than a whisper as the little hybrid pulled out carrying the irritating but interesting blonde as she drove off.

Julie's pitying voice brought me back to the conversation.

"It does because I know how much it hurts you."

My grip tightened on the phone. Why the fuck did everyone think they knew me or what I was feeling?

On an exhale, I said, "I have to go."

"Wait!"

I held the phone, but stayed silent. What did that say about me? The people I cared about had some kind of fucking power over me. I had Mother to thank for that.

"Ash, I want to see you."

My eyes closed, and it felt like my heartbeat slowed. Her coming around could only cause Sawyer pain. Though I wasn't sure how he felt about her anymore. We rarely spoke her name.

Teeth grinding, I said, "That's not a good idea."

"Why? Sawyer's surely moved on by now."

It was possible. Sawyer's new target was Shelly. That didn't mean his feelings for Julie had died.

"I can't."

Her reply was quick, like she'd had her rebuttal planned. "I stayed away and gave Sawyer a chance to do right by you. But he'll never love you the way I do."

She might as well had backhanded me like Mother did anytime I dared speak out of turn.

"I have to go."

This time I didn't wait. I hung up, rude or not. I didn't want to hurt her feelings. The truth was, I'd never loved her. Then it hit me. Sawyer probably felt the same way about me. He didn't want to hurt my feelings either. We were some sort of messed-up triangle. Sawyer loved Julie. Julie loved me. And I... The thought was too hard to process. But it made it easier to drive over to the townhouse.

I should have known better. When I arrived, Sawyer wasn't alone. No surprise there. The challenge in his eyes as he invited me to join his little sexcapade did me in as it always did. He was the ringmaster of his little circus, and I performed like he expected.

When I awoke, it took me a few seconds to recall where I was. It wasn't my room or Sawyer's. But I was definitely still in the townhouse. I turned my head. Sawyer took up most of the bed. I was glad he'd gotten the girls to leave shortly after everything we'd done.

He hadn't stirred as I headed for the bathroom. I needed a shower. The stinging hot water didn't make me feel clean. I scrubbed until my skin was red and raw, but I still felt dirty.

17

Willow

IT HAD BEEN A FEW DAYS, but my thoughts trailed back to the boy. Had I really said those things to him?

I should probably apologize. In truth, I was pissed at Kent. I'd been excited about going on a date with a cute boy, only to find out he wasn't interested in me.

"Willow." Celeste waved a hand in front of me. "Did you even hear what I said?"

I focused on her and shook my head. "I'm sorry. What did you say?"

The warm mug of coffee heated my chilled hands as she opened her mouth. A knock sounded, silencing whatever she'd been about to say.

"I'll get it," she announced and pranced over to the door in a shirt that barely covered her bottom.

Was she expecting company? It was Friday morning, but one never knew with Celeste.

When the door opened, the person standing there was

hidden behind a large bouquet. Immediately, my mind scrambled for what date had I missed. Was it her birthday? Or maybe that guy she left with the other day was sending her flowers? What secret was she keeping this time?

"These are gorgeous," she said, reaching for the stunning crystal vase they sat in.

There were flowers of various colors and species. Tulips, roses, pansies, and more. It was a hodgepodge of beautiful that forced you to smile.

Kent's face popped around the side. "And they're for Willow." He gave me hound dog eyes. "I'm so sorry. I hope you can forgive me."

I wasn't one to harbor ill will toward anyone and didn't immediately tell him to get out as he walked toward me. Mom insisted that being angry caused wrinkles. It's probably why I could get along with Celeste.

"Please don't hate me," he said, setting down the vase on the kitchen counter near where I rested my elbows.

"I don't hate you. I hate what you did."

His head bobbed. "I screwed up. But I still want us to be friends."

I sipped the coffee. We'd never been friends. I could easily say no. But I didn't have it in me. "Fine, but if you ever do something like that again..."

What was I going to threaten?

"I won't. I swear. Let me take you to dinner later and then we could go to the concert."

The rained-out one had been rescheduled for tonight.

Celeste stood a few feet behind him with raised eyebrows, waiting for my response.

"Yeah, okay."

It looked like he let out a breath he'd been holding as he held a hand over his heart. Then he came over, bent down, and kissed my cheek.

"Thank you."

I nodded.

"I'll call you later."

As he moved toward the door, I said, "I still don't have a phone."

He looked at me and then at Celeste. She pursed her lips and shrugged.

"Seven then?" he asked.

"Sure."

Once the door closed, Celeste dug into me. "I can't believe you won't just tell Dad to get you another phone."

She said it like it was no big deal. And maybe for her it wouldn't be. But Mom didn't work. It was his money paying for everything. Whether or not Celeste and Mom believed it, he wasn't exactly a fan of mine. He put up with me. I wasn't driven enough, and my choice of career path didn't meet his expectations. Mom had won the battle on that one. Still, I had student loans to look forward to paying after college. At least he co-signed to help me get them.

"It's okay." I lifted my shoulders and let them fall. "It'll turn up."

As much as I knew Mom loved me, there hadn't been an urgent call to my sister looking for me because her calls had gone unanswered.

"Do you have a date tonight?" I asked.

It was a good way to change the subject. There was nothing Celeste liked talking about more than herself.

"I'm hanging out with someone." The gorgeous guy with the delicious smirk came to mind. *Taylor*, I thought. "Though it's not a date."

"Maybe you should give up on Sawyer," I advised.

She glared daggers at me and I held up my hands in surrender. Then I picked up my abandoned coffee mug and poured the cooling drink down the drain.

"I've got to get ready for class."

I made it to the bathroom and was closing the door as she followed after me.

"Wait."

I didn't and grinned. For once, I'd snagged the bathroom first. I turned on the shower and ignored Celeste's protest. It was our apartment. Though I'd given her reign the last three years, today would be my day.

Besides, if all went right, I might get arrested and so be it. Tonight I planned to free the butterflies.

I thought about the beautiful bouquet of colorful blooms Kent brought me. And a stupid fantasy of a boy who enjoyed standing in the rain bloomed in my head. Why couldn't I get him out of my mind? Even if he played for my team, he was totally out of my league.

18

Past

WE WERE TALKING in the kitchen when Mother came downstairs.

"Sawyer," she said dryly. "Why are you here?"

She didn't hide the distain in her voice.

My best friend's grin only widened.

"Ms. W., you're looking good."

I could have choked as Mother rolled her eyes.

"You can go now."

My breath hitched. I wasn't ready for him to leave.

"But Ms. W., Ash invited me to stay over tonight." I had made no such offer. Panic clawed at my throat as I could feel Mother's glare on the back of my neck. "You know, to watch the playoffs."

"Ashton knows better. We have company tonight." Though that was true, Sawyer was never allowed to stay over... ever. "I'm going to run to the store. You need to be gone when I return."

I carefully kept my eyes averted. I didn't want to catch her punishing gaze. Sawyer had no idea the hell I would pay for his careless words.

"Bro, what's up with your mom? She's kind of scary most days, but damn if I didn't get a chill just now. What's her deal? Why can I never stay over?"

We'd been friends six years, and I'd dodged this bullet that entire time. Whenever he asked to spend the night at my house, I made an excuse why his house would be better. He had all the gaming equipment. There was no TV in my room. He'd understood or so I thought.

"She has a thing tonight."

"So? It's adult shit, right? Wouldn't it be better if I kept you company?"

Slowly, I shook my head. Tonight, *he* was coming.

"Fine, stay over at my house," he offered.

Sawyer had never pushed me to talk about anything. Why today? It felt like my Adam's apple doubled in size blocking my vocal cords.

"I can't," I managed to say.

"Why the fuck not?"

Sawyer didn't get it, and I didn't blame him.

"You have to go."

I closed my eyes, hating the weakness that overcame me. My will had been beaten out of me years ago. When I opened my eyes, they landed on the basement door.

Sawyer stepped in my line of vision. "What the fuck?" He turned and looked at the door. "What's down there? Is there some creepy dungeon?"

It was a prison of sorts. It just didn't have bars. Darkness held me in place.

"Ash." He was right there, holding my gaze and pinning me in place. "You can tell me."

"You have to go," I repeated. "Please."

The last was little more than a strangled whisper. I didn't want to tell him my shame. He was the only friend I had in the world, and I couldn't lose him because of my secret.

"If you don't tell me, I'll tell my parents your mom is into freaky shit. The cops and child services will show up."

His threat would come to nothing. My first year in school, child services had been called. My teacher said I was withdrawn. But it was when I pissed myself when the gym teacher put his hand on my shoulder that the school thought something wasn't right.

"Don't do this," I begged softly.

Hurt filled my eyes with moisture. Sawyer had been my safe place. He'd never made me feel uncomfortable before.

"I have to. You're shaking, and you look like a fucking corpse. You're looking past me as if I'm not here. Like that day I found you lying on the ground in the rain."

He sounded haunted. That day had been a blessing for me but a curse for him. After everything that happened, I was surprised he remained my friend.

I pushed away the memory. Recalling the squeal of tires and the sounds of his brother's screams wouldn't do either of us any good.

"They won't find anything. You'll just get me in more trouble."

Mother was good at causing pain mentally and physically, leaving only invisible scars.

"What trouble? Because I was at your house. You know that sounds crazy, right?"

He wasn't going to let up. I had to give him something so he would understand.

"For saying I asked you to spend the night."

His brows knitted together as confusion scrunched his expression.

"What is the big deal with me staying over? I get your mom is weird and super strict. But why..."

His mad math skills were adding things up as his words trailed off the path.

"Who's coming over tonight?" he demanded.

I shrugged because I honestly didn't know the guest list.

"But they aren't just coming to see her."

He isn't going to let this go, I told myself as I gave him a stiff nod.

"A girl?" But he knew better. He didn't wait a beat before moving on. "A woman?" There was hope in his eyes, but it dulled when I said nothing. "A guy? Someone's son coming over." That time he waited. Slowly, I swayed my head side to side.

"What. The. Fuck?"

That was what? The second or third time he'd said that. Each time he had it was like he was speaking different words as the meanings changed. That time had been slow and methodically as he finished the equation in his head.

He grabbed my shoulders and forced me to meet his gaze. His Adam's apple bobbed as he swallowed.

"No judgment, okay." He meant it. However, if I answered, would he still be my friend? I trusted him and nodded. "Do you want this?"

I hadn't expected that question.

"No."

Silently, he affirmed my answer. "Who is this asshole?"

So I told him what I knew, which was little. He was a wealthy judge from our district. Though he might have recognized the name, Sawyer was probably clueless on how the guy looked.

"Is he taller than you?"

"A little."

I wasn't sure where he was going with this.

"Good. I'll be back."

I sputtered out, "You can't."

"I can. It ends tonight."

He left, and I believed he'd be back. Later that night as I lay in bed, I kept looking at my closet thinking about the stories of monsters who lurked there.

My door opened, and I closed my eyes against the bright light that streamed in like a beacon from the hall.

"There you are."

The voice was like sharpened nails scraping over my skin.

"God, you're such a beautiful boy," he slurred as he walked into my room, closing the door behind him. "My wife would never understand."

He drew back my covers and found me flat on my stomach. I couldn't look at him. Fear and hate canceled each other, leaving me frozen in the space between the now and unreality.

"You are so pretty."

His rough fingers drew a path from my neck down, stopping to squeeze the little flesh that didn't cover bone.

"Ashton. Time to wake up. I can't wait to be inside you."

When he attempted to roll me onto my back, something came over me.

I came up swinging, connecting with his jaw. He stumbled back, tripping over his feet and landing on his ass.

"What the fuck?" he spluttered.

My irrational response to him was a borderline crazy laugh. The way he'd spoken the phrase Sawyer repeatedly said earlier now took on yet another translation.

He got to his feet, all gentleness gone from him.

"I suggest you turn around, boy. I paid a lot for that pretty ass, and I intend to get my money's worth." I lifted my chin, prepared to fight until he spoke his next words. "Besides, we both know you like it as much as I do. Your dick is always hard in my hands."

Shame was a paralyzing agent. My limbs locked up and my chin drooped. He came for me and I could do nothing.

Just as his hand cupped me to prove his point, a loud thwack sent him tumbling to the floor with his pants tangling him up. I hadn't heard him unzip them, but they were bunched around his calves as he wrapped an arm around his chest.

I wish I could say it was me who'd saved myself. But it was my avenging angel. Sawyer stood there with a baseball bat in a pose taken from a batter after hitting a home run.

"Keep your fucking hands off of him, you sick fuck," Sawyer roared.

"I think you broke my ribs, you punk," the devil wheezed.

"You better be glad that's all I did."

"What is going on?"

We turned, taking our eyes off the monster, though I heard fabric scooting over the floor.

"Call the police. That little shit assaulted me."

Sawyer cocked his head as if pondering the devil's request to Mother.

"It's actually battery. Most think assault because of cop shows, but that's more verbal. The threat, you know. Battery is physical. The act. So really it's assault and battery," Sawyer said, dripping with sarcasm. "And I'd think you'd know that with your fancy law degree, judge."

Mother cool as always said, "Why are you here, Sawyer? I think that's called breaking and entering."

He laughed. "And here I thought you would be concerned that this man has been molesting your son. But I guess what he said about paying you for the privilege is true."

"That would be none of your business."

Mother pulled a phone from her pocket. Sawyer too pulled something from his.

As Mother dialed, Sawyer did something and a recording began to play. I glanced at the monster as his words replayed. I recoiled as he called me beautiful. He liked to call me that a lot when he hurt me.

"That's called an iPhone. Dad likes to keep me up on the latest technology. So go ahead, call the police."

Mother made a move toward him. "Don't think about it. I have no problem bashing your head in. Hell, we could make it look like he killed you and we came to your rescue, but it was too late."

It was almost scary how serious he sounded. Mother paused.

"Let's call the police." As her lips curved up, I knew we were fucked. "But you know as well as I do, if I go down, he'll be taken away. Foster homes are riddled with predators. How will you save him then?"

"Yeah, she's right," the monster said, still huddled on the floor.

I'd heard this speech. Mother even showed me news stories of kids being rescued from places like that. She coined the phrase, *the devil you know is better than the one you don't.*

Sawyer wearily glanced at me as if in apology, then he turned his focus back on her.

"This is how it will work." He aimed the bat at the devil. "You will never touch him again or this goes to all the news stations." He pointed at Mother. "You will never pimp out your son again."

Mother's lack of expression never changed. "No police then."

"Not yet. But your continued freedom relies on his happiness."

"I can barely breathe," the devil said.

Sawyer gestured with the bat toward the door. "Take him to the hospital. Tell them what you like." He shrugged. "I have no problem telling the truth." He waved the small boxy phone with his free hand. "I have proof at my side."

Mother's cutting stare didn't affect Sawyer like it did me.

"Get up," she snapped at the man.

With her help, he stood, stooped over some, still covering the right side of his ribs with one massive hand. The one he liked to paw at me with.

I didn't exhale until I heard the front door close. I slumped on the bed, the weight of what happened pulling me down. Sawyer sat next to me and slung an arm around my shoulder.

In his eyes, I saw the kind of love I'd wanted from my mother all my life, unconditional and unyielding.

Tears spilled from my eyes, unbidden and unwanted. He said nothing to acknowledge them or shame me for them. He tucked my head on his shoulder as we stared at the open doorway.

"No one will ever hurt you again."

I believed and trusted him like no one before. But the truth was, I would be hurt again. Less than ten years in the future, he would be the one wielding the sword aimed at me.

19

Ashton

MY FINGERS BURNED as they always did after a particularly bad nightmare. I lost hours typing fast and furiously changing my past into fiction I could control. There was strength in words. Mine came more easily on the page.

My mouth was dry, and I felt the pangs of hunger, but I couldn't stop. I was caught up in the flow of the story as it unfolded on the screen.

My protagonist was Agni, a boy of seven, whose mother left him in the woods to save him from the dragons that were raiding their town. There he met Sujah, a boy no older than he, but there was a difference. One was fearful of the future. The other was fearless. After years of surviving on their own, they stumble into a dragon's lair.

A tap on my bare shoulder as I sat in boxers was like a lightning bolt. I struggled to hold in my reaction as I tugged off my headphones and turned. The door stood open, and I chastised myself for not locking it.

I gave Bryant my attention.

He held out something to me and told me one of our frat brothers told him to give it to me.

"Why?" I asked, turning it around in my hand.

"I don't know. Why do they do anything?"

"Thanks," I said to Bryant.

It wasn't his fault our frat brothers were idiots. Only he didn't leave. He sat on my bed.

"I asked her out."

Oh, so he was looking for advice.

"And?"

"And I'm not really sure. She didn't give me a clear answer."

His crestfallen expression soothed my eagerness to have him gone.

"You have a choice, give up or try again."

"Easy for you to say," he snapped. "The thing is coming with the thing."

He sounded moronic only because I'd warned him not to mention the Vanderbilt Club. He referred to initiation night.

"I'm pretty sure there will be women, lots of them, at least one for each of us. If I try again and she says yes, I wouldn't be able to go through with it." I shrugged. "It's not that I wouldn't be willing to give up going. But what if she only agrees to go out with me to be nice? And then I might have missed a chance, you know."

"Decide what's more important. One night with this chick or a night with some nameless girl who's probably doing it for all the wrong reasons."

He straightened and pointed to me. "You're right." He got to his feet. "Thanks."

My door clicked shut on his exit. Too bad all the words that had filled my head had quieted. Whatever I was writing was done for the night. I saved and closed my laptop. I could hear the muffled music when it was turned on.

Partiers had arrived.

I wanted quiet for the night. I pulled on jeans and put on a ball cap. I hoped to slide out into the night and blend in. I got into my car with no destination in mind and ended up on campus. Hunger led me to the café, but I was too late. It was closed.

When my first thought was to call Sawyer, I sat on a bench. That was the rut I was trying to get out of. He didn't need me. Why did I need him?

Around me the quad sat empty. Intermittent lampposts dotted the landscape, marking the paths and interrupting the darkness around me. It was the quiet that enticed me to stay.

I thought about Mother's house, rather my house. How many days had I longed for someone to talk to? These days, I fought to be alone. Funny how life turned out.

Quick almost silent footsteps caught my attention. I watched as someone entered one of the buildings. I wasn't sure if it was the shape and build or the strand of freed blonde hair like a floating arrow that had me following.

The shadowy hall was empty as I entered. I stood for a second listening for the sound of the church mouse I'd followed.

She was light on her feet, but the squeak of her sneakers on the tile floor as she came to a quick stop gave her away.

I too knew how to be silent. It was a skill born out of survival.

When I rounded the corner, she was entering a code into the keypad lock on the door.

I leaned on the wall with my arms folded, amused at her muttered curses when the pad flashed red.

"Breaking and entering."

The girl jumped a mile, clutching at her chest as if stopping her heart from bursting out of it.

"No—I mean, yes. Are you following me?" she spluttered.

I quirked a brow because she was amusing to watch.

"Call me a concerned student. You know, with crime on the rise."

Her jaw dropped, and I managed to suppress a laugh.

"I'm not a criminal," she said with her chin lifted. Then just as quickly, her eyes dropped to the floor. "Okay, maybe. But it's for a good cause."

Normally, I wasn't one to engage in conversation. My words were my own. But with her, they spat out like rapid gunfire.

"Saving the world?" I asked.

It was meant as a joke, but fierce eyes met mine.

"Maybe. They deserve to be free."

I narrowed my eyes, not sure where she was going with this. Then again, it was probably not her but old memories creeping out of the darkness and locked doors in my mind.

"Who?" I lashed the word out like a crack of a whip.

"It's not people or animals. And you may think I'm crazy, but insects have a right to live free too."

At first, I wasn't sure what to make of the girl. But there was passion that could rally troops in the way she spoke.

"What's your plan?"

My tiny warrior stood straight.

"Why? Are you going to turn me in?"

Her determination reminded me of someone else, but I pushed thoughts of my former best friend back into the closet.

"I might help."

That caught her by surprise. She stopped with her lips rounded as she'd been about to speak.

"I don't need help. I have the codes to get in."

There was something more. She'd been shaking like a leaf when she tried to unlock the door.

"Why are you so nervous then?"

"They've added cameras because someone might have freed other creatures from their cages."

She chewed at the corner of her lip as if I wouldn't guess the someone was her.

"And you think by wearing black and trying to tuck all of this —" I took the wayward strand of hair between my fingers and tugged the springy curl just enough so she could see it. "That no one will put together based on your size that it's not you."

She freed her lower lip and it protruded in a pout.

"What else am I supposed to do?"

I too was wearing all black. I turned my cap around and pulled the bill low to create shadows over my face.

"Tell me what to do and I'll do it for you."

Her mouth gaped. "You would do that?"

Why was I offering to commit a potential felony? A hint of a smile took root on her face and I knew not why, but that I would.

"Why not? You don't look like the sort of girl who would do well behind bars."

Her smile vanished as worry took over.

"And you would?"

I'd never been in jail. "I've had my share of bad experiences. Don't worry, I won't corrupt you." I pointed to the door. "Unlock and tell me what to get."

Her instructions were simple.

"I'll unlock the storage room and you free anything that's living."

I nodded and this time she unlocked the door easily.

Before she stepped into the room, I held up my hand.

"Wait. Is it possible they put cameras in the classroom?"

Her eyes widened as she took in the possibility. "I don't know honestly."

"So you stay here. Give me the code and I'll go rescue the prisoners."

Long lashes swept down as her gaze found the floor again.

"I feel bad. I should be doing this. I don't even know your name."

It had felt so easy talking to this girl, I hadn't even thought about the fact that I didn't know hers.

"Ash—ton."

I didn't know why I added the last part.

"Ashton?" Her eyes cast upward and locked on mine. There was something sweet when she said my name. When I silently acknowledged her question, she added, "I'm Willow."

"Well, Willow. Give me the code and let me launch this prison break."

There was weary reluctance on her face, but she finally gave me the code.

The classroom was dark except for the moonlight filtering in through the open windows. I used the slight illumination to navigate the room outfitted like a science lab. That made sense. I wound my way through the maze of high tables and ended up at a door in the back of the room and keyed in the code.

"Here goes nothing."

20

Willow

I COULDN'T KEEP STILL. It took longer than I expected it to. Would we be caught? And why was he helping me? It didn't make sense. Ashton...

His name sounded regal and as beautiful as he was. Then he appeared with nothing in his hand. Wait—his hand was covering something. Where were the butterflies? Then again, my poor instructions had been to bring out anything alive.

When he lifted one hand off the other, I jumped back, covering my mouth.

"This was the only thing alive in there."

My hands tented over my gaping mouth.

"We need to put it back," I said gently.

My breathing was a little ragged, but I tried to keep it under control.

"What's wrong?"

I looked at the hairy creature that nearly covered his palm.

"That's a tarantula. A venomous tarantula."

He didn't seem at all concerned. Though there had been no cases of human fatality from a bite, I couldn't chance letting it free.

Scared as I was, I held out my hand.

"You want me to put it back?" he asked, sounding utterly calm.

"I can. You've done enough. It was wrong of me to ask you to help me."

"You keep saying that, but I'm not complaining. I'll put it back."

"Her, not it. And I'll need to help you. Though she can't kill you, it still could be really bad." I stared at the docile creature. "Just don't jostle her."

I re-entered the code and walked in. I wouldn't leave him to do my dirty work. Plus, I didn't want him to get bitten. So I stood in plain sight of the camera and lifted the cage lid completely so he could easily put his entire hand in.

"Please be careful."

He nodded and slowly put his hand down. The spider didn't move for a second, and then crawled off and over to the small tree branch in the habitat she called home. I exhaled and covered the cage.

We said nothing and left. I'd given the room a cursory glance and didn't see the butterflies the professor said would be there.

Back out in the hall, I faced Ashton.

"Thank you."

I lifted on my toes, bracing my hands on his shoulders so I could plant a kiss on his cheek. I felt him stiffen too late to stop myself. I quickly let go and wished for a hole to crawl into.

"Thank you," I said again.

When he didn't respond, I looked up and found stone in his gaze. I rubbed my arms, longing for warmth even though it wasn't cold out.

"I'm—I'm sorry. I—I shouldn't have..." What shouldn't I have done? "We should go—" Did that sound like an invitation? "I should go. Thank you again. And don't worry, I won't mention your name."

His brow shot up. "My name?"

"I'm on camera. I'm sure they'll question me. But it's okay. We didn't take anything."

I'd made the mistake of looking for it when I walked in. My face had been far too visible. His hadn't been.

"You don't have to lie for me. I knew what I was getting into," he said.

I shook my head. "There is no way I would jeopardize your academic career for my crusade. Anyway, I should get back to my..."

Date was the wrong word. More importantly, I didn't want him to think I was on one. Why?

"Your—?"

"To the concert."

Stupid me had thought it was a good cover for me to slip out when Kent started talking to another guy. Clearly, I'd watched too many thrillers. I wasn't a spy or good covert agent.

Get moving, Willow. I willed myself to go, but my feet were super glued to the spot. His eyes held me with their long lashes. And why was it that guys had Maybelline eyelashes minus the makeup. It was totally unfair.

Just as I managed to pivot around, he said my name.

I swallowed before turning back around. He held something out to me.

"My phone," I said, practically lunging forward and swiping it from his hand. "Where did you find it?" I blinked. The answer was obvious. "Sorry, the frat house obviously. Thanks."

He nodded and finally I walked away. I wanted to hug him, but there was just something in his rigid posture that warned me I'd gone too far with the kiss. It had to be true then. He wasn't into girls, not that I would have a chance with a guy like him.

I tried to turn on my phone, but it was dead in the water. I shoved it into my back pocket and quickly walked across campus to where the outdoor concert was being held.

The music still played, but the crowd had thinned some. How long had I been gone? Kent stood facing the stage alone drinking from a long neck.

"Hey," I said.

"Where have you been?"

I shrugged it off. "Getting into trouble. How about you? Things didn't work out with that guy?"

As he launched into a diatribe of words, I couldn't get Ashton out of my head. *Don't be stupid*, I berated myself again. But every time I thought of him, my stomach did summersaults.

"Willow?"

I glanced up. Kent stood there looking at me.

"I'm sorry. Did you ask me a question?"

He smiled. "I talk too much, huh?"

I rubbed my arms, feeling a chill that wasn't there.

"No, it's not you. I guess I'm tired."

"Are you ready to go?"

"Kind of. Are you mad?"

"No, it's cool. I had a good time."

"Yeah, it was fun."

I stared out the window for the short ride to my apartment. Kent kissed my cheek, and I stiffened wondering if Ashton had felt the same. It wasn't that I hated it. It was because I was no longer attracted to Kent that way now that I knew there could never be an us.

"Thanks again for dinner," I said.

"I'll call you." He laughed. "I guess I mean I'll see you since you don't have a phone."

Before I knew it, I pulled it out and waved it in front of me. "Actually, I found it."

"You did."

"Well, someone did and gave it to me."

"Cool. I'll call you then."

I hopped out of the car, grateful when Celeste wasn't at home. I took a shower and forced myself to stop obsessing over a certain boy. Why me? Why did I have to like a guy who was so off limits? I'd easily accepted Kent for who he was. Then again, Kent hadn't looked at me like Ashton did. I couldn't explain it. It was like he really cared about what I had to say. And no, Ashton hadn't checked me out. I was being really dumb. I got in the shower and tried to forget about it.

After I finished and dressed, I went into the living room to find Celeste staring at something red in her hand while tracing something gold on it with her finger.

"What's that?"

She glanced up with a little jolt as if she hadn't noticed me come in.

"This is for you."

The envelope she held out to me felt like an omen the way her hand shook a little. I took it, but didn't open it right away.

"What is it?"

The long lashes she'd added to her eyes fanned down as she looked away from me.

"It's an invitation."

It was clear she wasn't happy about it. I still didn't glance down at it, keeping my eyes on her.

"From whom?" She shrugged and half-turned, but I wasn't letting it go. "Celeste, what's going on? Where did you get this?"

"It's an invitation to a Sigma party, all right. A courier dropped it off."

"A courier?" I asked in confusion.

She spun around. "A pledge all dressed up, okay."

A pledge. My brain was still a little foggy when I put the words *pledge* and *Sigma* together. That was when I glanced down. The envelope had a wax seal. The crest of the Sigma house was branded into it. I flipped the envelope over to see my name written in perfect calligraphy script.

"Open it already." Her words were no long timid. She sounded pissed with a dose of jealousy. "Clearly, you've been invited to one of their exclusive parties."

I sat because nerves got the best of me.

"We can go together," I said as I slipped a fingernail under a corner of the wax.

"It doesn't work that way," Celeste said sharply.

"Then I won't go. Sister solidarity and all that."

"Of course, you will."

Bitterness laced her every word, but there was determination behind it.

"It's just a dumb party," I said.

Her laugh came out half-choked. "The Sigmas are the future leaders of our world. If one of them invited you, it could be because they really like you or...?"

I waited a beat, hoping she'd finish. "Or what?"

"Or someone wants to bang you."

Her words weren't a surprise, yet they stole my breath anyway.

"Which is it?" I asked as if she had all the answers.

"I don't know. You tell me. Who have you been dating?"

She hurled the question at me like an accusation. Yet my mind flickered back to Ashton and our night together. Had he sent this so I would have sex with him?

"Well?" she pressed.

My focus snapped back. "No one. You should know that."

"What about Kent?"

"He's gay," I admitted.

She reared back a step and narrowed her eyes.

"How do you know?' But she didn't give me a chance for rebuttal. "He may have told you that to test you. I did some digging. The boy's got mad cash. His family is swimming in it.

And he seems to be at their parties a lot. He could be a member. Maybe he was feeling you out?"

Where, why, and when had she investigated Kent? My mind was spinning with all the reasons.

I shook my head vehemently. "No, I don't think so."

"Think or know?" she asked.

I took a moment, replayed his words in my head, and then stood my ground. "Know as much as anyone can know about a virtual stranger." I took a longer pause, and in a quieter tone asked, "So, this is for a hookup?"

She shrugged and pointed at my hand. "Open it and find out."

My hands shook harder as I tried to break the blood wax seal. It took me even longer to slide the thick parchment from the envelope.

It looked more like a wedding invitation than one for a frat party. I read it out loud.

"You've been cordially invited to the White Party, a night of firsts."

"White?" she asked.

Funny she'd honed in on that and not the firsts thing. I held up a finger and read on, which included the date, tonight, and time, nine o'clock. "Everyone in attendance is to wear white clothing."

I glanced up at Celeste, searching for clues. She was more in the know than I was.

She nodded to herself. "Makes sense. Every year they have a themed party in a specific color. Last year was blue, I think."

"That's it? That's all you know?"

Her eyes were charged with brewing anger. "I've never been invited. And people who are don't talk about what happens. I think it's a rule."

I felt like a fish as my mouth puckered and unpuckered before I spoke again.

"Okay, that's not ominous or anything."

"You shouldn't go," she suggested.

I glared up at her. "I thought you said I should go, and now I shouldn't?"

"Do they have a plus one?" I shook my head. "Then absolutely not. You have no idea what you're walking into."

"Can't you find out?"

She had connections.

Her eyes found her watch. "There isn't enough time. Like I said, no one talks. If they do, they'll get blackballed. To scour and find someone last minute when you need to find a white dress if you insist on going in the few hours we have is impossible. That's why they don't give you days to decide to keep things as quiet as possible."

Her withering stare bore into me. "So, what are you going to do?"

Was it a bad thing if a guy wanted to hook up with me? I'd been invited, not Celeste. I hated to think of it as a win, but wasn't it? And what if... what if Ashton had sent me that invite? I definitely didn't think it was Kent no matter what Celeste said. Who else could it be? I thought back to the parties. There had been Trent that first night. I was surprised I remembered his name considering how drunk I'd been. Then there was the cute guy from Sawyer's birthday party. It wasn't like they could force me to do anything. I could always say no.

"I'm going," I announced.

21

Ashton

MY NAME CAME out of her mouth like the crack of a whip. I shouldn't have answered the phone. It had been a number I didn't recognize, but the idea it could be one of my friends needing my help had been the deciding factor.

"Ashton, at least man up and answer me."

It wasn't fear that had me swallowing the bile that soured my stomach. I felt nothing for the woman who gave birth to me. It was the blinding prism light through the empty bottle of Louis XIII that was like a jackhammer in my head.

"Mother."

Saying her name was like a knife to the temple in more ways than one.

"You think you can do this to me?"

Her shrill words were spoken like nails on a chalkboard.

"It's done," I said, feeling the invisible frost on my tongue.

"After all I've done for you."

Though it was the first time I laughed in what felt like months, there was no humor in it.

"What? Treated me like a circus act. No more dog and pony show, Victoria."

"How dare you call me by my first name."

"When have you ever acted like a mother?"

"Don't be such a child, Ashton. I gave birth to you to have this life. I didn't give up my perfect body to be treated like a common—"

She'd wound up to the point of popping, I had to finish it for her.

"Whore."

She let out a frustrated yell. "This will not be the end of me. And I will fight you every step of the way."

In the background, I heard, "Miss, you are required to leave."

A tiny smile curled the edges of my mouth. Oh, how the mighty had fallen. I imagined her searching the background to see if the neighbors were watching. Knowing her, the cops had to be called to make her leave. She could have avoided all that if she'd left with dignity.

"That is my car."

I wasn't sure whom she was talking to, but I answered anyway.

"No, it's mine. But you took that too and bought me a used Dodge Challenger."

It had been a rust bucket. Her excuse to her friends why I rode around in a ratty car was to teach me life lessons. It hadn't bothered me. The car Dad had sent to us didn't interest me anyway. It took time since allowance was scarce, but it had finally become the car it was today.

"You didn't even like the BMW."

"That's not the point, is it? It was mine and you stole it like you stole my life."

She was quiet only a second.

"So now you're out to steal mine."

"No, Victoria, you own nothing. You're lucky I'm letting you walk away with all the clothes and jewels you bought with my trust fund."

"I earned that," she blustered.

If she thought yelling would make me change my mind, she was wrong.

"You earned jail time. You're lucky you're not getting that."

"You think you can hold that over my head forever."

There was so much to say, but I was done.

"I think this conversation is over. Goodbye, Victoria."

I cut off her rant by ending the call. I ignored every call back. What surprised me was that I didn't block her number. Part of me claimed victory in each call I sent to voicemail. Truth was, there was some part of me that hoped she would have apologized. If she wasn't a monster, there was no chance I was too.

I found peace in a bottle. It was becoming more and more my go-to. I was well on my way to drunkville when I stumbled out of my room. The noise coming from downstairs made me roll my eyes, yet another party. It didn't matter the day of the week.

"You okay?"

Bryant was coming out of his room and stood there as I caught my balance.

"Yeah, fine."

"You know what tonight is?"

I had no fucking clue. There was always a theme to give reason for a party. I shook my head.

"Virgin night. Funny, right? Like, my key isn't even in the basket. Is yours?"

My glare was answer enough. He held up his hands to ward off any venomous reply.

"Do you want to get out of here? I hear the Omegas are throwing a pool party," he offered.

What I wanted was to go back to the townhouse and get away

from these assholes and any stupid girl crazy enough to accept the invite to this party. But I never got what I wanted.

"Sure."

"I'll drive," Bryant offered.

As we descended, it was clear that the all black I wore contrasted with this year's theme color of white.

Just before I hit the final stair, I spotted her.

"Fuck," I muttered.

"What's wrong?" Bryant asked, halfway out the door.

I was several steps behind him and waved him on.

"I've got to handle something real quick. I'll meet you there."

His shoulders lifted in a shrug and he disappeared into the night.

I wasn't sure why I felt responsible for Willow, but I did. No doubt Willhouse invited her to get at me.

I pushed my way through the crowd. As I brushed against those I passed, the feeling of a thousand red ants scurring under my skin attacked my senses. For once that didn't matter, as my driving need was to get to her.

Even I could admit she made a pretty picture. Several of my frat brothers noticed too, eye fucking her from head to toe. She stood with a bunch of other people near a keg. Still, the cup in her hand worried me as Willhouse kept glancing at it and her.

"Don't drink that," I said, snagging it from her hand.

Some of the liquid sloshed over the side coating my fingers.

"What?" she asked, looking away from the guy who had been chatting her up, and glared at me. "What's wrong with my drink?"

It could have been my approach or the fact that the music wasn't yet turned up to ear-splitting levels, but we'd caught the attention of everyone around us.

Willhouse pushed off the wall and folded his arms over his chest.

"Yeah, Westborough, what did you put in her drink?"

He was saving face for the house and putting any potential rumors on me.

"Nothing," I heard myself say.

Sawyer and I had never attended the virgin party before, so I had no real idea what went on. We'd only been privy to the boasting about what we'd missed.

Willow held out her hand. "Then kindly give it back."

I did the only thing I could with all eyes on me. I drank it down and vaguely recognized a salty under taste in the beer.

Willhouse roared with laughter.

"Here, darling, let me get you another."

She gave him her sweet smile as he used the tubing kit attached to the keg to fill up a new cup.

When he handed it to her, Willhouse started a chant, "Chug, chug, chug."

She looked at me with those damnable innocent eyes of hers, and I shook my head slightly. Her brow arched, and the chant only got louder as she defied me. The cup went to her lips as her head tilted back. Her throat worked as she swallowed the entire contents.

I didn't notice I was toppling forward until a hand caught my shoulders. I spun around because that touch didn't hurt and found Sawyer.

"Ash, what's going on?" He glanced around. "This isn't you."

There was so much judgment in his glaze, I shook out of his hold.

"That's the thing. You really don't know me."

His arms fell to his sides as I blinked, trying to clear my vision from the identical Sawyer triplets I was seeing.

"What's really bothering you is you lost your lap dog. I wish you'd just leave me alone."

Sawyer's jaw tightened. "If that's the way you want it. Fine."

He strode off heading for the front door. When I turned back,

Willow was gone. A cup was thrust at me and I tossed back its contents, wanting nothing more than to find oblivion.

I stumbled toward a wall and pressed my back to it so I could get out of the milling crowd and figure out my next move. I knew something wasn't right when the party swayed like we were on a boat in choppy water. It felt like someone turned up the heat, and I swiped a hand over my brow.

Further evidence that I'd inadvertently drunk something I shouldn't was the instant hard-on I got when I found Willow standing near the base of the stairs. Her ass in that dress made it painful for me to look at her. My dick was so hard I could chisel stone into sculpture with it.

Willhouse was on the stairs handing out keys to the women waiting there. He gave everyone a random key from the small basket he held, all except Willow. He pulled a key from his back pocket and gave it to her.

Red dotted my vision, and I launched forward. No fucking way he was going to have what belonged to me. My steps hitched as I thought those words. I shrugged it off. I'd marked her safe from everyone here, including me. That was all I meant.

My hand was balled and ready to strike when I reached him. All the girls, including Willow, had disappeared upstairs.

"I will—"

Willhouse held up a hand. "Chill, brother. Your girl is safe. I gave her the key. Sawyer said it was okay."

My mouth went dry as I struggled for words. Sawyer had left. Then again, I hadn't watched him leave, and even if I did, he could have come back. Besides, he always got what he wanted.

"That's okay, right?" Willhouse snickered. "You guys share everything, right?"

His words were like the code to open my vault of memories. Flashes of Sawyer and me over the years and all the women we'd shared.

"Get out of my way."

Willhouse stepped to the side as I charged up the stairs like a bull.

"Like a virgin," someone sang.

I grimaced, but didn't stop. Willow deserved better than this. She probably had no idea what she'd really gotten into. Oh sure, Willhouse would have explained the rules and given her the option to stay or go, but she wouldn't know whose room she was entering.

I got to my door and raised my hand to knock. What the fuck was that all about? I couldn't make myself turn the knob. What if she was in there with him? I leaned on the frame, trying to make a decision when I heard her.

"Am I really doing this?"

I busted in, wanting to protect her from Sawyer's corruption. At first, I only saw her. She was pushing her dress off her shoulder and froze in shock.

Then I heard Sawyer's disembodied voice. It sounded so far away, I wasn't sure what was real and what wasn't. But his face solidified in front of mine.

That penetrating stare of his snagged my will, making me submit. He didn't have to say anything. His smirk was command enough. I knew my role, but I hadn't totally given up my voice. I looked past him to her.

"You really want this?"

But Sawyer flickered in front of me and I closed my eyes.

"I think they put something in my drink," I muttered.

Sawyer hadn't heard. Instead, he looked over his shoulder at her. That's when I noticed her mouth was moving.

"What?" I asked.

"Yes, I want this."

I turned back to Sawyer. His smirk was epic, and his eyes bore into mine. Though his mouth didn't move, I swore I heard him say, *you take the lead.*

Never once had I. But with her, that seemed important.

"Take off your clothes." Sawyer was speaking the same line he'd said a thousand times before to the girls we'd played this game with, but his voice sounded like mine.

He must have moved behind me, though I hadn't heard him. I didn't bother to look for him as the sight before me was rapturous.

Time held no meaning as she removed her bra, letting it fall on the heap her dress had made. I dropped to the tiny blue panties she wore. Her gentle curves made my mouth water. I wanted to feast on her breasts like a man starved. I had to fist my cock in submission as it tried to make a jailbreak from my jeans.

"Fuck," I groaned.

I hadn't been this aroused in my entire life.

When the blue cloth found the floor, I licked my lips. She wasn't bare there. A swath of golden curls covered her slit, and I wanted to taste her.

"Lie down."

Had I said that?

As she moved, a voice in my head commanded me to undress. I pulled the black tee over my head. Before I went to her, I turned for Sawyer. He wasn't there, and then he was, egging me on with a wink.

Eating pussy had never been a favorite pastime of mine. It required too much physical contact. Inevitably, the girl would want to touch me, and it would kill my mood instantly. But at the moment, I thought I might die if I didn't stick my tongue so deep in her cunt I could lick her ovaries.

I blinked. *What the fuck did I just think?* I shook my head and my dick throbbed, reminding me of my mission.

She lay there shivering.

"Are you cold?"

I still wasn't sure if it was Sawyer or me speaking, but I went with it.

Glazed eyes met mine, and she gave me a tiny head shake indicating no.

"Spread your legs."

I could have moved them on my own, but I feared if I touched her, the instant pain would kill everything. She would see it as a reflection of her.

Get out of your head, Ash! I thought.

I searched for Sawyer, needing reassurance. He wasn't where he had been. I swung my head around, and then I found him at the foot of the bed.

What are you waiting for? his stare asked.

The room swayed a little. His lips hadn't moved, but that was his voice in my head.

Willow's eyes were wide, and I wondered how long I'd been staring. She started to cover herself.

"Don't."

Slowly, her hands moved to her side.

"Reach above your head and hold on to the edge of the mattress and don't let go."

It sounded like me, but it couldn't be. I never spoke. Sawyer was the commander.

She nodded and did as she was told.

One knee on the mattress and it dipped under my weight. I moved into position and bent down to taste her as Sawyer practically dared me to. Fuck, it was liquid nirvana. I covered her pussy with my mouth like I was bobbing for apples, but let my tongue find her center and suck on the bud. She gasped, which only fed the beast that hid inside me. I licked her slit until I found her entrance and curled my tongue inside to taste her honey.

Stars in my eyes reminded me I needed to breathe and had me coming up for air.

"Hold on, baby, and don't fucking let go."

Sawyer would say some shit like that.

Her muscles quivered with need, and I took a chance. I slid a finger inside her as I sucked her little clit into my mouth. She writhed underneath me. Until she was coming, I finger fucked her and licked her until she was boneless beneath me.

Afraid my dick would explode if I didn't get inside her now, I think I said, "I have to have you."

It wasn't exactly a request, but I waited until she nodded in agreement.

I didn't bother with pulling my jeans completely off. I shoved them down far enough to free my cock. It bobbed in anticipation. I fisted it and rubbed it up and down her slit, covering it in her juices before plunging forward. All the breath was stolen from both of our lungs as we froze.

I was so far gone, any thoughts of what I should have done before pushing balls deep inside her were lost on me. But some part of me remembered she was a virgin. The tight hold her pussy had on my cock was another reminder.

"Are you okay?"

She nodded, then I was moving. She was so soft and wet I thought I'd died and gone to heaven. I stroked between her legs as the friction we created built something inside me I'd never felt before.

As her body tightened around me, I saw rainbows.

What the hell?

The room lit up in colors like one of those old-time disco balls was above me. For a second, I wondered if I was jerking off until a muffled scream sounded beneath me. Her pussy milked my dick until I was coming so hard I was sure I filled her up.

Spent, I crushed her beneath my weight as we both panted.

That's when I saw the unicorn. I rolled off her when it asked me if that was good for me. My back found the wall as I freaked the fuck out.

I thought I might have heard Willow's voice in the background, but other woodland creatures joined the unicorn and surrounded the bed. I closed my eyes, trying to block out what I was seeing.

A hand touched my face, and I jerked my eyes open. For a second, it was Willow, but Sawyer's face replaced hers, though she spoke through his mouth.

"Are you okay?"

I closed my eyes again, praying it would all go away. When I opened them, Sawyer was still there. This time it was his voice I heard.

"You've always wanted to fuck me, and now you have."

I scrambled so fast off the bed, I lost my balance. Pain blossomed on the back of my head, and darkness took everything away.

22

Willow

THERE WAS no time for me to process what I'd just done. One minute he was inside me like for real, then he was staring off into space like he was seeing ghost. He'd scrambled off the bed so fast, my first thought was what had I done wrong.

Naked and crouched before his still form, my heart was beating so fast I could hardly catch my breath.

"Ashton?"

There was a small cut on his head, but it hadn't bleed all that much. I shook his body, wondering if I should call 911. How embarrassing. Before I could go for my phone, his eyes opened and held me in place.

"Kiss me."

He cupped the sides of my face and drew me down. His lips were soft as he only exerted gentle pressure. When his tongue licked the seam of my mouth, I opened for him. I hadn't been kissed a lot, but this was far better than anything before.

When he pulled back, I savored the taste of him on my

tongue. I could already feel something in my heart for him. It wasn't love, but it was a hell of a lot of like.

"You kissed me back," he said.

Wasn't I supposed to?

My confusion was compounded by the reverent way he stared at me. By his look, I had to be the most beautiful thing in the world.

His smile faded, turning quickly into a frown, and he let go.

"You're going to pretend it didn't happen, aren't you?" I opened my mouth, but clamped it shut when he spoke next. "Typical Sawyer."

He thought I was Sawyer. My heart plummeted as several questions lit up my brain. Did I look that much like a dude? Who had he thought I was when we had sex?

His eyes rolled and not from a potential concussion. He got to his feet in all his naked glory. I got a really good look at his penis and, damn, it hung there, long, thick, and heavy. Semi-hard, I guessed, but what did I know?

"Maybe you're not even here." He swiped a hand over his eyes. "Whatever was in that drink has fucked with my head."

I sat back as he lay down on his bed. Not real? The ache between my legs said it had very much been real.

His words replayed in my head. Someone had spiked his drink. A cascade of images flooded my mind all the way back to the drink he took of mine. Next was his voice telling me not to drink it. He'd practically begged me with a pleading gaze, but I'd been annoyed he'd interrupted another boy from talking to me when he didn't want me for himself.

I glanced up to the bed and found his eyes closed. I knew practically nothing about concussions, but I'd remembered something about not letting the person sleep.

On my knees, I crawled over to the bed.

"Wake up, Ashton."

At the same time his eyes popped open, I felt something oozing out of me and down my leg.

An indulgent smile played on his lips. "Willow, you shouldn't be here."

I'll admit, I wanted to cry. Though I wasn't sure what he believed about what happened to us, his message was plain and clear.

He reached out, but stopped shy of touching me. His fist balled. "Don't cry. It's just these guys are assholes, and I don't want anything to happen to you."

I wiped angrily at the tear that spilled from my eye as his shut again.

"You can't go to sleep," I said, trying to hold it together.

My feelings were all over the place. I wanted to ask him if he remembered us having sex or did he think it was Sawyer. But did I really want to know? My first time would be something I could never forget and to know it was a lie would hurt far too much.

He'd shut his eyes again and rolled to the side, giving me his back. I reached for his shoulder and shook him some. He yanked out of my hold, and panic filled eyes lanced me.

"Please don't hurt me."

I froze and not just because of what he said. It was the child-like voice that freaked me the fuck out. Was he just tripping on some drug? I really knew nothing about him. Then, his eyes slammed shut and he held them that way, so I knew sleep hadn't claimed him. His body started to shake. I glanced up at his face, but he'd rolled away from me again.

What should I do? I pushed at my hair, which had curled at my nape. I probably looked like a hot mess.

He still shook, so I assumed he wasn't asleep. I found my phone, which thank God had reception, and searched the word *concussion*. As much as I wanted to leave and forget this night happened, I couldn't leave him until I knew he was okay.

According to my Google search, he hadn't shown any of the

visible symptoms like slurred speech or vomiting. The only thing was the loss of consciousness or maybe he'd just passed out from the drug or alcohol he'd taken. And he had held a conversation with me. I found that a misnomer was not letting a concussion victim sleep. It said they could.

I let out a breath and decided what to do. I badly wanted to flee, but what if he did start throwing up whether from a concussion or something else? If he choked and died, I could never live with myself. So I found my clothes and put everything on but my underwear, which I'd used for quick cleanup.

He hadn't used a condom pinged in my held. What had I been thinking? Truthfully, I had been a little drunk myself. Add in a dose of fear that I was about to lose my virginity to one of the hottest boys on campus and I'd lost my damn mind.

When I turned to look at him curled into a ball, my heart broke for the beautiful boy. I feared that if nothing else that he'd said and done tonight, there was truth in that fear coming from a little boy inside him. The pain in his words trumped any hard feelings I had about him not knowing who I was.

Besides, if he'd drunk my drink because he knew it had been spiked, he'd saved me yet again. How could I blame him for any of it?

I spent the night watching over him. My eyes drifted shut a few times as I sat in his chair, but his muttered, terrified words would wake me up. As the sun came up, hours later and he hadn't hurled or retched, I was pretty sure he'd be fine.

Part of me wanted to stay until he was up. Cowardly, I didn't want to face him and what he would say.

After checking to see if he was breathing one last time, I left. I took my time closing the door, not wanting to disturb him. Then I tiptoed like a dumbass to the landing. When I heard a door open behind me, I double-timed it down the stairs. Before I could reach the door, someone called out.

"Hey, you're Ashton's girl, right?"

Okay, part of me preened at the notions until parts of last night came back. I turned around to find Jason, the cute dark-skinned boy I'd spoken to at Sawyer's birthday party. I hadn't seen him last night.

He saddled up to me, leaning his forearm on the wall as his eyes dipped down and back up again. The huge grin on his face said he liked what he saw. Some girls might be pissed at being ogled. For me, it was validation I didn't often get.

"He claimed you as his, but if you're not—"

Ashton claimed me? What did that even mean? I was more confused than ever. When I still didn't answer, he prodded me some more.

"It's your choice. I could take you out instead."

He was cute, but I needed time to figure this all out. "I'm his."

His lips pursed, but didn't turn into a frown. "Figures. Wait here for a second."

He held up a finger until I nodded. Then he disappeared through a doorway. Should I leave or stay? Before I could decide, he was back holding a black envelope.

"You should have this."

He set it in my hand. This one didn't bear my name. Instead, a gold crest was embossed on it. I stared at it, unsure what to do.

"It won't bite," he joked. "You should come. Otherwise someone else will take your place. And—" He put a finger to his lips. "You can't tell anyone. I could get kicked out if you do. It's just, I like you and him. I would hate for him to be forced to do something he doesn't want to."

He held my gaze as if trying to tell me more. But lack of sleep and a weird night, I couldn't read between his lines.

"Later," he said and jogged up the stairs, leaving me.

I closed my hands over the envelope, but didn't open it. I needed to leave before anyone else saw me doing the walk of shame, most of all Ashton.

23

Ashton

I slapped at the phone, wanting it to stop. Finally, I gave in and blindly accepted the call before I managed to pry my eyes open.

"What the fuck, Ash? Did you miss practice to avoid me?"

Groaning, I moved the phone from my ear so I could get a good look at the time. It was well past two in the afternoon.

"Ash," Sawyer said again.

"It's not always about you," I said.

Though I wasn't sure he understood me because it sounded a fuck of a lot like I had gravel in my throat.

"You know what? Whatever."

Before he could hang up, I said, "Wait." Then I rubbed at my temple. Last night was a mystery. I remembered stopping to see Willow, then a fight with Sawyer. Everything else was a blank space.

"What else have I done wrong?"

Some of what Chance had been saying to me about Sawyer

not being himself rang true from the lack of confidence in his words.

A flash of his face with his signature smirk flashed in my head. I wasn't sure if it was a memory of last night or what.

"When did you leave last night?"

I could imagine his expression screwing up in the silence that proceeded my question.

"Right after we talked."

Another flash of Willow's face as she smiled at Willhouse, taking a key from him.

"You didn't come back?" I asked.

"No." I pinched my temple. "Why don't you remember?"

I couldn't tell him. I had to deal with this on my own.

"It's nothing."

I ended the call and slowly rolled to a sitting position. Oddly, I didn't feel hungover, yet half my night was missing.

The messed up thing about it was I was pretty sure I'd been drugged. Rage bunched my muscles as I stood spoiling for a fight. I wasn't angry because of what happened to me. I was pissed the fuck off because I hadn't been the target. Willow had been? I needed to find her and make sure she was okay. I had no idea if Willhouse succeeded in getting some GHB in her system because I recognized that salty taste too late.

The air conditioning kicked on and a cool breeze alerted me that I was naked. I didn't sleep naked ever for a very good reason. I pressed the heel of my palms over each eye, willing the night before to come back.

Nothing.

I got up and noticed a little blood on my sheet, but one look in the bathroom mirror and I spotted dried blood on my forehead. What the hell happened last night?

Ignoring the sheets for now, I made showering and dressing my first priority before I beat a path to Willhouse's door. I banged my fist on it and got no answer. I double-timed it downstairs and found him and a couple other guys huddled near the useless fireplace.

I barreled forward, my thudding footsteps alerting them I was on my way.

The smug bastard turned and a grin the size of Texas split on his face.

"Nice night?"

The guys who stood behind him snickered.

I answered him with my fist. He saw it coming and had tried to dodge, but I'd course corrected and my knuckle connected with his jaw. It was the second time I put him on his ass.

Our frat brothers moved to hold me back.

"Don't fucking touch me!" They held their hands up like the prey they were and stepped back. "If you hurt her, I swear I'll kill you."

Willhouse held his jaw as he sneered at me.

"I didn't touch her, but I imagine you did."

I didn't like the smug look on his face. If I stayed any longer, I might have killed him. Besides, he wasn't going to tell me the truth about anything. I was glad I grabbed my keys. I stalked out of the room, knowing I needed to find Willow.

I hadn't been sure why I'd sent a message from her phone when it had been given to me. But it meant I was able to call her. When she didn't answer, I left her a message.

"I need to talk to you. I'll be at the spot for a while."

I'd missed class and didn't care. The last thing I wanted to do was to see people. My hatred of mankind was only amplified by the assholes I lived with.

There were only a few I considered worthy of the air they breathed. Chance, Kelley, and even Sawyer and his brother Finn were among them.

After parking my car and making my way around the pond to the place where the tall grass could shield me from the world, I also realized my tribe had grown to include Lenora, Brie, and even Shelly, the girls who had slayed my friends. But there was one more life that had begun to matter to me as well, Willow. I wasn't even sure how or when that happened.

As I sat, I knew it to be true. I feared she wouldn't show because of last night. Had any of my so-called brothers done something to her?

Her face full of innocence danced in my head. The image of her lying down with her hair fanned out all around her.

"Hey," a serene voice above me said.

I glanced up, noting it wasn't as bright as when I arrived. Clouds had come in and I wasn't sure how long I'd been sitting there. But still the sun haloed her form.

"Hey."

She tucked her hand under her short dress as she sat ladylike. There was no way else do describe her. She had grace in a way my mother could never hope to achieve.

"You wanted to talk to me."

I didn't want to think of Mother or compare her to Willow, so I kept my eyes trained ahead.

"I, uh—wanted to check on you."

"Why?"

I felt her eyes on me, yet I couldn't look at her. What if I'd been the monster of her nightmares, not any of my frat brothers?

"Last night. That party. I want to make sure nothing happened..." I hesitated because what if she'd chosen to do something with someone? Was it my business? I fisted a hand in the dirt and forced myself to be cool. "I just want to make sure you're okay. That nothing happened against your wishes."

She sighed, and because I didn't dare meet her eyes, I couldn't interpret it.

"I take it you don't remember anything."

I shook my head.

"Are you into drugs?"

My head snapped in her direction, confused by the change in topics. "No."

She bobbed her head. "Why do you think you don't remember last night? Too much to drink?"

Though I needed to know her answer to my question, I felt like she needed the truth from me.

"No, some assholes thought it would be funny to spike my drink."

Her face was blank. "How do you know that?"

I swallowed and glanced away. Though I felt compelled to be honest with her, some truths were only for me. How I knew about GHB, otherwise known as the date rape drug, was something even Sawyer didn't know.

"I've had it before," I admitted.

When next she spoke, there was steel in her voice.

"Your friends get off on drugging people."

"No, but one in particular has a grudge against me."

I faced her glare. "And you're not angry?"

"I took care of it. With any luck, the asshole's jaw is broken and they will have to wire it shut. Then I won't have to hear him speak for weeks."

Was that a grin on her face? I was hard-pressed not to mirror her smile.

"But I need to know. Did anything happen last night?" I asked again.

Though her face didn't lose any softness, her expression turned sad.

Fear lanced through my heart and I pressed on. "Did I or anyone else do anything to you last night?"

She held my gaze as her hand lifted. Automatically, I flinched and watched her hand fall.

"No, nothing happened last night. I left shortly after you took the drink from my hand."

The way her eyes bore into mine, I knew she'd connected the

dots about which drink was spiked. But I couldn't bring myself to say it out loud.

"Good." I nodded more to myself and repeated, "Good."

Then I followed a bird swoop down and land gracefully in the pond.

Out of the corner of my eye, I watched her shift, so she too was facing forward. She folded her hands on her lap, though she wasn't holding still. That's when I wondered if she was being honest with me. I closed my eyes, dreading what I was about to say.

"I know I asked before, but I have to again. If anything happened, even if it was me, would you tell me?"

24

Past

"Ashton," Mother called sweetly. "Come into the kitchen, please."

She'd never been nice to me a day in my life and had treated me even worse since everything went down.

I'd been on my way out the door. "I'm going to Sawyer's."

"About that," she said. "I need you here tonight."

I narrowed my eyes as she waved me over to sit across from her.

"Come, let's be adults."

She indicated the amber liquid in the glass tumbler that sat in front of me. She brought hers to her lips.

"Drink. I know you do over there."

She was talking about Sawyer's house.

"What do you want?" I asked, not feeling charitable.

"Ashton, things don't have to be like this between us. We can help each other. Drink."

I didn't trust her.

"Oh, come on. It's a little brandy, to cool my nerves. I've never asked you for a favor before, and maybe this will ease the way between us."

That was true and the dare in her eyes made me stupid. I would wonder later why I was still so desperate for her to love me. I drank some. It tasted a little salty. I hadn't had brandy before, as Ashton's parents were big fans of vodka and tequila.

"Don't be shy," she urged.

I drank more and she did the same.

"Now, I really need you here tonight. I have guests coming. I really want my son to be here. They are looking forward to meeting you."

I only remembered snatches of time after that.

First was being led into one of the guest rooms. There were two, maybe three people waiting there from what I saw through the haze that blurred my vision. One was female as she squealed in delight.

"Oh, he's delicious," she remarked.

I couldn't see their faces because they wore masks.

I had a sensation of falling. Then I woke up with the woman bent over the bed with my dick in her mouth, a man wearing a dog mask grunting behind her.

The next thing I remembered was being on all fours as a familiar punishing pressure moved in and out of that horrid place inside me. A woman giggled, but I couldn't turn to face her let alone breathe as my head was jerked up and down on whatever stole my breath.

Tears leaked from my eyes as I prayed for darkness.

I woke later with little memory of the events. Mother ordered me from the door to clean up like I'd created the mess in the room. There was a smirk on her face and shame in my heart. I hurt everywhere. By the time I made it to my room, I ignored the

messages on the cell Sawyer had gotten me. I would take whatever happened that night to my grave. I would never tell a soul
how stupid I'd been, especially after all he'd done to save me.
Instead, I curled into a ball and thought about death as a real
option for the first time in my life.

25

Willow

IT WOULD HAVE BEEN selfish to tell him the truth given his haunted expression.

"No. Nothing happened," I said.

But I wasn't selfless either. A part of my ego was bruised that he looked relieved by my answer.

"Would it have been such a bad thing if something did happen?" His imploring eyes dug more words to blurt out of my mouth. "You know, between you and me?"

His brows pinched. "I'm not the guy for you, Willow. You deserve better."

If he'd stabbed me, it would have hurt less. How many times had I heard a version of this? Frustrated beyond reason, I said, "What is so wrong with me?"

I started to get to my feet, not bothering to hold my dress down so I wouldn't flash him in the process. It wasn't like he hadn't seen the goods, even if he didn't remember.

"Wait."

There was so much pleading in his voice, I sat back down and faced him, but kept my mouth firmly shut.

"You're beautiful and any guy who doesn't see that is an idiot."

Even more exasperated, I let loose a snarky reply. "You sound like my mother. Did she call you?"

The last part was desperate levity to hide my vulnerability for admitting my lack of self-esteem.

His chuckle didn't match his expression. "She didn't, but she sounds like one of the good ones."

The fact that he hadn't thrown Mom in with some kind of quip led me to believe that maybe his mother was part of the reason such a beautiful man looked like the weight of the world rested on his chest.

"She is." Silence fell heavy between us. Despite that, there was something about him, and that implored me to open up more. "I don't know why this even bothers me. I'm used to it."

His brow quirked, and it was as if he wanted me to unload on him.

"Have you ever felt invisible?" He surprised me by nodding, but not adding to the conversation. "I've felt that way ever since my so-called sister came into my life." He didn't have to speak to question me further. An arched brow did that. "Our parents married when we were about twelve. Ever since, people look right through me to her."

"Celeste?"

Color me shocked, he knew her name? Then again, invisible. I nodded.

"She's pretty, but she has nothing on you," he said.

Talk about a bad case of blushing. I was as ripe as a tomato, but that didn't stop my reply.

"Tell that to all the guys that dumped me for a chance to go out with her."

Did I really just tell him that?

"Dumbasses, all of them," he said with a faint smile.

"Yeah, well…"

It was almost like I could see him reaching out but holding back even though he hadn't moved.

"Trust me, I know how you feel. But for different reasons. I don't mind being invisible. At the same time, I had to walk away to find myself."

"Do you have a brother?" I asked, wanting to know more about him.

His eyes shifted away to stare out into the distance.

"No. But he's like a brother."

He could only mean one person.

"Sawyer?" It came out so softly, but where we were, our voices only had to compete with the sounds of insects and small animals that inhabited the area.

His head whipped back in my direction. I shrugged.

"Does he know?"

I knew I'd gone too far when any compassion he'd held for me disappeared into a frosty glare.

"We're just friends." His words were like stones dropping into a river.

His vehemence was only further proof of his feelings.

"You know what, I'm sorry. It's none of my business."

"You're right about that," he snapped.

He ran a hand through his hair.

I couldn't even get mad for the way the conversation turned ugly.

"Yeah, I should go. I have a meeting with my professor."

I was fairly sure she'd seen the footage of my failed attempt at rescue.

His eyes widened. "You've been caught."

I shrugged. "Don't worry, I won't give you up."

"You think I care about that? You can tell them about me."

I shook my head and scrambled to my feet. "This was my grand plan. I'm not getting you in trouble."

I dusted myself off and he got to his feet.

"I'm going with you."

I had to crane my neck back to look at him.

"No. And that's a firm no." At his frown, I added, "I really appreciate you wanting to go to bat for me, but I can handle this."

His stiff nod looked reluctant, which unfortunately made me crush harder for him. *Stupid.*

I'd almost completely turned away when I shifted to walk backwards.

"And thanks," I said.

His head cocked to the side. Damn, he was a beautiful man.

"For what?"

My heart raced in my chest. Though I'd woken unsure about the previous night, all that had changed.

"For caring about what happened to me last night."

My graceful walk away fumbled as my foot landed in a patch of uneven ground and I pitifully pinwheeled my arms to gain my balance.

Then he was there, hand blazing on my back as it appeared like he'd dipped me in some old-time dance. His face was right there. Our eyes locked, and I couldn't stop my mind for wishing he would just kiss me.

When I swallowed, the spell broke and he righted me. His hands fell away so fast, I was sure he'd been burned by the heat that had flared between us.

"I should go," I said and practically jogged to the path that led back to school.

I wanted to look back, but I also didn't want to be disappointed by what I might see or not see in his expression.

26

Willow

SUNSHINE FED MY SMILE. All my doubts were gone. I'd lost my virginity to a good guy. And it didn't matter that he didn't remember. His memory loss was due in part because he'd saved me from being in the shoes he currently walked in. As messed up as that was, I could look back and know that the guy I'd given my most precious gift wasn't a douche.

Seeing that I was walking into a meeting where I could very well be expelled, I had to hold on to something good.

I pulled open one of the heavy double doors and crossed into the coolness of the air-conditioned hallway. I wondered if this was what it felt like for prisoners on death row as I walked to the unknown. I was scared and anxious at the same time to get it over with.

Faces blurred as I held my head high and kept moving forward. Ash was never far from my thoughts and not on purpose. My body ached with each step, reminding me of what we'd done. Flashes of him above me, muscled body moving with purpose. Something built so deep inside me, I'd cried out when it was set free.

My fist held in the air a second before I knocked on my professor's door. *I can do this*, I told myself. I exhaled and rapped at the door twice.

"Come in," came a voice from inside.

I entered the well-appointed office. It was tidy but had a lived-in feel.

"Miss Young, have a seat."

I sat in the only free chair in the room and crossed my legs at the ankles, folding my hands on my lap. Before now, I'd only been in trouble at school a couple times in my life. Each time, I was scared shitless. Though I'd never been in trouble at Layton. Funny thing was, I wasn't afraid now.

"I'm sure you know why you're here." I kept my mouth closed and didn't even nod. "Before we get to that, I'm curious why you chose entomology as your major."

Because bugs couldn't hurt you, emotionally at least.

"Insects can save our world."

She nodded as if I'd answered correctly.

"In order to study them, there have to be sacrifices," she said, starting down a trail that led to a parental-type lecture.

"There are plenty of dead bugs outdoors," I cut in, eyebrow lifting in challenge as I mentally fist pumped.

"As a scientist, you realize that there are so many variables outside of a controlled environment. We can't draw accurate conclusions unless we can limit the unknowns."

I leaned back in my chair. It wasn't as though I was afraid physically, but she had been correct with her assessment and I'd all but outed myself as the culprit if she had any doubts.

"We've seen the tapes," she said.

Finally, I gave in and nodded.

"Fortunately for you, it only shows you coming to return the arachnid." She paused, giving weight to her gaze on me. "I will ask you once for the name of the individual with you."

I might as well have waved a white flag for how fast my reply came.

"He didn't do anything wrong."

At least I sounded convincing.

"I beg to differ, Miss Young. As of right now, the evidence would suggest you caught *him*." She paused, and I inwardly groaned. I gave her the clue that it was a guy and not a very tall girl. "If you are unwilling to give me his name, I'll have to assume you two were working together and consider recommending expulsion to the dean as your punishment."

I wrung my hands on my lap, knowing how disappointed Mom would be in me.

"It's not his fault."

Though I'd spoken softer, I'd held my ground.

Her lips flattened into a thin line. My stomach bottomed out as I waited for the words that would abruptly end my senior year.

"Your record is stellar. You are a good student. In fact, I'd been talking to a colleague of mine at Harvard about an open research fellowship he has available I thought you'd be a good fit for."

My eyes widened. For a second, my heart leaped, only to plummet because I knew what she was about to say next.

"I can hardly recommend you for that spot if you can't stomach the death of a specimen."

Maybe I should have kept my mouth shut, but I didn't.

"What's my punishment?"

It had come out as dry as my tongue.

"I'm not going to recommend expulsion. However, I can't grant you access to the lab after class hours anymore."

Which meant, if I couldn't finish an assignment during class, I would get a failing grade.

"I'm also going to fail you for this current lab. However, I'm feeling charitable and will give you an opportunity to raise that failing grade to a B at most."

I had to pass this class. It was a requirement. If I didn't, I couldn't graduate. Next semester, I needed to take another class where this one was a prerequisite in order to fulfill my requirements for my major.

"What do I need to do?"

She sat back with a squeak of the chair. The sound rivaled the thunderous beating of my heart.

"I require a ten thousand word essay. The topic will be how insects and Shakespeare's plays are alike."

My jaw hung open. "You can't be serious." I hated writing. Technical writing about scientific findings was okay. But English papers about long dead literary figures or creative writing papers gave me hives. "What does Shakespeare have to do with anything bug related?"

"That's for you to figure out, and I expect it on my desk in two weeks."

I'm sure I looked like a Venus flytrap, jaws agape and predatory as I held my tongue in outrage.

"This isn't fair," I spat.

"Life isn't fair, Miss Young. In scientific terms, we call it survival of the fittest. You chose a path, and I'm being very generous not completely failing you or getting you kicked out of school. Do the paper and maybe you'll learn a lesson or two."

She'd made it all sound easy as she sat there wielding power like she was a god. That was what was wrong with the world. No one truly had freedom, including the insects that could point to a way to save our planet from human overconsumption and waste. I stood and closed my eyes for a second, reining in my emotions.

"Thank you. You'll have my paper on time," I said with all the dignity I could muster.

I fled her office in a panic. I didn't know much about Shakespeare. What I'd read in high school hadn't stuck in my head. I'd done whatever assignment given and then tried to forget the hours of my time spent writing bullshit that didn't matter.

When I pushed through the double doors of the science building and took a deep, cleansing breath, I nearly choked when I spotted Ashton. He sat on a half wall that lined the steps leading to and from the building to the path.

Marching over to him probably wasn't the best idea considering my mood.

"Why did you come? I told you I didn't need you here."

Venom laced every word and I didn't wait for his response. I kept striding past, but knew he was following me. I cut through the buildings and into the wooded area that eventually led to the man-made pond he seemed to favor.

"What happened?"

His deep voice sent a shiver through me despite the baking heat.

"You shouldn't have come. My professor wanted me to give up your name and I didn't. You fit the profile of what she probably saw on that video."

My breath picked up as I fast walked into the tree canopied shade.

"You could have told them," he said.

I spun around with the force of all my pent-up anger from my meeting.

"You can't save me this time," I hurled out my words like a lash across his cheek. Some of his concern dimmed as his jaw tightened. "I'm sorry. I didn't mean that. I'm not mad at you. I just don't want you to be hurt because of me. And I'm pissed I'm being forced to write some craptastic paper about bugs and Shakespeare."

"That's your punishment?" He tried to hold back a smile, but his lips twitched.

"It's not funny. I hate writing." But I found some of the tension leaking out of me.

"I can help you."

It was my turn to laugh. "Really, how?"

"English is my major with a minor in journalism."

I was stunned again. "Seriously?"

"Yes."

I blinked a few times and then said, "I appreciate the offer, but I need to do this."

"You weren't the only one in that lab that night. Let me help you."

Words like *valiant* and *chivalrous* bounced in my head as I stared at him.

"Thanks, even though I don't think butterflies are over romanticized, I'm sure I could come up with some parallels between them and Romeo and Juliet. They both had short lives." I shrugged.

He didn't move as we stood almost facing off as if he could change my mind.

"You could. But since you brought it up, do you have any other options?"

Though it wasn't a debate, I took him up on his challenge.

"Okay." I crossed my arms over my chest. "Butterflies are pretty, don't get me wrong. And they say when you meet someone you really like you get that feeling in your gut. Then there are fireflies. What isn't romantic about standing in a field at night with someone you love as fireflies light up the field? And they do it to attract a mate. But honestly, I think the true romantics are dragonflies."

One perfect brow lifted as he, like so many others, was clueless about what makes dragonflies the ultimate romantics.

"Oh, come on, the heart shape," I said. When he only stood there, I filled him in. "When dragonflies hook up, the male grasps his chosen female by the neck, bringing her abdomen to his—" I wave a hand. "—you know, so they can join together. When that happens, they form a heart, though the more technical term is the mating wheel."

I left out the part about how aggressive the males are to stave out any other guys from getting his woman. But it's kind of hot how possessive they are.

"Do they stay together forever?" he asked.

"Not exactly, but most insects don't. The males do hang around long enough to protect their woman from other males until she's fertilized. Otherwise, another male will come along and remove his sperm and replace it with theirs."

Ashton broke out in laughter, and I couldn't stop from laughing myself. His smile could light up the world, especially since he didn't often wear one.

"And that's romantic?" He tried to hold in his chuckling, but it didn't work.

"Stop." I couldn't either, giggling before I finished. "Considering everything, yes. They choose a woman and are forced to fight off any other guys to have her. And when he gets her, his job to become a father isn't done. He has to stay and protect her."

"His investment in future dragonflies."

Standing there as he gave his deadpan answer, I couldn't stop the blush from forming. I looked away and then back into his gaze.

"Well yes, still. A heart, come on. That's love all the way."

When our laughter died, he said, "You should write about that. I could give you a few Shakespearean quotes, like '*The fault is not in the stars to hold our destiny, but in ourselves.*' Though that is a modern take on his words."

His eyes never left mine as he recited the words.

"Wow." There was a lot of power in that sentence. "It's beautiful. What play is that from?"

"*Julius Caesar.*"

His stare was unreadable. Or maybe I didn't believe enough in myself to take the chance.

"I guess that could work for the male dragonfly," I admitted.

"More so than butterflies?"

"Yes."

I licked my suddenly dry lips, wanting something I didn't think he would give, despite all that happened the other night. There was an undeniable pull toward him inside me so strong, I wondered if he felt it too.

"I could send you more," he offered.

"Yeah, that sounds good."

The air was charged and buzzed over my skin. Yet the silence with only the insects to fill it soon became awkard.

"I should, um—go." I hiked a thumb in the direction of home. *Tell me to stay. Take two steps closer and kiss me.*

"Actually, I have somewhere to be too."

This was it. Now or never. Though I wasn't the make-the-first-move kind of person, I found myself taking the two steps forward. "Thank you."

My lips tingled in anticipation. The question was, would he let me kiss him?

Clumsily, I rose on my toes. He tensed when my hands landed on his pecs. I still wasn't tall enough to reach him. He would have to bend down some. The moment seemed to stretch, but he moved just enough. I rose just a little higher to reach him.

27

Past

THE SUN WAS high and bright in the cloudy sky. I lay staring into the infinite blue as if I could see all the way to the stars hidden in the daylight.

"So, where do you think Sawyer is?"

I didn't look at Julie. She was tanning, or that was the reason she'd unhooked her top, claiming she wanted her back to be free of tan lines.

"No telling," I said.

"He's probably with yet another girl."

She let out a loud exhale of breath.

There was no good response. If I agreed with her, I would be betraying Sawyer. He was in love with her even if she didn't know it. If I disagreed, I'd be lying, and she'd know it.

"Doesn't it bother you? I mean, your reputation is tied to his when you're nothing like him."

Sawyer was everything I wasn't, and I envied him for it.

I didn't hear her move. When her skin pressed against mine, I looked up as she edged me over with her hip to fit on the lounger with me. From the sky, my eyes lazily moved down to find her face. It was obvious why Sawyer crushed on her. She was pretty, very much so.

"So—what do you think of my boobs?"

I wasn't shocked by her question. She was always very straightforward. Automatically, my gaze shifted. She hadn't put back on her top and all I saw were tits.

My first thought was her father. I glanced toward the double door that led inside her house, expecting him to walk out and drown me in their pool. But her parents weren't home.

She took my momentary distraction to clasp my wrist and bring my hands to cup the warmth of her soft flesh. Then she pressed her lips to mine.

As brief as it was, she slowly pulled back and bit at her bottom lip. "You like?"

All I could think then was Sawyer and how much he would hate me if he found us like this. I snatched my hands away to rest on my lap, hiding the evidence of my reaction. Her cautious smile inverted before flattening into a thin line.

"You don't like me, do you?" she asked, all the confidence drained from her.

I wasn't sure what I should feel and kept my hands in place to cover my hardening cock. It had responded favorably to everything she'd offered.

"I can't—" I cut myself off before I told her all the reasons why, which began and ended with Sawyer.

Abruptly, she stood and gave me her back. She took three steps forward and dove into the pool, disturbing the tranquil stillness of it. I gripped my dick to get it back under control.

No matter what was going on, I would never betray Sawyer in a million years. I couldn't understand why my body reacted to Julie. Quickly rationalizing it away, I decided it was because there had always been a girl between Sawyer and me. And metaphorically speaking, Julie had become that girl between us.

Her head popped above the surface, leaving her hair slicked back. I couldn't take my eyes off her and licked my lips, trying to get ahold of the numerous emotions running through my head.

"What's up, good people?"

I snapped my head around in time to see Sawyer coming through the gate that separated his property from hers.

"Sawyer," Julie said dryly.

He didn't notice her tone. His eyes had found her discarded top on the ground and a sly grin rose on his face.

"So, we're skinny-dipping?" he asked.

I stood on instinct and walked over to him to block his view. Even looking back, I wasn't sure why I'd done it.

"Just lay off, okay," I said at the same time Julie said, "I'm surprised you found time for us."

He didn't miss her dose of sarcasm.

His eyes focused on me as he spoke loud enough for my ears only. "What's her problem?"

There it was, the accusation in his eyes.

"Nothing. She's just mad you weren't here," I blurted without thought.

That was partially true.

His grin returned. "She's jealous."

His head tilted, mulling over the idea.

"You guys can go." We turned as one to find Julie with a towel wrapped around her. "I have a date to get ready for."

Her eyes found mine, and I quickly glanced away.

Sawyer was too caught up in what she said to notice.

"Tell me you saw her tits. What are they like?" he muttered to me under his breath before what she'd said hit him. "Wait, a date? Who is this guy? Do I know him?" he asked her.

Julie turned on her charm, which she was damn good at.

"Why should I tell you? Do you tell me every girl you hook up with?"

Sawyer sputtered and walked past me to step in front of her. Though they'd been friends, he'd become increasingly tongue-tied around her. It was almost funny, but there were other emotions wrapped up in my feelings about the two of them together.

"I'm trying to help you out," he pleaded.

She laughed. "No, you're not."

"Tonight, my house. Party. Don't bring your date," he offered. He glanced over his shoulder at me. "This is our time. Graduation. It should just be the three of us."

Normally, I understood what he meant. But I didn't think he would want to share, not Julie. I wasn't sure I wanted to complicate our friendship. What if she realized she wanted him too? Would I be mad because she would take him away from me or that he would take her?

"Just the three of us?" she asked.

They looked at me for confirmation. I closed my eyes and nodded. It would end up a night I'd never forget.

28

Ashton

IN THAT SPLIT MOMENT, I reflected on a time with Julie when she'd kissed me. I hadn't been the frog turned prince. I twisted my head just enough that Willow's kiss landed at the corner of my mouth.

She pulled back. Her frown mirrored Julie's from that past time and I had a second to regret. I wasn't sure what I felt for Willow except that I cared enough about her not to bring her into my complicated life. She, like Julie, would never understand what Sawyer meant to me and what I owed him.

Though Sawyer was in love with someone else, my feelings hadn't changed.

"I should go," she said again.

"Do you want me to walk you home?"

Her smile, like the sun, had the power to warm my skin.

"You're cute, but I'll be fine." She pointed to the sky. "It's still light out." She pulled her phone from her pocket. "And I haven't lost it yet."

She licked her lips before pressing them shut again. Then she gave me a little wave and headed deeper into the dense man-made woods.

I stood there watching her retreating form and ran a rough hand over my head.

My phone buzzed, and I pulled it out. There was a text from Chance.

Where are you? Coach is pissed.

Fuck. Practice. I was late again and would miss it if I didn't hustle over there.

One hundred one-armed push-ups, another set of clapping push-ups, then after what felt like a million stadium stair climbs, Coach released me to walk alone to the locker room. It was empty as everyone else had long since left.

The hot shower was a welcome respite, and I stayed there until the water cooled. Even after I turned it off, I rested my forearm on the tile and put my head there.

"Was it worth it?"

I lifted my head and glanced over to where Sawyer stood outside with his arms stretched out to rest on the edge of the stall I occupied as if he needed holding up. I blew out air, resigned to forestalling the oncoming confrontation.

"What?" I asked tiredly.

"Coming late to practice to avoid me."

My arm had dropped so I could cover my dick. Again, I wasn't sure why I'd done it. It wasn't like he'd even remotely looked in that direction.

"Do I need to remind you that it isn't always about you?" I said in my defense.

That was when I noticed how tired he looked. I wondered when the last time he slept.

"Can we call a truce? I need my best friend."

I closed my eyes, feeling like the biggest shit ever. Something was definitely going on with him. I nodded.

"I got my dad on my ass and something's going on with Shelly. I'm worried about her," he said.

"Shelly's got a boyfriend." Not that he wanted to hear that.

"Thanks, like I didn't know."

At least he wasn't mad. In fact, his lips twitched.

"Do you think I could get dressed before we finish this conversation?"

He snatched the towel that hung over the half wall and threw it at me before glancing down at my hand. I'd caught it midair.

"Don't worry about shrinkage. I hear most guys have that problem in water," he joked, leaving the shower area.

A burst of laughter that felt like forever in coming busted out of me. I almost shouted *stop thinking about my dick*, but the words died in my throat. Our friendship hadn't repaired enough to go there. I sobered and quickly dried off, wrapping the towel around my waist.

He sat with his arms resting on his knees, fists pressed into his eyes. I scrubbed a hand over my mouth.

"Do you think I can move back in?" I asked.

It wasn't just because Sawyer needed me. I'd had enough with the Sigma house and all the shit it stood for.

"I never accepted you'd left, not for good anyway."

His easy smile was too quick and lacked all the enthusiasm he normally had in abundance.

"What's going on with your dad?" I finally asked.

I'd let him talk and tell me how much or how little he wanted. I didn't ask questions, because what he needed was for me to listen. He never had trouble speaking, but what most people didn't know about him was that he felt like those that mattered never heard what he had to say except for me until lately. I'd failed him there, and he'd been doing a lot of stupid and reckless things I recognized now as attention grabbers. That was what my former therapist would have called it. Though I hadn't done many sessions. The university psychologists were over worked and underpaid. I'd felt like a number and not a person.

Back at the townhouse in my room, it was business as usual. I found myself falling back into old patterns. Sawyer needed me, and I jumped back into the familiar. I lay on my bed early two Saturdays later waiting for the guys to leave for our game.

I felt guilty. I hadn't seen Willow and had only traded a few texts. I'd given her some more Shakespearean quotes, but that was it.

"Are you ready?"

Sawyer had stolen my thoughts. What would it be like without him? I'd tried and failed to do it on my own. What would happen when we graduated in the spring?

"Yeah," I said, moving my legs over the side as I sat up. "Don't look so happy about the game."

His lack of enthusiasm matched my own.

"You know how I feel."

"You don't want to be quarterback," I finished for him.

"I don't have a choice either. Dad and his master plan to be president."

I thought about the conversation I had with my father. "Does your dad know that mine has the same lofty goals."

They weren't exactly friends, nor did his father know that the senator of the great state of New York was my father. But he knew they were on opposite sides of the party line.

Sawyer shrugged. "I don't exactly talk politics with Dad."

Chance moved into the doorway and slung an arm over Sawyer's shoulder.

"Hey, before we go, do you have the necklace? I'm going to give it to her tonight."

I went over to my chest of drawers and opened the top one, pulling out the box. I hoped he liked the changes. I handed it over.

"Fuck, brother," Chance said and I couldn't read his expression.

He walked over, pulled me in with a quick tight grip on my shoulder, and then released me.

"It's okay, right?" I asked.

His voice broke. "Okay? I owe you. She's going to fucking love it."

"You don't owe me anything," I said.

Sawyer came in. "Let me see." Chance offered him the box. "Moon and stars and shit. I get it." He looked at me. "Didn't know you had it in you," he said to me. Then to Chance, he said, "Remind me not to be in the house later. She's going to bang your brains out tonight."

We laughed, the moment over.

"Let's go kick some ass," Chance announced.

Out of the three of us, Chance actually liked playing football or maybe it was the scholarship that came with it.

I stood, and we left the townhouse piling into Sawyer's BMW. He put on some old school NWA "Gangsta Gangsta" and Dre's "Nuthin' But a G Thang." You would have thought the car had hydraulics the way Sawyer rolled up in the parking lot.

We got a few brows raised from some of our teammates, but Sawyer didn't give a shit. He popped some shades on and exited the car like a G. Chance and I traded glances before laughing. I was pretty sure the press van in the lot was the reason for Sawyer's antics. He didn't want to be his father's lap dog and would do anything to prove he was his own man. I put my cap on and followed Sawyer like a good dog.

Things went well for Sawyer with us winning in spectacular fashion. Unlike last game, he got his bell rung several times and had been checked out for a concussion.

We ended up at a huge house party. I'd settled into a rut. Following Sawyer's lead meant copious amounts of alcohol. As usual, he had pussy on the brain, and I thought I had enough.

"Hey." The guy I'd thought had been Willow's boyfriend waved me into a room.

Honestly, if I'd taken the time to really think about it, I probably would have guessed about what he wanted. He'd been staring at me all night.

"I'm Kent."

I tried not to make any assumptions. That was a dangerous thing. I had a lot of experience with them.

"What do you want?" I asked.

Truth be told, when he closed us into the room, the more my head toyed with the idea of figuring out what I wanted. I needed to know.

Was I what the monster claimed me to be?

Who had I been attracted to that night at the party so many nights ago when Willow had been too drunk to string four words together? Or had it been him?

"I thought we had something in common," he claimed.

I frowned as he went on to tell me that his brother was hosting the party. I checked out of the conversation a second until I heard him say, "Though you were looking for that guy."

There it was again, but I had to ask. Maybe he wasn't referring to Sawyer.

"What guy?"

"I think his name is Sawyer…"

He rambled on, but I found myself hating that everyone read me so well.

"What about him?"

"I've seen you watching him and he left with some girl."

I gritted my teeth. "And?"

He cocked a brow and folded his arms across his chest. "You're into him. I get it. He's hot."

When I didn't respond right away, he closed the distance between us, raising my hackles.

"It's not like that," I said.

He kept coming, and it was becoming all too real.

"It isn't? You want him, but you have options."

"Options," I sputtered.

When he stopped less than an inch away and pressed his mouth to mine, I ruled out that he was talking about other girls.

Kissing was something I didn't do regularly and gasped at the sudden contact. He took advantage, sweeping his tongue into my mouth.

I lost my breath and not because I enjoyed the contact. I was taken aback when all my choices had been stolen from me. It was automatic when instead of shoving him away, I punched him. The saddest thing about it was the resigned look he gave me, like me hitting him wasn't unexpected. That's when I realized I had no idea what his story was.

"I'm sorry," I spewed out as he wiped blood from the corner of his mouth. "I'm really sorry."

I fled the room, confused by the encounter, only to feel claustrophobic in the hallway. There were too many people brushing against my skin. I might as well been stung by a thousand bees for all the pain I was in. The monster I thought I buried was resurrected. That's when I saw Sawyer ducking into a bathroom with Shelly. I should have let it be, but he was my safe place, which I needed more than ever.

When he finally let me in, I knew I'd walked into a pivotal moment between the two of them. Yet, I couldn't leave no matter what it would cost me in the end. When you love someone so unconditionally, the consequences of what they needed from you didn't matter even knowing I could never have what I wanted. Like Vegas, I left what happened in the bathroom between us in the past, not to be brought up again.

Though I did walk away with answers I hadn't had before, that didn't stop the heaviness in my chest when Sawyer and I had a talk as we walked on campus the next day.

"It can't happen again," he said, warning me off Shelly as if.

It was exactly what he'd said after closing a door on a chapter in my life months ago. Finally, I brought up the topic he hadn't once acknowledged. That graduation night with him, Julie, and me, three years ago. We'd been high off of God knows what. Lines had been crossed that would never be crossed again. He'd made that clear as he spoke.

"Ash, don't go there."

I wanted it out in the open for once. "Why? It happened."

He and I had a moment that might had solidified the feelings I'd been holding onto for years.

"It shouldn't have."

The shame the devil had engrained in me had me spitting out my next sentence. "Because you are ashamed?"

"Yes."

There it was.

"But not because of the reasons you're thinking. I was supposed to protect you, not use you like that asshole."

My heart kicked up a beat as I looked at the only person to ever love me. When he first spoke to me all those years ago, all my doubts about life disappeared. He'd been the only home I'd given my heart. As he continued, I held back on my world crumbling in front of me. Even though I'd come to my own conclusions last night, I knew things between us were forever changed. I needed to learn to slay my own dragons.

He continued to talk, and I caught a few words here and there.

"It was a mistake." That was like the final nail in my coffin as my heart, along with my world, vaporized. I could picture the useless organ turning black with each word he spoke. "You can't let the past shape your future. Besides, what guy have you kissed…"

An inappropriate laugh left the empty shell that was me as I remembered Kent and his kiss. I'd gotten confirmation of one thing from it.

"You have?" he asked, drawing his own conclusions from my reactions.

"No, this guy, he..."

I found myself unable to finish that sentence.

"He kissed you?"

I nodded, remembering that moment over again.

"And?"

A part of me didn't want to tell him. He'd draw conclusions I didn't want him to. But it was Sawyer and I couldn't lie to him, not after everything.

"I don't know. He took me by surprise."

His rye smile should have lightened my mood, but I'd died inside. I didn't see that I would ever love someone like I'd loved him.

He chuckled. "What did you do?"

"I punched him."

He stopped and doubled over with laughter.

"See. You're not bi either."

He wrapped an arm around my shoulder, like everything was right in the world when mine had toppled over. But the time for sharing was over. I had to accept that he would never love me the same way I loved him. Still, he was right about one thing.

We'd made it to the parking lot when a voice interrupted my thoughts.

"Are you the asshole who hit my brother?"

29

Willow

MUSIC JAMMED out of my tiny Jawbone speaker as I twirled around my apartment feeling lighter than ever.

"What's got you in a good mood?" Celeste asked.

"My paper is done," I sang.

"I've never known you to be happy about writing a paper."

I didn't let her sour mood bring me down. I'd done it on my own for the most part and thought it was pretty good. I gave her a smile, showing lots of teeth as I thought about Ashton. He'd sent me some quotes, some I'd used, others I'd found on my own. Though I hadn't seen him since that day when he hadn't let me kiss him.

The me from a few weeks ago would have been devastated by his rejection. The today me couldn't be mad at him. There was just something so beautiful about his soul. He'd shown me selfless kindness every time we'd met, never asking for anything in return.

That didn't mean my crush had disappeared. I still liked him.

I also knew realistically it would never happen. So in a way, I'd moved on.

My phone buzzed in my pocket and I drew it out, grinning at the screen.

"Wow, now you have to tell me," Celeste probed. I caught her gaze as she asked, "Who is he?"

I bit my lower lip.

"Seriously, you're not going to tell me?"

Instead of answering her, I widened my grin.

"That's not fair," she continued. "I told you Taylor's name."

She had, but nothing more about him. She had her secrets. Why couldn't I have mine too? I danced toward my room, and she followed, of course.

"You've been acting weird since that white party. What happened?"

I lifted my shoulders in reply. I thought when I lost my virginity I would want to shout it from the rooftops. But there was something so private, I wanted to keep it to myself. Then again, I wasn't a good liar and didn't want her to know the part about Ashton not remembering.

"Fine. If you're not going to tell me, at least spill if you are meeting a guy."

It was a borderline smile with my lip between my teeth. It was stupid to keep it from her.

"It's not an actual date," I admitted.

"Okay, I can work with that." Then she rummaged in my closet. "We so need to go to the mall soon."

She flipped through clothes as I stood and glanced at the text again.

30. Same spot.

It was such a nonconsequential word, but it wasn't really a word, but a number. Still. Time was ticking down.

The shorts my well-meaning sister had picked out were a

little tight and the yellow halter shirt showed too much of my belly, but she'd convinced me I'd looked great.

The sounds of crickets played as I made my way to *our spot*. When had it become that? The sky was a rainbow of colors from gold to dusty pink as the sun dipped into the horizon.

"You finished it?"

I clutched my chest. Ashton's deep voice scared the crap out of me. He lay hidden in the tall grass. I was lucky I didn't trip and fall on him again. Still, I grinned thinking about the heavy weight off my chest.

"Yeah. I finished."

Even I heard the pride in my voice.

"Are you going to let me read it?"

I made a place in the grass to sit next to him, feeling shy all of a sudden.

"You don't have to," I said.

Though I valued his opinion, insecurity crept in. He was the English major. I couldn't read his expression with it covered in shadows from the dimming light.

"I want to," he said.

Taking a deep breath, I flipped through the screens on my phone to bring it up from the email I sent my professor. I handed it over and waited for his fingers to brush over mine. Somehow our skin didn't touch. I leaned back on my hands to hide my disappointment and found the sky, afraid to see any reaction from him while he read.

He didn't skim as much time passed. I'd been thinking about my plans for later that night when he spoke.

"It's good. I really like your use of 'All that glitters is not gold.'"

I sat up and quietly clapped at his high praise.

"Yeah, I thought about our talk and really thought that worked with how dragonflies don't mate forever, kind of like Romeo and Juliet, time was short. At the same time, just because what's beautiful might be short-lived, doesn't mean one shouldn't try."

The area began to light up with fireflies, creating a perfect mood as the crickets continued with their nightly chorus. Only this was not a date, I reminded myself.

In the fading light, his eyes held mine like I was the apple of his eye. I'll admit, it stole my breath, until I remembered the non-kiss in the woods.

Then it happened so slowly and unexpectedly, I can't say which of us initiated the contact as we met somewhere in the middle.

His lips were as soft as I imagined. Caught up in all the sensations, I closed my eyes and must have opened my mouth, because his tongue stroked over mine and delicious things happened in my belly as butterflies took flight.

Oxygen was no longer a thought as long as I could breathe in his air. It wasn't quick, nor did we rush. He took his time exploring me as I did him. He'd tasted like a sweet apple freshly picked from a tree if I didn't know better.

The need to touch him overwhelmed me. Our contact so far had only been mouth to mouth. I definitely felt resuscitated, but I needed more. I brushed a hand over his cheek, prepared to cup the back of his neck to draw him closer.

That contact changed everything. He pulled back so fast, I nearly lost my balance. What had I done?

Falling back into old habits, I apologized, "I'm sorry," and took all the blame.

Then again, the alarm on his face had me checking where my other hand was.

"I shouldn't have done that," he said, widening the gap between us.

Hurt feelings put my defenses up, erecting a wall to protect my heart.

"We shouldn't have, especially since I have a date tonight," I said.

He stilled halfway to getting to his feet and then sat back down. "Date?" he asked.

"Yeah, you know, when two people go out together to enjoy each other's company."

His tongue darted out of his gorgeous mouth and licked his lips. Why should I want to know what was going on in that beautiful head of his? But I did.

"I know what a date is, though I've never been on one."

That killed some of my anger. "Seriously?"

His shoulders lifted and fell in answer.

"Well, if this is how you treat girls, I can see why."

My petulant tone broke through him, though I should only be angry at myself.

"Willow, I like you, I do. Things are just complicated right now. It wouldn't be fair to you..."

My heart soared and took a dive in the same second. *He liked me.* My inner self did a little dance and maybe a twerk or two until I remembered the second thing he'd said. *Things are complicated.* That could only mean one thing.

"Isn't that my decision to make?"

It was a desperate attempt to change things around, which was stupid considering my date.

"I need to get my head on straight," he said.

Red flag, Willow. Let him go.

Yet, I nodded even though I didn't understand and decided to just put it out there.

"You're in love with someone else," I said.

I didn't mention Sawyer by name. That had only gotten him to shut down in the past.

He pursed his lips tight and revealed nothing.

I nodded again and got to my feet. "For the record, he's

missing out." His jaw worked, but he didn't look at me. "Thanks for everything." When he still didn't acknowledge me, I said with finality, "Bye, Ash."

His head jerked up, but I was already turning away. I wasn't sure what came over me to not use his full name. Something about it felt right.

In little time, I made it back across campus, to where a black and white movie drive-in style played. Blankets littered the field in place of cars.

I found Derek with his black-framed glasses waiting for me. He had popcorn and beer and kept up a steady conversation about life back then and now as we enjoyed the show. Problem was, I couldn't stop thinking about the kiss that had blown my world into smithereens.

A tap on my shoulder brought me to the present. Derek wore a hesitant smile and said, "You left me there for a second."

"Sorry."

I was. It wasn't fair for him.

"That was fun. Can we do it again sometime?"

"Yes, we should... do it again."

He helped me to my feet and didn't let go. In fact, he walked me all the way to my apartment. In his hopeful eyes, I could see he wanted to kiss me goodnight, but I couldn't.

"Thanks again for tonight," I said.

Our hands fell away and I gave him a little wave before going into my apartment without so much as a brush of lips on a cheek. I touched mine, which hadn't stopped tingling from hours before.

After closing and locking my door, I flopped on my bed. Was Ashton thinking about me? Probably not. He was in love with Sawyer, but apparently, that didn't mean he didn't like girls. He'd said he liked me. What should I do with that?

When a text came, I read it several times before answering.

30

Ashton

DAYS LATER, I still didn't know why I'd kissed her. Except I had. I'd needed the confirmation. She'd been the third puzzle piece I had to fit together to see the picture of my life clearly.

Sawyer took my feelings as some twisted form of hero worship. Maybe there was some of that, but that thinking diminished how I felt. And denying it hadn't gotten me anywhere, not that admitting it had either.

Then there had been the kiss with Kent. He was a good enough looking dude, and because I recognized that, I hadn't been sure what that meant. Then there was pretty Willow. I'd acted on instinct and kissed her. It had been a shitty thing to do.

What had I learned about myself? Sawyer was right. I wasn't gay or even bi. It was a relief, not because I would have been ashamed at either revelation. More that I'd questioned who I was for so long, having an answer was a relief.

I'd never been interested in any guy ever outside of Sawyer, and with him it had always been different. There was a connection between us that was deeper than the physical. The fact that I'd felt nothing when Kent kissed me confirmed that guys didn't do it for me.

However, nothing had been far from what I felt when I'd kissed Willow. My dick had instantly risen to the occasion, like it had with Julie all those years ago.

Sawyer hadn't been around either time, and I couldn't blame my body's readiness on him.

Although I was pretty sure I had the answers I needed, a thousand questions still plagued me.

I took the steps down into the usual underground space hollowed out beneath the frat house. Initiation night into the Vanderbilt Club was tonight.

Open lockers lined the small dark room I'd entered. We'd been instructed to deposit clothes and dawn the robes for the first meeting.

Sawyer came in as did Lance. I traded glances with my friend. We were both surprised to see Kent's brother as a potential inductee. He had the money and family power. Still, that wasn't the only criteria to be chosen.

No one spoke. Sawyer left before me, and I started to follow. Lance brought up his arm like a bar to block my way.

"My brother's not a fag like you."

I didn't give a shit what he thought of me, but I didn't like that use of word.

"He isn't," I said, because though Kent was gay, he wasn't a fag. "But you are."

I took hold of his arm and shoved it down, pushing him back out of my way at the same time.

He stumbled back a step, and I left taking my time. I did listen in case he tried to rush me, but I wasn't afraid. I gave him the same dead stare I'd given Willhouse when I dared him to try me. Lance trusted his instincts and left me alone.

I followed a narrow hall that led to a large cavernous room. It was circular and shrouded in darkness. An inlayed marble floor was a pattern of ovals that outlined the perimeter. Many robed figures had already filled spots. In the low light, I couldn't see Sawyer's face and chose a place halfway toward the back of the room.

Within minutes, all the spots were filled. A booming voice filled the room.

It spoke of loyalty, unity, and ended on trust. It wasn't exactly in my nature to trust. He went on to say that we would be given a gift.

A line of women walked into the room and the circle we formed. They corralled around to stand one by one three feet in front of each of us. Then together they dropped their robes. Someone gasped, and there was no doubt in my mind it had to be Bryant. His dream was about to come true as it became apparent what our gift was for the evening.

The woman before me was as perfect as a human could be. Her breasts were heavy and rounded. Her stomach was flat with hips full enough to grab ahold of. Yet, there wasn't a twitch beneath my robe.

"Follow me," she said in accented English.

I refocused on her and closed the distance between us while I'd pondered what it meant not to have a reaction. She was beautiful for sure. Shouldn't I want her?

She grabbed my wrist, and it took everything in me not to snatch my hand away. Her hold sent stabbing pain lancing through me. My heart rated increased as ingrained panic from so many years ago welled up inside me.

"I have something you need to hear," she whispered.

That got my attention. What would she need to tell me?

As if she'd heard my thoughts, she added, "It's about your parents." When she said their names, my interest was piqued. I removed my hand, but followed her to one of the rooms beyond the circle outline.

We entered a room, small but large enough for a bed with straps that hung from posts and plenty of space to walk around it. There was also a small chest of drawers in a corner. The only other interesting thing to note was the door on the opposite side from the one we entered.

By the time I made eye contact with the woman, raising a brow in question, a voice came from the small speakers high in the corners near the ceiling.

"Trust goes both ways. If we are to share our secrets with you, you must trust us the same. This test is the first of many and not a terribly hard one. Take a load off. Give yourself over to the pleasure we bestow unto you. Let yourself be bound and believe that we will not take advantage of the power you grant us this night."

My past had never been far from my mind even after so many years. Though I had nothing to prove to this society or my father, who was a member, I had something to prove to myself.

You can do this.

Because I'd yet to react to the woman watching me, I doubted anything could happen. I sat on the bed before exhaling a breath and lying back. My mind trailed to Sawyer. Was he too giving in to the rules of this test?

The woman who'd not given me her name came over and began to strap me in.

"There is a woman who knows your mother. She has answers to many questions you may have about her."

I took slow breaths, trying not to let my fear get the best of me, and concentrated on her words.

"Why do I care?"

To her I must have sounded like I was in pain the way I'd gritted out the words.

"You will learn the truth about your father."

Neither of the so-called people who'd given me life had ever been parents to me. So, why was curiosity growing inside me?

"Why would you know anything?" I asked.

She glanced up above the door. I craned my neck, but didn't see anything. Though I imagined there must be a hidden camera that she was well aware of.

"They want you to know."

They could mean anything, but most likely the Club.

She pressed a paper into my hand and left that wrist unbound as she moved to cover my eyes with a blindfold. Everything went dark. If not for my free arm, I might have thrashed about to get free.

She bound my ankles and came back. I knew not by sound, but by the faint floral scent she wore.

Her breath fanned over my ear as she spoke.

"You've been granted another gift. It will not be me who takes care of you tonight."

Breathing too fast, a dizzying sensation rocked through my body. It left me a little light-headed, and I had to remind myself this game was about trust. Given that I had a free hand, I could leave at any time. I wasn't sure how long I could wait to find out if I would lose to panic and old memories or if I could win this round.

31

Willow

WHEN I WALKED IN, Celeste was there waiting in the living room to ambush me with what she held in her hand.

The black envelope was so distinctive, there was no mistaking what she had.

"When did you get this?" she asked like she had every right to know.

There had been a time when I would have cowered against her demands. But all the reasons why had faded away since I'd met Ashton. He'd helped me fight against my insecurities. He'd found me attractive and not lacking. Though I still held a major crush on him, I was actually okay with not having him.

I'd gone out with Derek a couple of times and he was growing on me.

I moved forward and plucked the invitation from her hand.

"It's none of your business," I said and kept moving forward to my bedroom.

She might have been briefly stunned that I'd talked to her

that way after years of silent compliance. She was still only four steps behind me when I entered my space.

"Well," she said, with a dramatic pause to follow. "It seems you don't need my help anymore."

I held up the envelope. "Why were you going through my things?"

She stared at me like I had two heads.

"I was looking for my earrings I let you borrow and you never gave back. And there it was in the top drawer."

I sighed. Okay, she hadn't been snooping.

"Fine, but why did you take it out? Did you read it?"

I wasn't sure why I was pissed.

"No. I didn't have to. Are you going?"

I hadn't been sure, and tonight was the night. On one hand, Ashton's mixed messages were confusing. He'd told guys at his frat I was his. He'd had sex with me, but didn't remember. Lastly, he'd said he liked me and kissed me, but in the same breath warned me he wasn't the right guy for me.

"Is this how you plan to lose your virginity?"

There had been many reasons why I hadn't told her about that yet. It had been my secret that I could replay in my head and not analyze the reasons why the night wasn't as magical as I'd wanted it to be.

"I'm not a virgin anymore."

Her eyes bugged out. "What? Why didn't you tell me?"

I didn't want to lie or tell her the truth, but I shrugged.

"Are you okay? Was he good to you? You don't have to tell me if you want."

Celeste had many layers. Today, she was showing me the kindness I knew was inside her with her genuine concern.

"He's a good guy," I said.

Thinking about him brought a grin to my face.

"That good, huh?" When I only gave her another half-shrug, she asked, "Are you guys together?"

"Not exactly."

Her expression turned sympathetic, which only made me feel pathetic.

"Is he going to be there?"

She pointed at the envelope I still held.

The truth came out of me in the form of a nod.

"If you really like him, you should go."

Her declaration took me by surprise. I wasn't expecting her to give me that advice. She seemed so weary about it.

"What do you know about it?"

She shrugged. "Not much, other than if you don't go, there will be another girl there to take your place."

That had been the warning the guy who'd given me the invitation at the frat house had said.

"It's not like I'm his girlfriend," I protested, not sure why.

"Well, your chances will only get worse. He's going to be with someone. Either you or another girl. And what if he and another girl hit it off outside of him screwing her?"

The crude way she spoke made me wince.

"Just because I go doesn't mean things will change for us."

"No," she admitted. "But you being there can lock him down from being with someone else." She paused. "Look, I'm going to be honest and say that if you go, be ready to screw him because that's what this is about."

I thought about our first time, which he completely didn't remember, a side effect of the date rape drug that had been intended for me. Though I didn't blame him, more like hero-worshipped him for taking it to protect me, the idea that we could be together and he would remember enticed me.

There were so many more questions I had for Celeste, like *how did she know?* But if I was going, I had to get ready. It would take a good portion of time to tame my hair. My wild curls had gone mad from the short rain we'd had earlier that morning.

"Go shower and I'll get my flat iron ready," she said.

I did just that. While she worked, I tried to broach the subject of how she knew what went on at that party. She remained tight-lipped. I didn't press because she was doing me a favor with my hair. I didn't want to piss her off and have it half-done.

She studied her handiwork when she was done.

"He's going to die when he sees you."

I bit my bottom lip as a small smile grew on my face.

"You really think so?"

I hated the insecurity, but it was a very real thing.

"Willow, you're gorgeous, even without makeup. Something I would kill for."

She was being far too kind, but when I turned, the girl in the mirror was someone I'd only wished I could be. I wasn't a model, but I did feel pretty.

I turned and hugged my sister. I had a love-hate relationship with her. In this moment, I loved her very much.

"Thank you," I said.

Celeste offered me a dress that was more her style. It would cling to every curve and imperfection, which wasn't the reason why I turned her down. Tonight was about Ashton seeing me for me. Yes, it was some sort of sex party, according to Celeste, but we didn't know for sure. He'd said he liked me. So tonight, I would be me.

When I walked out of my room five minutes later, Celeste nodded in approval.

"It's good," she said.

The sundress Mom had bought me last summer played to my body type. It was loose, but not overly so. It hinted to my shape, but wasn't like cling wrap.

"Do you want a ride?"

I almost said I would drive when I remembered alcohol would likely be involved. Though I was sure I wouldn't drink anything after last time, never say never. Ashton would be there, and I trusted he would take care of me. He'd proven that over and over again. I took Celeste up on her offer to drive.

She looked like a proud parent when she dropped me off, and I thought of Mom. I doubted she'd be proud knowing what I was about to do.

The frat house didn't look as imposing as it had other nights. Without the muffled music and steady stream of people entering or exiting, it looked like any other mini mansion on that particular street.

Per the invitation, I was required to enter a side entrance. A tall woman with a thick accent was waiting by the door.

"Invitation?" she asked.

I handed it over, trying to place her origins. She didn't sound Southern let alone American.

"Put this on." She handed me a blindfold and didn't give the invitation back.

Maybe this was how they kept things so secret. I hadn't thought to take a picture of it. Then again, did I really need a souvenir of tonight's events?

I settled the silky mask over my sleek hair and let the darkness take me. This was beyond anything I'd done before. The trust I was giving on the pretense that Ashton would be here only confirmed how far my crush had gone. What if he wasn't here? What if the guy had lied?

My heart kicked up as I was led down with a firm hand on my shoulder. That was strange. Basements weren't a common thing in Oklahoma. Something about the soil or water table prevented such a thing from being added to almost all houses or businesses. Clearly, money ruled all because I was most definitely headed down. The air got cooler with each step.

The space was large as we took several turns. I wasn't sure I could find my way back in an emergency.

Though I couldn't see, I knew instantly when I was herded into a room with others. My blindfold was removed, and the same tall, imposing woman with a short crop of bleach blonde spiky hair stepped in my line of vision, blocking my view of the room full of other women. They weren't college students.

"Take off your clothes and put on this."

Russian. Yes, she sounded Russian.

I took the hooded gown thing she handed me, unsure what I'd do next. The women around me were in various stages of undress, uncaring if anyone saw them. As much as I wanted to be brave, insecurity and fear of the unknown took hold.

"You don't undress, you go," the woman directed, pointing toward the hallway.

"Just do it," a whispered voice said behind me.

I tried to turn, but the herculean woman glared at me. I bobbed my head, figuring I could still back out.

When I turned to face the other woman who'd spoken, she was naked. I quickly shifted my gaze away.

"It's okay. I'm used to it." Her accent was fainter than the woman in charge. "It's not so bad. Most of the guys are very good-looking."

She spoke like it was a job, and maybe it was. I opened my mouth, then clamped it shut. If I said anything, she would know I wasn't with them. I wasn't sure if she'd stop giving me advice.

"There are worse things than fucking some rich boy," she added.

Her smile was faint and looked forced. I nodded. From the murmured conversations, everyone had an accent except me.

She put on the robe, leaving me to make up my mind. Should I stay, or should I go? These women were probably professionals. The likelihood of Ashton hooking up with one and making her his girlfriend was slim.

An honest-to-goodness growl formed in the back of my throat. Reasonable or not, the idea of anyone else touching him irritated me.

He wasn't my boyfriend, but maybe Celeste was right. If I had a chance in hell at making him mine, it was now.

A fear spiked in my gut, but I slowly took off my dress, leaving my undergarments on. I put on the sheer robe over my head and took off my bra and panties as if no one could see. Then I curled my arms around my middle and shrank into the shadows.

"It won't be long. And most don't take much to get off," my new friend said.

We laughed softly, me more out of nerves. There were still a lot of unanswered questions. I told myself to be brave and fearless. This was America. I could still say no and walk away.

The large Viking-like woman walked back in. "Time."

I wasn't the first to step forward, but when I moved, her arm lifted and a finger pointed at me. "You stay," she ordered.

The one woman who'd given me advice gave me a sympathetic smile before filing out with the rest. Though it was my second dose of pity that day, I wasn't mad at her.

I hung back in the small locker room-like area, really seeing it for the first time. A large noise I recognized as a voice piped through a microphone filtered into the space where I stood. Though I could hear it, I couldn't make out individual words.

Since I was alone, it would be so easy to get dressed and leave. But Ashton's face popped in my head. I wasn't sure how I knew, but I had a feeling he would prefer me over a stranger. That wasn't conceit, far from it. It had been the look in his eyes after kissing me like he'd surprised himself.

I had no idea how long I waited, but just as I started to talk myself out of staying, the large woman returned.

"You. Come," she ordered.

You never know what you are capable of until you do something you never thought you could do. The first step was the hardest. After that, every step got easier.

The dimly lit corridor we traversed gave nothing away other than we weren't walking straight. The curved walkway held nothing on the walls. Nothing but closed doors on the left. We stopped in front of one.

When it opened, one of the women from the locker room stepped into the hall. She nodded at the leader, who then pointed at the open doorway.

A man in a dark robe lay flat on the bed. Just as I noticed he was bound there, the woman shoved me into the room with no directions. She must have assumed I would know what to do.

When the door clicked shut, I jumped.

"Who's there?"

His prone form hadn't given away who he was, but his voice did.

I opened my mouth, but a voice from a speaker beat me to saying something.

"Tell her what you want."

After a quick look above in search of the hidden camera, my gaze quickly came back to him to search for any cues as to his feelings about being here. I watched his body visibly relax. Troubling though was he didn't speak right way.

"Are you there?" he asked after a few long seconds. "Say something."

If I spoke, would he ask me to leave?

"I'm here," I whispered.

His head shifted in my direction, but he was as blindfolded as I'd been. I inched forward, my fingertips itched to touch him.

"Is it your choice to be here?" he asked.

"Yes." The word was nothing more than an exhale of breath.

His arm shifted, and I noticed he wasn't completely bound. As his hand made its way to his blindfold, I moved to stop him. I practically had to straddle him to press his wrist back to the bed. I didn't know what came over me. But I didn't want him to see me yet.

I pressed my lips to his. Though my torso hovered over him, my center had landed right on his cock.

"Willow?"

Stunned for a second, I almost answered. Instead, I swept my tongue over his. He kissed me back, turning my insides on fire. He hardened beneath me, groaning in my mouth.

"Willow?" he asked a second time.

The last time he'd thoroughly taken care of me. It was my turn to repay the favor. I crawled down his torso, pulling up fistfuls of fabric as I moved. I desperately wanted to see him.

Then it was there in all its glory, long and thick. I marveled how it could have been inside me. Yet, my mouth watered. Something about this man made me want to try things I'd never done before.

I'd let go of his wrist in favor of wrapping my hand around him. Before I could, his hand snaked out and took mine. He threaded his fingers with mine as I stared at him. Though he'd said my name, did he really know who I was?

I brushed aside that insecurity, letting his actions give me more courage to settle myself between his legs. Then I used my other hand to hold his dick up. I wrapped my lips around the crown and attempted to suck more of him down. He shuddered, his hand tightening in mine. I took both as a good sign.

Things ended before they really got started. He tugged my hand so his cock popped free of my mouth. He pulled me forward until I landed in the same position I'd started out in. Then the blindfold was gone and we stared at each other for a long second before he cupped the back of my head, drawing me to him. We were kissing again, this time deeper and harder as his dick pressed between my thighs.

I panted when we broke apart.

"You want this?" he asked.

In answer, I sat up, resting more firmly on his hardness. Then I tugged the robe off me in one fluid motion.

His eyes bounced between my gaze and my breasts. He reached out with utter reverence, palming one and stroking the pad of his thumb over one beaded nipple. His touch lit a flame the moisture between my legs tried to put out. I dropped my head back, enjoying all the sensations created.

Too soon, his hand glided down my side and took ahold of my hip where his fingers dug in. The firm way he held me might have been bruising, but all I felt was his intense need for me.

He ground his hips, rubbing his cock where I needed him most.

On instinct, I lifted. His desire matched mine as I raised his dick to stand so I could impale myself on him. He stretched me to the point of pain. That didn't stop me from riding up and down his length slow and steady at first.

He helped by taking control and guiding me in a pace that suited us both. His thumb somehow made contact with my nub and I cried out, unable to stop myself. My breathing became ragged as I clenched around him, feeling that pressure building to a feverish pitch.

"Fuck," he cried out as I came with the force of a rocket.

Then it was all him, thrusting up and losing pace as I continued to spasm around him. Then he lost it. His head craned back, the veins in his neck bulging as he found his release. I collapsed on top of him, unable to think.

His hand landed on my back seconds later as if he hadn't been sure he wanted to touch me. That was my first clue that like Cinderella my magical night was coming to an end.

"Did I hurt you?"

Still trying to catch my breath, I shook my head in the crook of his neck. I felt him softening inside me, and weirdly I didn't want him to pull out yet.

I rested my hand on his chest as if I could touch his heart like he had mine. But reality came crashing in like a tidal wave.

"Are you on the pill?" he asked.

It wasn't exactly the conversation I'd wanted to have, but as I thought about it, a practical one. Had I really just had sex with a guy I barely knew without protection again?

"No." I was back to speaking in hushed tones.

"I can give you the money for the morning after pill."

I shifted to stare at him wide-eyed. It wasn't as if I wanted a kid. But we'd just had sex. I didn't expect him to profess his undying love. Yet, I yearned for something more than a clinical conversation about the ramifications of what we'd just done. I felt tears build in my eyes.

"It's okay. I think I can manage," I said before moving off him so fast you'd thought we were on fire.

I grabbed the garment I'd worn in the room, putting it on in such a hurry, my hair no doubt stood on end. Then I was out the door quicker than he could call my name. Embarrassment fueled every step until I found the locker room, which was open. Otherwise, I might have been running in circles for days.

I got my clothes on and ran into the woman in charge of this weird sex party.

"Done?"

I nodded. She reached over, took an envelope, and handed it to me. I almost gave it back, knowing full well I wouldn't be attending another party. Instead, I let her blindfold me and lead me out.

Once I was outside, she unmasked me and then disappeared behind the closing door. Before leaving, I peeked inside the innocuous envelope and found cash, leaving me to feel cheaper than the McDonald's dollar menu.

32

Ashton

WHAT HAD I SAID?

She'd run like a scared rabbit, leaving me to scrub a hand down my face before trying to get up to go after her. I'd really screwed up. My legs and arm tugged against the bounds, reminding me that I was secured to the bed like a prisoner. Though I worked fast to free myself, when I entered the hall, Willow was nowhere to be found.

For the first time, I felt one step closer to something I'd been searching for all my life. *Me.* She'd given me that gift even when Sawyer hadn't been able to.

In absence of her returning my messages, I'd gone to our spot many times hoping to find her. She'd never come. I'd resorted to scoping out the building where I knew she had classes when I had a chance, and still no sighting.

Even at football games when the crowds packed the stadium, I imagined her there somewhere. Though what would I say? The last time I'd royally screwed up.

"Westborough."

I snapped my head up and saw everyone in the huddle staring at me. I nodded. Somewhere in the back of my mind, I'd heard the play. Sawyer clapped his hand, we got into position, and he counted off before the ball was hiked into his hand.

He shovel passed the ball to me. Having spent my entire life avoiding being touched, I was uniquely suited to dodge and slip through walls of muscle on the field. I found the small holes and pockets and ran like hell when I saw freedom ahead of me. You'd think my life depended on it when I hustled as the crowd cheered.

All of the noise around me quieted as I focused on the end zone ahead of me. I should have remained focused, but a vision of Willow above me filled that silent space. The bliss on her face as she'd come broke through the drugged haze of memory and dream that long ago night. I'd seen her face like that before. The other night hadn't been the first time we'd been together.

My steps stuttered before they were out from underneath me. As I face-planted into the turf, I'd had the presence of mind to secure the ball beneath me. Bodies fell on top of me. The opposing team didn't just try to get the ball from me, their blows were meant to harm. Punching to my side and face almost had me blacking out. By the time I was excavated from the bottom, my ears were ringing.

Sawyer shouted, but I couldn't make out the words. He held out two fingers in front of my face. I held up my middle one. He grinned, but there was relief on his face. For the first time in all the time I'd known him, hope for something that could never be didn't spark inside me. I gave him a small smile and followed him back to the huddle.

"Finish this," he said, gaze aimed at me.

We were on the one yard line. I'd gotten that close. I nodded, though my brain still rattled like a bobble head unable to focus. What kind of ass had Willow thought me? Why had she lied when I asked if anything happened between us that night? Her only reason had to be to protect me.

When the play began, I had one motive. Not to win the game, but to end it. I had so much making up to do, I wanted off the field. I took the ball handed off to me and leaped over the defensive line and dove for the end zone.

Our victory only delayed me getting off the field. I had no plan other than to find her. Even if she didn't accept me, I had to apologize for it all.

Looking at every face in the crowd that I could see proved fruitless.

"What's up with you, man?" Sawyer asked later that day.

"Nothing."

"You don't seem yourself. You had that score and you stopped."

Though I'd relied on Sawyer most of my life, I couldn't depend on him anymore. One more semester and we would go our separate ways. I kept Willow to myself.

I shrugged and watched him try to hide his disappointment.

"Okay. If you want to talk—"

The nod I gave him was returned with a sad yet understanding one.

I'd stopped blowing up her phone and told myself she'd probably lost it. Besides, she had every reason to hate me.

When I wasn't thinking about Willow, I thought about the cryptic message the woman at initiation night had given me. There had been no word from the Vanderbilt Club either. I had no idea if I'd passed their test and didn't care.

Days turned into weeks until the holidays were upon us.

Chance's girlfriend popped in my open door.

"Dinner's ready," Brie said, tapping me on my shoulder to get my attention.

"Thanks. I'm not hungry right now."

"You know if you ever want to talk…"

Everyone always wanted to talk when all I wanted was quiet. But Brie was a psych major, so her offer didn't annoy me.

"Thanks," I said.

She left, disappearing downstairs where a number of voices were laughing and talking. I'd promised Sawyer I wouldn't run again. That didn't mean I wanted to play fifth wheel between the couples downstairs.

If Willow were here, it would be different. She made me smile in ways I never thought anyone could. But maybe things were better this way. She had a chance of happiness. Who was I to bring her into my fucked-up world?

It was only a few days later, I scooped up my bag with a black envelope I'd received that morning tucked inside. Thanksgiving was here. The house wasn't yet empty. Sawyer was taking Shelly somewhere. I heard Chance and Brie behind his door as I walked down the hall. I left, not wanting things to get awkward. This was the one holiday I'd always spent with Sawyer until now. Everyone knew I was leaving. No need to drag it out.

I can't say I arrived in merry England sober. The jet I'd chartered was full-service. Considering the price of the flight, I took advantage of all the amenities except the stewardess who all but threw herself at me.

My destination looked like a palace. I walked into the private boarding school and facilities for the wealthiest people in the world's stowaways. It was a bullshit excuse for rich people to quietly hide away their problem children.

"Fuck if it isn't Ash."

I smiled at Finn, who looked a lot like his brother, Sawyer.

"Don't act like you didn't expect me," I said, dropping into a leather armchair in his private living room.

"Sawyer will be here tomorrow. Why didn't you hitch a ride with him?" Finn was smart as fuck. One of the smartest people I knew. It didn't take him long to puzzle it together. "Oh, he's bringing his girlfriend. Shit, brother, that sucks."

He knew like everyone else. I'd done a poor job at concealing my feelings to everyone but Sawyer. He'd either ignored me or had his head in his ass. Besides, the last thing I wanted was his pity.

"It is what it is. I'm fine with it. She's good for him."

They weren't sarcastic-laced words.

"Whatever you say, brother. Are you hanging around?"

"Nah, got places to go."

I had nowhere to be exactly. That wasn't exactly true. The black invitation gave me an option. "I'm going to Prague, actually." He nodded. "I would appreciate it if you kept that to yourself."

I hadn't told anyone, and I wanted it kept that way.

"Yeah, man, your secret is safe with me. I would go with you, but I'd slow you down."

Finn was the first person to make light of his situation. Instead of sulking about the distance his parents put between him and the rest of his family, he'd accepted his fate and was making it better despite them. He was a clear reminder that you could do anything when you put your mind to it.

"How do you do it?" I asked, needing some advice.

"What? Deal with this?"

His finger lifted, and I watched in amazement. It shook as it moved side to side, as if his arm had spread wide to encompass the room. I didn't ask how yet. I let my gaze take in the palatial room as he wanted. It was fit for a king with a huge four-poster bed on one end and an entire living room with sofas and a huge TV on the other.

"You're right. It's too small," he joked.

I had to laugh at that. "How do you deal with being on your own?"

"Oh, that." He sobered some. "It's been like that so long, I'm not sure what it would feel like to live back home. I'm not even sure I would if I could. If my father were to be believed, he only has one son, not three. Tomas prefers dick over pussy, though he'll do either, I'm broken, and Sawyer loves pussy, which in my father's eyes is pure gold."

Willow popped in my head, and I could see her saying *All that glitters isn't gold.*

I nodded as I pictured her in that field with the sun haloing her pretty skin.

"But you're not alone. Give Sawyer time," he was saying.

"It's not him. It's me." The frequency in which Willow invaded my thoughts scared the shit out of me. I wasn't ready to have feelings for anyone else. I wasn't sure I would ever be ready for that. "I've relied on his being there for so long, I can't see what life looks like without him."

He sighed. "I get it. Give yourself time." I could almost see him rubbing his hands together as he switched topics. "I've been reading the shit you've been sending me and, damn, it's powerful stuff."

The story I'd been writing that was loosely based on me I'd shared with him.

"That kid, Agni, is a badass."

"That's all Sujah."

Finn shook his head. "No way. Sujah awakens something in Agni, yes. He teaches him shit, like how to survive. But Agni will be the one to save the world."

Though I hadn't seen myself as a fictional writer, I tossed ideas to Finn, and he was opinionated enough to be honest about his feelings on where I saw the story going. I didn't know how many hours past until an attractive nurse knocked on the door.

"Mr. Cargill, are you ready?"

Finn's eyes glittered as he smirked at me and winked before he said over his shoulder, "Give us a few more minutes."

I shook my head after she left again. If there was one thing true about the Cargill brothers, they all liked sex a lot. That probably had a lot to do with their parents being very open about it from when they were little. It wasn't a taboo in their home and something their parents discussed more openly as the brothers got older.

"So that," I said and tilted my head toward his hand.

He lifted the finger again and grinned.

"Father's money is paying off."

I got up without fear and locked my finger with his. "Good for you, brother."

It was the closest thing we had to a handshake in all the years I'd known him.

He winked at me. "Before you know it, I'll be walking."

"I look forward to that day." Before shit could turn sad, I said, "I'll let you go to your nurse," and left the question of what the nurse planned to do hang in the air.

"No rush. She'll be back." In a slightly quieter tone, but still loud enough to hear, he added, "She sucks dick like a champ. I swear, if I had a gold medal, I'd give it to her."

That made me laugh, and not because of what he said, but why. Finn wanted me not to think about all the bad shit going on in my head, so he'd said something completely off topic to catch me off guard.

"Then I should really go. I wouldn't want to come between you and your nurse," I jested.

"Like I said, she'll be back. They always are. But you, brother, you stay. Crash on my couch. I'll tell my brother I'm busy and for him to show his girl around London."

It would be too easy to say yes.

"Nah—I'm actually looking forward to some alone time."

What I really wanted were answers. That black invitation held a promise of some.

33

Willow

A DAY before the Thanksgiving feast, I was being smothered by my mother. When she released her hold, it was only to free her hands to grab the sides of my face.

"Willow," she crooned, staring at me as if she hadn't seen me in years. "I missed you so."

Her hands stroked down my hair before I was finally freed.

"I missed you too, Mom."

On the other side of the room, Celeste was getting similar treatment from her dad, only less hands-on.

Mom appraised me. "Have you been eating?"

She asked the question in a way I wasn't sure if she thought I was too fat or too skinny.

"Enough," I said passively and changed the subject. "How are you doing?"

"Oh, you know, charity dinners and meeting with clients keep me busy."

Of course, she wasn't talking about her work, which she

hadn't done in years. Rather she was my stepfather's arm candy, and Mom was happiest in that role.

Warning bells went off in my head. If I didn't get her off this current topic of conversation, she would be giving me the third degree about my own love life, existent or not.

"Is there anything I can help with for tomorrow's meal plans?" I offered.

She shifted and draped an arm around my shoulders. "Oh, honey, it's being catered. I'm making your father's favorite home-made apple pie, though."

For a second, I thought she was talking about my dad until I followed her eyes over to Dan.

"He's not my father," I muttered under my breath.

The smile plastered on her face didn't falter even as I stood, muscles tensed.

"Don't say that. He loves you like you were his own."

I turned my face away from where Dan was still talking to Celeste, not at all looking pleased. He hadn't even acknowledged my presence, per usual.

"He tolerates me because of you."

Mom faced me, giving me that *don't make trouble for me* look.

"That's not true. He pays for your college."

I ground my teeth because Mom was stuck in her fantasy world.

"Funny, because I have a ton of student loans to pay back that say otherwise."

Mom pursed her lips and I mirrored her expression, crossing my arms over my chest for added weight.

"Well, he pays for your room and board. That's something."

I glanced heavenwards, praying for patience. We'd only just arrived, and I didn't want to fight with her.

"He isn't paying for me. Celeste wanted to live off-campus, and the place she found there wasn't much difference in cost for a second bedroom."

Mom sighed, but still managed a small smile. "It's something. Be thankful."

"I am. I'm sorry. It's just he's not my dad, okay. That doesn't mean I'm not grateful for the things he has done for me. Mostly, I want you to be happy."

Before I could draw her into a hug to make up, she had me in one.

"You will always be the most important thing to me," she said into my ear and kissed my forehead before letting me go.

Dan looked ready to blow, and Mom stepped over.

"Why don't you girls go get ready for lunch?"

She smoothed a hand down Dan's arm as his face lightened from a fiery red to pink.

I threaded my arm through Celeste's and pulled her free from the stare down she was having with her father.

"What's going on?" I murmured as we turned the corner on the stairs on the way up.

Her eye roll seemed to go on for ages until we entered her room. I shut the door as she flopped onto her bed like the world was ending.

"So?"

I stood there, arms folded, which seemed to be my favorite pose when I was at home.

"I told him."

She stared at the ceiling and I exhaled a breath as I sat next to her.

"He didn't take it well?" I asked.

That was an understatement, but I wasn't sure what else to say. Dan had plans for his only daughter, and she wasn't living up to his expectations.

"Talk about meltdown. You'd thought I'd told him I was pregnant, not that I hadn't applied to a master's program."

I laughed. "That would start Armageddon. Don't joke like that."

My laughter died as she bit her lip.

"Wait? You're not pregnant, are you?"

She glanced away.

"Shit, Celeste. Who? What? How?" When her gaze rolled in my direction, I amended my statement. "Okay, forget the how. Though I'm seriously wondering how because you're on the pill."

"Like the pill is hundred percent."

Her sarcasm didn't stop my mind from racing. If big Dan found out, whatever guy had knocked her up was going to enjoy a permanent dirt nap. Mom may have loved the guy, but he scared the crap out of me. He was only a big teddy bear when it came to his daughter. And even that was limited, considering the murderous gaze he'd given her not ten minutes ago.

I lay back with the weight of everything and turned my head to face her.

In a gentler tone, I asked, "What are you going to do?"

She shrugged. "Tell him, I guess."

The him must be the father-to-be. "Who is he?"

A picture of a baby-faced guy with a killer smile that could combust any girl's panties popped in my head.

"Taylor."

I remembered the guy who didn't have to speak to get her to follow.

"I guess this means you're giving up your crush on Sawyer."

Her shoulders rose and fell again. "I guess, unless he's into single mothers."

I didn't comment that she'd practically admitted having the baby was a done deal.

"Are you going to tell your dad?"

Her head jerked back in my direction.

"Are you crazy? If, and I mean if, I do this, I'm not telling him anything until after graduation. He'll cut me off once he finds out."

Not that I wasn't concerned for her, but the conversation I'd just had with Mom popped in my head. If he stopped paying her bills, I would end up homeless too.

"I'm here for you whatever you decide."

I held out my hand, and she took it. Then we both stared at the walls. I couldn't help placing my free hand on my belly, remembering my night with Ashton. What would I do if I was the one with a living being growing inside me?

That thought only made me wonder what Ashton was doing? I hadn't decided how mad I still was with him. Despite that, I couldn't help wondering where was he and who was he with? Most of all, I wondered if he thought about me at all after I ran off.

My phone had become a doorstop when it had fallen out of my pocket on my mad dash home after leaving the frat that night. That was probably a good thing. I'd be depressed if he hadn't called to check on me. Now I'd never now.

With Dan pissed at Celeste, I didn't think it was a good idea to bring up that I needed a replacement.

34

Past

A HAND SHOVED down my boxers before I was fully awake. I hadn't had time to brace myself as I was pulled up to my knees and he shoved himself inside me. My insides felt like molten lava as I strained to get away.

"That a boy. Fight me. I love a good fight."

His forearm became a noose around my neck, constricting my airways and stealing what little strength I had.

My eyes burned, but I refused to cry. I bit my lip hard until I felt a trickle of blood seep onto my tongue.

"Damn, boy." His hot breath fanned over my neck, filling my nose with the smell of bourbon, a smell I would never forget. "You're like a fine wine. You get better with age."

I couldn't respond. I was doing my best not to pass out from lack of air while he ripped my insides to shreds.

His free hand wormed down into my shorts and grabbed my withered dick. With impossibility, blood rushed to the damn thing against my wishes.

"You like this boy, don't you?"

My consciousness was slipping. I'd only managed a few sips of air.

His rough hands were like sandpaper across my skin. Still, I grew closer to the edge of darkness and pleasure. In that moment, if I'd had a gun, I would have shot myself. I hated every inch of my skin from every tug and pull until I spilled with no choice of my own.

My vision was foggy at the moment of his guttural groan in my ear as he emptied himself inside me.

He sagged forward, pressing me into the bed, further cutting off my oxygen supply.

At that point, I didn't care. I longed for death. It was better than the hell I was living. When he rolled off and out of me, my body once again betrayed me. I gulped in copious amounts of oxygen. So much so, I felt my light-headedness begin to fade to normalcy.

He picked up a tumbler from my nightstand and stumbled out of the room. He hadn't closed the door, and I heard a mumbled conversation. He had to be speaking to my mother. Guests weren't allowed upstairs. Apparently, paying ones were.

"I said the money's in the account," the devil slurred loud enough for me to make out his words.

"Good. Now go. I have to get my beauty sleep," the monster answered.

I would come to learn the slight giggle in her tone meant she was flirting. I fisted the sheets and willed back the moisture that threatened to rush from my eyes. There was no use in crying. It would only spur the demon. And she was coming.

"Come on now. Clean yourself up. This room smells."

When I didn't move fast enough, a sharp pain landed across my back stealing my breath. I opened my eyes and spotted the cane she didn't need for walking as she slapped it in her open palm. I practically fell out of the bed, but jumped to my feet when she arched the instrument of my destruction above her head.

She hadn't always used an object to strike me. Now that I was nearly as tall as she was, it was more and more her go-to form of punishment.

"You're such a nasty little boy. I don't even understand what he sees in you. You better be grateful. If not for him, you'd be begging on the streets. You'd end up whoring yourself for scraps of food. And don't fucking cry. You act like you're the only one that has to suffer a little to live. Get over yourself and clean this fucking mess. Change your sheets too."

She tapped her palm with the cane, and I remembered my manners.

"Yes, Mother."

The crack across my cheek cleared my brain from the nightmare I'd been living to the real hell on earth.

"You sound like that crazy boy in that movie *Psycho*. Don't call me that."

Mother had been a slip that should have stayed in my head. It was something I chanted a thousand times, but knew better than to utter. "Yes, ma'am."

"Better, and don't think about sleeping until this room and that filthy body of yours is spotless."

"Yes, ma'am," I droned like the robot she'd programmed me to be.

It hurt to move, but I did my best to disguise my discomfort as I pulled the sheets from my bed. It may have been well past midnight, but the truth was, I would have slept on the hard floor than on those sheets anyway. Damn, if something like a raindrop fell from my eye before I could stop it.

35

Ashton

It felt like I was jerked into the world by my throat as my eyes popped open. I rubbed at a phantom ache around my neck, wondering when the past would stop plaguing me. The nightmare predated Sawyer intervening.

The call from my mother the night before must have brought it on. For the next few minutes, I replayed it in my head.

"Yep," I'd said into the receiver.

"Don't be a little shit, Ashton. That house was as much mine as yours."

Mother.

"It was never yours," I'd said, furious at myself for not checking who called before I answered.

"You wouldn't be alive if not for me."

I'd rubbed at my ear from her ear-splitting shriek. She had to be feeling the effects of being without money.

"That was your problem, not mine."

"I could ruin your life," she'd warned.

You already did, *I thought*. "*I could do the same. You'd probably look good in an orange jumpsuit.*"

"*My lawyers will stop you.*"

"*Let them try. And while you're pissing away the little money you might have left, remember you're going to grow old with no one. Who's going to take care of you then?*"

I'd ended the call and put a block on her number.

The heels of my palms pressed into my eyes, annoyed I'd spoken to her. I pinched the bridge of my nose using pain to help wake me up.

I stretched as I assumed the upright position in my pod on the plane. I hadn't used a private plane, the trip not as planned as I would have liked. I hated the pretense of first class, but I wouldn't have survived in the cramped seats next to strangers who could incidentally touch me. It would have been a hell far worse than the one I'd survived all those years ago.

With only a duffle, I didn't have to wait at baggage claim as I shook the remnants of sleep from my body. My driver was waiting with a sign baring my given name on it. I followed him to a black Mercedes sedan and assumed a rigid position in the back seat. This wasn't a vacation, even though the Thanksgiving holiday loomed.

The Bohemian feel of Prague didn't make the city any less like I'd stepped into a fairy-tale book. I was the furthest thing from being any sort of prince.

The private car I'd hired pulled up in front of a canopy that read *Café Jewel Bar*. I gave the driver a questioning look. He only exited to open my door and waved me toward the bar. Our communication had been stilted to gestures since I spoke no Czech and he very little English.

When I walked in, the space was smaller than I expected. I was immediately greeted by a friendly staff member who said my surname.

I nodded and followed him past the tiny bar area into a small space that served as the hotel lobby area. I dropped my leather duffle onto the sofa and stood in front of the small counter the guy moved around.

"It looks like you have a single room."

I nodded. No matter how underwhelming the place looked so far, it would be fine.

"We have you in the Onyx room." He handed me an honest to God key. I stared at it a second before following him up a steep winding staircase a couple of flights. There hadn't been an elevator or at least one not big enough for people. It was a good thing I was in shape. The dizzying ascent could be hazardous to anyone not.

"Here we are," the pleasant man said in a thick Czech accent.

The door was at the top of the flight of stairs. He held out his hand for the key, and I had to wonder why he'd given it to me in the first place if he was only going to ask for it back. Not wanting to make an issue of nothing, I dropped it into his open palm. He used it to open the door and held his hand out for me to enter.

I'd never felt so big in my life until I stepped into the tiny room. I took up the space between the door and the twin-sized bed that butted up against the wall. Then from the hall, as there was really not enough room for the both of us, he gestured to the left, my right, and I spied a small but updated bathroom at the end of the tiny room.

"There is a robe and toiletries." I nodded. He pointed to the desk. "There is the remote to control the heat or A/C, whatever you prefer."

His congenial smile was the last he gave before disappearing down the stairs. I closed the door to the room before inspecting my accommodations.

Despite the lack of square footage, the room was decorated with luxuries. I could see why it was described as a boutique hotel. Some might find the room claustrophobic. Sadly, I enjoyed the small space. When one was alone, a larger area would only accentuate that fact.

I dropped my bag onto the desk that sat opposite the bed, leaving a single path to the only window in the room. I leaned my forearm on the glass, looking down at the cobblestone streets, and wondered if this could be my future home. Time would tell as I would be here a few days through the holiday.

That only brought my mind back to why I'd come here in the first place. The cryptic message I'd been given by the Club from the woman with the scrap of paper to the invitation. When I'd opened the black envelope, it read...

How can you trust us when you can't trust yourself? Go to Prague and get a taste of our reach. We can give you the answers you seek when no one else can.

What did they want me to know and why? The exclusive group didn't need me. I was a nobody whose future didn't include politics or the CEO position for any Fortune 500 companies. I was a writer. If not for my trust fund, I'd be considered a starving artist. It couldn't be money they wanted.

I slipped the scrap of paper from my pocket and stared at it again. There was a number. I hadn't yet called it, and wasn't sure what I was going to do despite making the trip here. With no home to go to and Sawyer spending his holiday with someone else, there weren't better options.

The bed was surprisingly firm and didn't completely collapse under my weight as I left the view in favor of staring at the wall. I'd avoided the black-framed mirror over the bed, not wanting to see the face that looked so much like my mother's.

I leaned back to the wall and rested my arm on a feathery soft, black cylindrical pillow. It was then I noticed that all the accents in the room, even the tile I could see into the bathroom, were black. Made sense, I was in the Onyx room. It might have been fate, considering my mood matched the décor.

How had I gotten myself to this point? Why had fate placed

me in the hands of a sadistic mother? Had the apple fallen far from the tree? I was so fucked up, the world would be better off without me. Too bad I no longer saw death as an option. I had to live if nothing else than to prove to that crazy woman that she no longer controlled my life. She didn't think I could be anything, and that was what drove me now.

Before I could move forward, I needed to know the past. There had to be something there that could make sense of the whys of things. I put my cell on the desk and reached for the phone instead. I studied the numbers a second longer before placing the call.

The meeting was set at a smoky bar across the street in a half an hour. I made the trek there long before then. I was ushered to a table in the back past a display of very appetizing desserts and tried to convey I was waiting on someone. When the guy nodded like he understood, I let it go.

The place wasn't packed, but many of the tables were taken. I took that as a good sign as I perused the menu.

"Ashton."

I glanced up to find a thin woman who appeared roughly the same age as my mother. She stood behind the empty chair across from me. I nodded and began to stand. Mother hadn't taught me a lot, but she did stress manners.

She tucked a strand of lifeless brown hair behind her ear as I held the chair out for her. Despite time, which hadn't been very kind, I could see that she had once been very beautiful.

When I sat, she said, "You look very much like her."

Her saying that only reminded me why I hated my appearance so much.

"My mother?"

She smiled. "Yes," she said shyly as her cheeks pinkened.

I wasn't sure where her embarrassment came from, but was certain at some point I would discover why.

"Sorry, I'm Susanna."

We exchanged a quick, limp handshake before I drilled her for the reason I was there.

"How did you know her, my mother?"

Some of her pleasant expression faded. "We met when she attended college, yes?"

I knew very little about the woman who gave me life. She wasn't exactly chatty with me. I shrugged and she nodded as if she understood. I wanted to rush her, eager for the mystery of Mother to be exploited. She had every advantage over me. Though I spent our time in that house either as a victim or housemate, she knew my habits more than I knew about hers.

The waiter came over to take our order. My appetite had been lost the moment the woman sat down. I ordered a drink and tried something with Becherovka in it. After she ordered in her native tongue, leaving me to guess what it was, I pushed ahead.

"You mentioned attending college with my mother."

The woman across me looked as though her life was hard. She didn't seem like a college graduate. For now, I would give her the benefit of the doubt.

"She did. I didn't."

When she didn't elaborate, I kept probing, trying not to get frustrated with the dribble of information she was giving me. I kept hanging onto the fact that I'd been led here for a reason.

"So, how did you meet her?"

She glanced out the large panes of glass that were embedded in the grand doors that faced the street. My guess was in the warmer months, those doors would be opened to let fresh air in.

"We met at a job."

The last word came out clipped and only heightened her accent. She'd practically spat the word out.

I clenched my jaw, wanting to rush her. I held back because the fragile woman before me looked like she would wilt and close into herself if I let loose on the spray of curse words I wanted to shout.

I leaned forward in my seat. "You didn't exactly seem surprised to get my call. I suspect you were waiting for it." She nodded. "I assume there's something you are supposed to tell me."

She blinked and I sat back as water pooled in her eyes. She trembled as she wiped the offending moisture away. Then she faced me squarely in the eye, leaving me to feel sorry for her.

"She and I worked in the same business."

I suspected what *it* was even before she said it. Mother was good at one thing as far as I saw.

"Sex," I supplied.

Her curt nod and quick glance away were the confirmation of her shame.

"And," I said, trying to convey to her that I held no judgment. I was only here to learn why I was here.

She jerked her head back and surveyed me. I shrugged, hoping to relieve her of whatever guilt she felt. She cleared her throat and continued.

"She was in it to pay for college or so she told me. I—I had other reasons." She didn't explain and I didn't ask. It wasn't my business. We all had our crosses to bear.

I clasped my hands on my lap and tried to be patient with her slow as molasses tale.

"What does this have to do with me?" I challenged.

"You're proof that her plan worked."

Anything I might have said died in my throat. "Plan," I uttered, not exactly surprised, but yeah a little.

She blew out a breath and told me a version of the story Mother had already shared with me. Her father had a debt to his boss, and Mother ended up the payment.

I wanted to feel sorry for her, but I couldn't. Instead of protecting me from a similar fate, she inflicted the same horror on me.

Susanna's flat eyes refocused on me. "I remember thinking

she was about to cry, after telling the story, but she laughed. I'll never forget the scary smile that formed on her face. She said it wasn't all bad after the first time. Eventually, the boss man brought her little gifts or gave her money. That's how she learned the value of pussy."

Disgust rather than sorrow filled my veins. Her father had sold her and she had sold me. We were a class of monsters that didn't need to breed.

"You mentioned a plan," I said to get her back on track.

There was nothing she could say to soften my heart toward the woman who bore me.

"It started when we were sent to work a party." Her eyes cut over to mine. "That's the first time she met your father."

I didn't want to react, but I did. I leaned back in the seat as if I could put distance between us despite the wall behind me.

"You look like him too," she said.

"You know my father."

She nodded. "I'll never forgot how lost he looked at that party. We girls tried to cheer him up, but he turned us down."

Up until that point, I'd just assumed things about my parents, like my father's infidelity. Yes, I knew Mother had probably manipulated the situation, but it sounded like a hell of a lot more if I was here.

"There's a but, right?" I asked.

Her head shook slowly side to side. "No, Victoria tried too and failed."

When my mouth hung open, she continued. "Like I said, she had a plan and almost gloated about it." She paused a beat. "She'd found out that his wife was going through uterine cancer treatment and decided to exploit that. She did everything she could to research him. She was obsessed to have his child when she learned that his wife wouldn't be able to. I got the feeling she'd been searching for the right rich guy she could marry."

This wasn't new information. My mother had proven herself to be an opportunist at every turn.

"It took a while, but she was determined to sleep with him. Apparently, her scheme worked."

The waiter came over and put a dinner plate in front of her. He placed my drink down, which I'd completely forgotten about. When he left, she pushed her fork around the food as I picked up my highball glass.

"Weeks later she was so excited, she bragged she'd finally gotten him into bed. She laughed when she admitted how apologetic your father had been about it. He took the blame, saying he'd had too much to drink. He claimed he'd never cheated on his wife and wouldn't do it again."

For so long, I hated the guy, only to learn he'd been somewhat of a victim of Mother's manipulations as I had.

"And she got pregnant?"

She shrugged, but her eyes landed on me. "I moved back here shortly after. But looking at you, I guess so."

It wasn't hard to believe, but why had someone wanted me to know this? Had my father orchestrated this meeting? His sudden interest in my life and the timing of this information didn't sit well with me. He wanted me in his life, so he claimed. He was running for president. And here I was.

Susanna began eating her food as I received a text.

Willow sent me a text with a turkey emoji and a couple of grinning faces.

36

Ashton

THE CALL I made wasn't one I expected. My hand hung in the air, prepared to knock on an unfamiliar door. What was I doing? Why was I here?

I'd barely pulled back from my quick two taps against the door when it opened.

The woman who stood before me contrasted Susanna in every way. The Czech woman had been a tall waif. The female in the doorway with a grand staircase behind her was petite and carried just enough weight not to be considered fat, but far from thin.

"Ashton," she greeted. "Please come in."

I stepped inside a foyer with high ceilings and a museum-worthy chandelier. Before I could look around, I met the woman's eyes as she took my measure.

"I'm sorry. I'm being rude. It's just—"

She stopped like a red light blinked on my forehead. I finished the sentence for her.

"I look like him?"

My father.

"A little, especially your eyes."

His wife's smile was pleasant enough, but we both stood as if unsure what to do next.

"I'm sorry. It's just you remind me of Will when we first met." She quickly turned away and began to move down a long hall. "Would you like something to drink?"

I silently dropped my bag near the door. Despite coming here, I wasn't sure how long I would stay. Just as she turned to see if I was following, I moved in that direction.

A formal sitting room was off to the left. We followed a hall all the way to the back which opened to a what had to be called a chef's dream kitchen. A large family room was just beyond that.

"What would you like?" she asked, standing near a double-sized refrigerator.

I wanted a drink, but a glass wouldn't do. A bottle would be on order.

With kind, motherly eyes appraising me, I answered, "Water, please."

"Still or sparkling?"

I might have frowned. "Either."

Water was water, right?

She handed me an Evian almost too frosty to touch. I twisted off the cap and drank deep. I had a feeling I was going to need it.

"Will's not here," she began. "I asked him to give us some time alone."

"Why?" I hadn't thought the word, just said it.

As we both stood there trying to figure each other out, I watched as she put more distance between us. I'd towered over her.

"I've wondered about you for so long."

I held my breath. It seemed all my preconceived notions

about everything was wrong. I assumed she'd only found out about me recently.

"If your curiosity is satisfied, I can leave now."

Her faded smile made me feel like an ass for how rude that sounded.

"That's not why I called," she said.

The call had come almost immediately after I left Susanna. It was as if she had a tracking device on me.

"Why did you?"

She looked down at her clasped hands as I fisted my own at my sides.

"Will told me you put the house he'd gotten you up for sale. I worried you didn't have a place to spend the holidays."

Her kindness shouldn't bother me, but it did. Where was she all the years I lived like a prisoner under Mother's thumb?

"Why do you care?"

I held her gaze until she adverted her eyes.

"That's fair. I deserve that." She stood up and her abrupt movement had me straightening my spine. "None of this is your fault, of course. But you must understand my position. You were the evidence of my husband's infidelity. As much as you were innocent, meeting you would have destroyed the fragile relationship I was working to repair with Will."

It wasn't that I couldn't see her point, but that didn't explain her summons despite her *let's play family for the holidays* reason.

"Why now?"

I shoved my hands with stiff arms into my pockets, certain of what she was going to say.

"I know, and I feel terrible that somehow I played a part in what—"

"In nothing. You weren't there."

My body tensed. I was ready to bolt. I didn't come there to be reminded of why my life was fucked up.

"No, but if I hadn't been selfish, you could have lived here with us."

My laugh was such a shock to us both, she jumped.

"You have no reason to feel guilty for any of it. I asked him to take me away and he didn't, enough said."

Her silence to my revelation was only fleeting.

"You need to see something."

She left her perch at the end of the counter and beckoned me to follow after her like a chastised puppy. I found myself two steps behind her as we ascended the winding staircase.

At the T-junction landing, we headed straight down a wide hall. About halfway to the end, she stopped to open a door on the right. She stood just outside and held a hand toward the entrance for me.

I turned and nearly sucked in air. The room was large, of course, and the painted blue walls with decorative waves stenciled in matched the clouds of the sky on the ceiling. The centerpiece of the room was a very expensive replica of a wooden boat that held a twin-sized bed. It was probably every little boy's dream, and if I could remember an unjaded moment of my childhood, maybe it might have been mine.

"He never had any intention of leaving you there," she said, breaking the silence.

Her words held no meaning as I focused on the built-in at the end of the room. The custom shelves and desk filled a wall in grand fashion to equalize the anchoring bed.

Though it wasn't the shelves that had captivated me. It was the framed photos spaced out like artwork that held my attention. I hadn't realized I'd moved in that direction until one such frame was in my hand.

There hadn't been a lot of pictures of me about the house I'd grown up in. The few only materialized when Father was expected for a planned visit. Then they would disappear behind closed cabinets not to be seen again until he returned.

I didn't recognize the boy in every picture. The one smiling or playing baseball or whatever sport for the season. The only reason I knew all of them were me was because of the birthmark that had started out like a freckle and eventually changed into a mole. On an annual visit to the doctor, no doubt required by my father, Mother had asked about the damn thing. He'd explained that moles were common even in babies, but had a tendency to evolve over time. Since I only had the one, he didn't think it was necessary to test for skin cancer.

She spoke, reminding me of her presence into the past I'd sunk into.

"He came home after that visit and told me he planned to bring you here. I balked, of course, and made threats of leaving him if he did. He wouldn't back down until I reminded him that he'd barely been on the Hill long enough to make a name for himself. When was he going to have the time to raise a son? I threw it in his face that he'd end up leaving me and a nanny to take care of you."

Slowly, I set the frame down, feeling as though it might break in my hands if I held it any longer. I didn't turn around, though anger vibrated through me.

"He still didn't give up. He had this room designed and papers drawn up with our lawyers," she said.

"He didn't come." I folded my arms protectively across my chest as if I could hold in all the hurt when he left me with that woman.

"It wasn't like he could just take you. Legally you weren't his. There were channels."

Her voice shook. No matter her tears, I had a lifetime of unshed ones. I wasn't buying it. How could he have this waiting and not one time had he brought me here? As far as I knew of my parents' conversations, he hadn't asked to take me for a visit.

"What stopped him?"

"Me. I reminded him how awful it would be as a mother to have your child taken away."

What she was really saying was she'd guilted him because she'd lost the ability to have a child. She used the only card she had left to stop him.

"He finally saw reason. Probably because he knew how much I'd wanted to be a mother all my life. A child is such a precious gift. That's when he ordered his lawyers to start managing the money he gave her for your care. I didn't know—"

Her sentenced was choked off.

"I was left in the hands of a monster," I finished, turning to face her.

She'd covered her mouth with a hand and nodded vigorously. When she released her hold, she added, "How could I know that a mother would be so cruel?"

The laugh I spat out was clipped and sounded villainous.

"Cruel isn't exactly the word. That suggests that occasionally she was other than that. When she wasn't."

"I'm so sorry, Ashton."

"What are you sorry for? You didn't make her sell me off when I was no longer an easy payout." Her sob was cut off by her hand again slapping over her mouth. "I guess sold is the wrong word. I was rented out."

"Ashton," she cried out as I moved for the door.

The trip down memory lane was about to end in disaster. I'd say something I couldn't take back, or break every piece of furniture in the sham of a room. Its purpose was so he could pretend he was a father, when he hadn't been one at all.

"I have to go," I announced, making my way into the hall.

The brusqueness of my tone was just the undercurrent of rage I felt.

"Ashton."

That time the voice wasn't soft and feminine. I glanced up to see my father leaning one shoulder on the wall. How long had he been standing there?

"I'm leaving," I said.

He pushed off and stood to block my path. I should have gone around him. The hall was large enough. But I wasn't as unaffected as I acted. Between Susanna's story, his wife, and that shrine of a room, every notion I had about my father was shattered.

His hand landed on my shoulder. I blamed the fact that his skin had touched a barrier for why jolting pain didn't light up my neural pathways. Though when I stiffened, his hand fell away.

"It's getting late. Stay. Not in there, of course. Take your pick of rooms. I'm sure you have jetlag from your overseas flight."

It was like I'd taken an uppercut to the jaw. I took a stumbling step back. He shouldn't have known where I was.

"You sent me to Prague? Was this your plan to somehow get me here?"

I felt betrayed yet again. When his wife had called, I hadn't told her where I was coming from and hadn't used a private plane. Only his brows were as furrowed as mine were in confusion.

"I did." I turned around and faced the woman behind the man as she said, "I set it up."

"The Vanderbilt Club?" I asked.

She shrugged as I clenched my hands, trying to put all the pieces together. How much did my father know?

"My father had been a member. Will is. I know what goes on. And I needed you to know all that I do. The truth," she said.

What was the truth? If anything, I was more in the dark than I had been before.

"It isn't easy to find out your husband cheated, especially when you'd been fighting for your life. I hired someone to look into *her* and watch him to see if he would see her or anyone else again."

"Stephanie."

Dad sounded like he'd be strangled.

"Will, I had to know. Your word wasn't good enough." Her focus moved from over my shoulder to back to me. "The detective found Susanna. For money well spent, I met with her and she told me all she knew about Victoria. Will made no other missteps after that and I eventually forgave him. When he told me you wanted nothing to do with him, I found a way to put that information in your hands to find. He's as innocent as you or me to a point. She seduced him with words of friendship and pretended to be a confidant. She worked on him as I pushed him away. I was selfish in my pity for not feeling like a woman. I opened the doors for her to use alcohol and loneliness against him. So you see, it's my fault really. If you want to be mad at anyone, let it be me."

Nothing in the world was black or white. From everything I'd learned up until this point, we all had shades of victims and villains in our past. Wasn't I a villain for sending my mother in the cold? Shouldn't I have been the better person? I'd also never given my father a chance. He had a story too and it wasn't so clear-cut as I'd thought.

"None of us are right or wrong," I said, deflated from the heat of anger.

"You've done nothing wrong," my dad said.

Dad. The word had slipped so easily in my mind. It wasn't like I was going to hug him or even call him by that name. But it had felt like the broken part in me over our non-relationship had unlocked. That maybe I could give him a chance.

I met his eyes, prepared to still walk away.

"Stay... please," he begged.

The longing in his voiced felt genuine.

"Stephanie's made dinner."

"She cooked?"

Not sure why that popped out of my mouth. It was surprising.

Mother and Sawyer's mom hadn't exactly been in the kitchen unless it was to eat.

He laughed, breaking some of the tension. "Yes, she cooks, all the time in fact. We can eat turkey dinner and talk." He held up a hand when I felt my spine straighten. "Not about the past, unless you want to. I'd really like to hear about your future."

Any lightness I'd started to feel, fled.

"I'm not interested in politics or heading a Fortune 500 company," I admitted.

I waited for him to frown, but it didn't materialize.

"That's good. I wouldn't recommend either." He chuckled some and added more when I only stared at him. "I just want you to be happy no matter what it is. Go backpacking around the world if you like. I just want to get to know you."

It wasn't as though the hell I'd been living in disappeared, but it wasn't quite as hot. I followed them down the stairs, trying to figure out how drastically my life was changing. I fingered the edges of my phone. I hadn't heard back from Willow. I'd replied to her text, but I wasn't good at words. She hadn't responded, which led me to believe that she'd accidently texted me or once again I'd said the wrong thing.

37

Willow

HOW STUPID HAD I been to text him?

Mother had an older phone. We'd switched out the sim card, and the first thing I'd done was send him turkey emojis.

It had been a little past midnight, marking it officially as Thanksgiving Day when I'd done it. I blamed the wine we'd had with dinner. Mom kept pouring to smooth the tension between Dan and Celeste, and I'd gotten a little more than tipsy. So much so I was pretty sure I'd accidently dumped said phone into the trash when I'd been helping clean the kitchen. Or that was one theory. I'd lost the replacement and hadn't found it in my room or Celeste's.

Dan's foul mood hadn't changed all weekend, so there was no way I was going to bring it up that I'd destroyed or lost yet another phone.

"What is it with you and phones?"

I glanced up at Celeste who was pacing. She'd been fidgety and wanted back on campus. Now that we were there, she stared at her phone, willing her unborn child's father to return her message.

"Maybe you should send him an S.O.S. or a message in a bottle," I teased.

"Funny," she said, but her expression was far from humorous.

"Mom says scowling can create premature winkles."

Her eyes only hardened on me. I held my surrendering hands up. "Okay, I'm just trying to lighten things."

"Maybe you should call your boyfriend."

Boyfriend? I had no boyfriend. Derek and I had only been out a few times over the last few weeks. I hadn't even let him kiss me yet.

She laughed before I could correct her, only it wasn't from amusement. "Oh, that's right. You don't have a phone."

She went back to glaring at hers, probably willing it to ring with the other ninety-five percent of her brain.

Just as I opened my mouth to explain things, the doorbell rang. We both jumped out of our skin, having been living in silence except for our brief conversation. She moved before I could. She did a damn good impression of the Flash as she headed for the door.

It was like déjà vu. The door opened to a bouquet hiding the man who held it. For a second, I thought Kent had returned. But I hadn't spoken to him in forever, happy to leave that relationship in the past.

The flowers shifted and there stood Derek. Celeste deflated while I waited for my heart to skip a beat.

It didn't. No flutter in my belly either no matter how much I willed it to come.

"Willow, your boyfriend is here."

Her proclamation was unnecessary, and I flushed. He was less than a dozen feet away from where I was on the couch. When he gave me a beaming smile, I decided not to correct her and poten-tial embarrass him. I got to my feet and met Derek halfway.

"They're beautiful," I said.

The colorful tulips were a relief. For some reason, roses would have felt more serious when I had to confront the fact that this relationship really wasn't going anywhere despite the title. In fact, Derek and I hadn't discussed the subject at all.

"You're beautiful."

He leaned in and instinctually I turned my head, letting his kiss land there.

"None of that here," Celeste said, dismissing us.

Damn, if I couldn't have kissed her for that, even though she was so engrossed in her phone, I was surprised she'd seen the move.

"I tried to call you—" he began.

His nerdy but superhero in the making looks weren't enough to make my heart go pitter-patter.

"Yeah, I lost my phone," I said hastily.

"She does that a lot."

Celeste had spoken as if she was an active participant in our budding conversation, when in fact she was only half here.

"Oh," Derek said. "I was hoping maybe you'd like to hang out. There is a thing."

"What thing?" Celeste asked. "And can I come?"

That surprised me. I didn't think she wanted to go anywhere until she'd spoken to *the* guy.

"Actually, it's just a bunch of couples," he replied.

"Oh," she said, never looking up from her phone. "Well, go then. Leave me be."

I wasn't sure how I felt. Then again, it was better than him going into my room. We would have to confront the state of our non-relationship when I had yet to decide what to do. Give it more time maybe? I'd been telling myself that for weeks.

When I followed him outside, I was surprised to see the sleek vehicle at the curb. It didn't seem like Derek. I wasn't a car lover and didn't know the make by the side view. When he opened the

door for me, I slipped into soft leather seats and spotted the
Jaguar symbol on the wheel. As he went around to enter the
driver's side, I glanced up to our apartment window and spotted
my sister.

She was probably as surprised as I was to learn Derek was
most likely loaded. I hadn't aspired to have a rich boyfriend, but
apparently I had one.

When we pulled up to mini-mansion row, I shouldn't have
been surprised. But the looming Sigma house wasn't where I
wanted to be. Would Ashton be in there?

"Is everything okay?" Derek asked, when I didn't make a move
to leave the car.

I thought back to all the parties I'd recently gone to there. I
hadn't seen Derek there. Maybe... maybe not? I took his hand and
let him help me out of the sports car.

We walked in to a subdued crowd. Pairs of people were
lounging on the leather sofas as a game played loudly on a
mounted TV I hadn't noticed before.

If anyone asked, I wouldn't have been able to tell them if
someone muted the sound or if white noise had filled my ears. I
could only say everything seemed to go quiet as all eyes turned
my way.

"Guys," Derek announced, his arm like a vise around my
shoulder. "This is my girlfriend, Willow."

Embarrassed by his introduction, I berated myself for not
correcting Celeste earlier. My mortification only increased when
we didn't get the normal response like a chorus of greetings. Only
a few girls said hi back. The guys glanced at each other and then
over at Ashton who occupied a space at the end of one couch
with a girl so close to him she was practically on his lap.

My cheeks burned under everyone's scrutiny. I spotted Jason,
the guy who'd given me the signature invitation to the underground party.

However, it wasn't him who spoke. It was Trent, the guy

Ashton had saved me from who'd dared to disturb the growing awkwardness.

"Isn't that—" he began.

"Leave it." Ashton's snarling words took everyone by surprise.

"He speaks," Trent mocked. "And we should listen. But he should know—"

"Let it the fuck go," Ashton pressed.

The dimwit looked around for support, but no one was going to back him against Ashton. He brought his glass to his lips to play off his shutdown.

Derek didn't have a clue what was going on, and I was grateful when he offered to get me a drink. We walked into the kitchen.

"What's that about?" he asked.

He had every right to know. "Can we talk somewhere else?"

He nodded as he snagged a bottle of water and held it to me. I relieved it from his hand and followed him back into the room filled with the sounds of the sportscast. I couldn't look at anyone, fearing what I'd see. I felt eyes on me, but wasn't sure whose.

Upstairs, Derek's room was neat, though it felt like it had been made that way for my arrival. Everything was a bit too orderly to be real. Or it might have been the rose petals on his perfectly made bed that caused nervousness to fill my gut.

"Is there something going on between you and Westborough?"

I blinked, wondering who that was until I remembered Ashton's last name from the back of his jersey.

"Oh," I breathed.

He took my relief and gave me back suspicious eyes. I licked my lips, wondering if I had the courage to say it. He'd been my one shot for a boyfriend. I didn't have any other prospects at my door. I thought back to how that had seemed so important long ago and took a deep breath.

"Not currently. I'd never do that. But in the past."

He exhaled and scrubbed a hand over his unruly hair. He let out a blustering noise that might have been a laugh or a cough.

"It figures. Guys like him—"

My jaw tightened. I wanted him to finish that sentence and get on to the part about girls like me.

His pacing stopped dead in front of me and he abandoned his previous sentence.

"You screwed him?"

I didn't like his tone, but I tried to think about how I would feel in his position.

"I had no idea you knew him or belonged to the same frat."

Because if he had a room in the house, he was a card carrying member.

"Yeah, well, my idea of a girlfriend doesn't come here to get screwed."

My hand flew out so fast, I couldn't stop it. I shocked myself by the sound my hand made against his cheek.

He rubbed the cherry red print blossoming on his face.

"I deserve that."

"You do," I snapped. "And before I go, I'll set your mind at ease. I've only ever slept with one guy... *ever*," I added with emphasis.

He reached for me. "Wait. Please."

I whirled around and slowly shook my head.

"There was never really any more than friendship in our future."

"Is that why you wouldn't kiss me?"

There was no point in lying now. I nodded.

"But friendship is off the table. I can't be around someone who slut shames," I said and was out the door, ignoring his pleas for forgiveness.

I pulled it closed, and when I glanced up, the girl Ashton had been cozied up to stood in the empty hallway.

"I think it's time for us to talk," she said.

38

Ashton

I sat with my head in my hands as I replayed the last ten minutes.

Ever since she'd walked in the door, I almost regretted coming to the frat house. I was there because I'd done Sawyer a solid. It had been the first time I'd felt like I could save him. I couldn't totally be sorry for coming because I'd gotten to see Willow.

The only problem I had now was needing a favor from Sawyer as I balled my hand at my side. Would it be manslaughter or first-degree murder if I killed the guy she was with? I settled on premeditated murder since I was contemplating it when Julie cut into my thoughts.

Leaning in way too close to my side, she whispered, "Who is she?"

Her hand slid down my arm making my skin crawl.

"No one."

My lie had nothing to do with the possessive way she took

hold of my hand. It was just none of her business, and I knew she would make it hers if I gave her so much as Willow's name.

The seductive smile Julie tossed me had as much appeal as rotting food. She stood and held out a hand. The only reason I took it was I wanted to leave. It was a bonus she led me upstairs.

"Which one?"

I was surprised she'd known I had a room. Then again, how much had Sawyer told her before they stopped talking altogether?

I aimed a finger toward the room on the right at the far end of the hall. Her smile grew as did my relief.

She walked into the room I'd called home much of this semester, her eyes drinking in every sight.

I lifted the cap I wore as a shield and ran a hand through my hair before resetting it backward on my head. I stood by the closed door until she turned to face me.

"Wow, better than I imagined."

The place was tidy. The cleaning crew had done their thing.

"Julie," I began.

Her grin had more teeth than I thought possible. She moved toward me.

"You don't have to say it. This is perfect."

I took a step back when she got too close. She wasn't the safe harbor she'd once been. Her smile dropped, leaving a frown on her face.

"What's wrong?"

"It's not going to work," I said without explanation.

I wanted her gone, and I knew what I had to say would hurt her. Still, I wouldn't spare her feelings.

"Why not? Sawyer has obviously moved on. You don't have to feel guilty about being with me."

She reached up and I caught her hands, moving them away from my face. Her expression darkened.

"It was never Sawyer holding me back," I said.

I knew that now. I'd only thought I'd loved her because Sawyer did and he'd been my compass for all things normal.

She freed her hands from mine and stepped back. "What? You're still hung up on him after everything? When will you see he'll never love you the way I do?"

Our friendship had been real, and for that I'd be thankful. I wouldn't tear her down, but she needed to face reality.

"You don't love me any more than I love you," I said.

"That's not true." She ate up some of the distance between us. "How can you say that?"

I let her come within inches of invading my space.

"Think about it. You went to college, and after the first few weeks we didn't hear from you. You stopped calling, not the other way around."

Her hand dropped to her sides. "I just thought..."

I didn't complete her sentence for her. When her eyes met mine, there was pain and maybe a little regret.

"I was protecting myself. I didn't want to hear about you with anyone else," she supplied.

"You weren't saving yourself for me either."

She turned away from me. "I've never loved someone like I loved you."

I did sympathize with her. My feelings had been so twisted, I'd felt the same way she had about Sawyer.

"You were in love with the idea of me. Trust me, I can never be what you want," I said.

She faced me with a renewed sense of purpose.

"You deserve love too."

I could argue with her, but what was the point?

"So do you." I shook my head. "And it's not with me."

"How can you be sure?" she asked.

The breath I let go was filled with something I wondered if Sawyer felt. Exhaustion.

"I know how I feel, Julie. We can only ever be friends."

She nodded, and my next exhale was filled with relief.

"She doesn't deserve you."

Julie had never been stupid. I didn't bother trying to take her off the scent.

"It's the other way around," I said, moving away from the door and letting her take hold of the knob.

"You know how to reach me when you realize the mistake you're making."

It was out of childhood friendship I let her have the last word.

My temples ached with the memory of that conversation. When the knock came, I sighed. Had Julie come up with a new angle before she would finally leave?

I opened the door as her name left my tongue.

Though the woman before me wasn't her. Two sets of eyes burned brightly on me as I dragged Willow close and pressed my mouth to hers. I slid my hand possessively down to the small of her back, tugging her inside to close the door on the pair of glares from those who didn't want us to be together.

I let her go, unsure of my welcome despite her melting against me.

She took a few steps back as we silently appraised each other. A gut-wrenching need burrowed deep inside, awakening something that had never been before. The clarity I'd long since determined only sharpened with her so close.

"Are you with Bryant?" I asked.

The question should have been redundant given her lack of protest to my caveman impression at the door. But I needed verbal confirmation.

Her confusion cleared up a second later. "Oh, you mean Derek. I forget you guys call each other by your last names."

I should feel bad. Bryant had been a needy friend. He'd spoken about a girl he was into. The truth was, I hadn't known it was Willow and had connected with her before I knew she'd been the girl of his dreams. I wasn't selfless enough to give her up for him. Maybe if I'd known before, I would have never gotten to this point.

"Yes, him. Are you together?"

She glanced at the door at my back as if she could see through it. A frown turned her pretty lips into something I feared. Was she about to let me down gently? Was her appearance at my door simply to clear things up before she moved on with him? Mentally, I closed my eyes and fisted my hands. Outwardly, I held her gaze, waiting...

"No. I told him as much."

The tightening in my chest loosened and I could breathe.

"And why are you here?" I asked.

Again, it was an obvious question that I needed her to answer.

"For you."

Her bold statement deserved a decisive answer.

Instead, I began with, "I'm not..."

A what? A monster? I was or at the very least a product of one. A good guy? I didn't know what that meant. For so long, my only role model had been Sawyer. He'd been a father, brother, best friend, and my sole desire. I'd bound my life to his without a preserver.

"You're not a what?" she asked, her shyness coming back in soft-spoken words.

Her beautiful eyes fastened on mine like hooks reeling me in.

"I don't know how to be—" There was that pause again creating a wall of awkwardness. "A boyfriend."

I let the blunt word be the sabotage that it was. She was too good for me and deserved a guy who would know how to treat her like the treasure she was.

"And I don't know the first thing about being a girlfriend."

Her eyes once again shifted over my shoulder a second before returning to mine. There had been something between Bryant and her, but she didn't elaborate. I wasn't a masochist and didn't probe her for an explanation.

"So, what next?" I asked.

According to Sawyer's playbook, I should fuck her brains out and worry about the rest later. But I wasn't Sawyer and she wasn't a throwaway girl.

"We try and see where things go."

She took a step forward, and I held my hands up. Anything that came next would be a signed, sealed, and delivered agreement. She needed to know what she was getting into.

"I'm fucked up, Willow. There's so much shit you don't know about me."

She invaded my space like a conqueror. Her fearlessness bore fruit as she placed her tiny palms against my own. Like before, her touch didn't elicit pain, though I'd admit only to myself a tingling sensation that shot up my arms and down my spine.

"No one's perfect, not even me," she explained.

But she was perfect to me. I didn't let the past control my present. I boldly went where I hadn't gone before. I bent down and kissed her. This time it wasn't a reaction to external elements. This time it was very much premeditated. I'd been unable to keep my eyes off her Cupid's bow like I'd been hit with an arrow.

The kiss didn't exactly go right. She'd gotten to her toes faster than I could reach her. Our mouths collided in a lovely mess, all teeth and lips. Neither of us apparently experts in the art. We pulled back and laughed.

It was my turn to show no fear.

I reached out and tipped her chin up. "Let's try that again."

Using my free hand, I slipped it around her waist, drawing her close and lifting her to her toes. There was a smile on my lips as this time our kiss connected like magnets. The pull so great, I deepened it by sliding my tongue over hers and enjoying her taste.

My cock swelled to epic proportions, pressing closer to her, eliminating the little space between us. She moved in despite having felt my desire. My hand slid from her back to her ass. It may as well have been a choreographed dance how effortlessly we moved. She wrapped one leg around me and I hoisted her up, turning and pressing her against the door.

There in the cradle of her legs, my dick found its way home. I wanted inside her like a man starved. I let my free hand roam up her ribcage. I used my thumb to outline the curved underside of her breast, before roving over the hardened peak of her nipple.

She let out a gasp that broke our connection. I dipped my head to nip at her taut nipple through the fabric that covered it.

For once I wasn't a student in need of instruction. I'd learned all my lessons well and graduated with a master's in the art.

As much as I wanted to unfasten my pants and plunge inside her, I needed to kneel before her and pay homage to the gorgeous woman before me. I reluctantly let her slide down until she was standing on her feet. She looked as hesitant as I felt at breaking our connection.

"Are you sure you want this?"

I gave her an out. Little did she know the consequences of her answer because I wasn't just talking about sex.

She nodded, and I got to one knee. Her eyes widened, but I let my hands do the talking.

Touch was a basic thing to some. But for me, it was a gift I'd long since been denied. It was something to trail my fingers from her ankles to her inner thighs, taking my time and never letting my gaze leave hers.

The *blow in the breeze* type short dresses she favored gave no problems as I moved the fabric up to her navel. There before me covered in blue cotton was the object of my cock's desire. I leaned in and ran my tongue over her most sensitive part. That wasn't enough. I needed to taste her. I hooked my fingers into her panties and dragged them down her legs. Then I used one hand to move the dress up again and let my other to get to work.

I licked between her folds until I found the pearl I sought. She shivered in my hold as I sucked her hard clit into my mouth and used my fingers as a prelude to my cock. When she began to shake and lose her balance, I shifted one leg and then the other over my shoulders, leaving the dress to halo my head.

Once she was on board, I went all in, tongue going deep, seeking that spot that would get her off like no other.

She cried my name, pride swelling like my dick, which could drill holes into the floor.

"Hang on, baby."

The words had come without conscious thought and flitted away as she removed my hat and dug her nails into my hair like she was on one hell of a ride. The shock of momentary pain didn't stop me cold like I would have guessed. Her mulling cries for more fueled me on until her pleasure coated my throat. I hungrily devoured every drop.

Though she was boneless, barely able to stand, I put her on her feet until I could get to my own. Then I lifted her and made for my bed.

39

Willow

THOSE BEAUTIFUL EYES of his drenched the inferno that threatened to consume me. Every muscle in my body had become liquid. Yet, I'd never felt more alive until that moment.

As he stood above me, he reached back, grabbed a handful of his shirt, and whipped it off. I found myself studying the hills and troughs of his muscled chest. I reached out but held there, afraid to touch him. There was something about touching that affected him in a way I hadn't discovered yet.

When I felt his fingers circle my wrist, I watched as he placed my palm over his heart. I took advantage and explored the hardened plains. It contrasted with the soft kiss that came a second later as he urged me down onto the soft mattress.

A moan left my lips when his mouth explored my neck, sending shivers to course through me. He tugged up fistfuls of my dress to get to my breasts. With newly acquired courage I'd used to knock on his door until now, I whipped the sundress over my head.

He moved one side of my bra down and latched onto one nipple. His suckle soaked my core with need. As if he knew my body better than me, his fingers circled that area below until I threw my head back with a gasp. His probing fingers dipped inside my inner walls. My body trembled as he worked magic and his burning kiss found my mouth again, hungrily devouring me from the inside out.

Though I thought I might die if he didn't get inside me at that very moment, another need was stronger. I levered up and pushed him back so that he was standing again. There in front of me was the object of every need I had. I worked at his fly as he watched, freeing his cock, and pushed his jeans down his legs. His powerful thighs flexed as he kicked them to side. His cock stood long, thick, and proud, his skin burning in my hand as I circled it. I pumped down once then twice before dipping my head. I wet my lips before sucking the head in.

His hand landed on my shoulder and gripped it tight. I took that to mean I was doing something right. I did more than the last time, taking a page out of some of the dirty novels I'd read. I kept my hand tight around the base of him as I took him as far as I could into my mouth. I worked a rhythm between my hand and mouth. Just as his panting worked into a crescendo of sorts, he shoved me back, parting my legs and guiding the head of his dick right where my desired was centered.

When he pushed in, I fisted the sheets on either side of my waist. He leaned down and took my mouth in a bruising kiss. I let go of the sheets in favor of scoring his back to draw him as close as I needed him to be.

His long, slow strokes were the most amazing torture. Every touch of that secret spot inside made my thighs quiver as I tried to hold it together. I bit my tongue so the entire house wouldn't know what he was doing to me.

As I drew near, I tensed up. His breaths came faster, and I realized tightening my inner walls had preformed magic. A small smile curled my lips. For all the pleasure he was doing to me, I had power too. I did it again making him lose control.

His weight pressed onto me as his speed picked up. My breath hitched in my throat, and I let loose the moan I'd held back. My hands dropped from his back and he twined his fingers of his left hand into mine. His right found the swollen button between my legs. I squeezed my thighs, and my legs wound around him, digging in as I was so close to losing my mind.

"Let go," he said, his voice barely a gritted whisper.

I hadn't realized I'd been holding back. But his words did something to detonate my orgasm. I spasmed around him, his strokes only heightening the pleasure. Then he was spilling his pleasure inside me.

When a cry burst from me, he covered his mouth over mine, the kiss stealing the last breath from my lungs until I lay in an exhausted heap.

With one last grunt, he stilled, his body pinning me prisoner for only a few seconds. He rolled to his side, taking me with him. His cock softened but stayed buried in my heat.

"Are you okay?" he asked, eyes soft on mine.

I nodded, still trying to catch my breath. Yet, I leaned in and kissed him gently. It was my way of saying all the things I couldn't put into words.

My eyes opened, and his stare made me a little self-conscious. What was he thinking? Had I done everything right?

"As much as I want to, I don't think we should stay here."

My heart took a nosedive for my stomach. My head must have done the same thing, because his finger lifted my chin until I was staring into his unfathomable eyes.

"I want to take you to my place."

I frowned. "You don't live here?"

"Not really." As if that answered it. "Anyway, it's only a matter of time before a party gets underway. You don't mind, do you?"

He was still inside me and I really didn't want that to change.

My gaze only had to drift to the door, reminding me of the girl and everything she'd said. Then there was Derek to consider. I may not want to be in a relationship with him, but I didn't want to hurt him any more than I had. That only made me wonder if he'd heard me. I closed my eyes, holding in a curse.

"Sure," I answered.

His stare made me feel like the fifth wonder of the world. Had he heard my disappointment? Or maybe his invitation had only been polite?

"I don't have to," I blurted.

I searched his eyes for some truth he might not say. Insecurity sucked.

"I want you to, but you don't have to."

I covered my face with my hand and shook it, embarrassed I couldn't take his words at face value.

"I'm messing this up, aren't I?" I asked.

When he pried my hand loose, I again caught him looking at me in that strange way like I was something new. His eyes only glanced at his hand holding mine, but I'd caught it.

"You're not," he said, but it almost sounded like a question.

I gave him a plaintive smile. He brushed tendrils of my hair from my face. His movements were slow, like he was unwrapping a gift. I felt special with every touch.

"Let me get something to clean up. Then I want to take you home to meet everyone."

That was significant, watering my grin until it rooted and became full-blown. His soft kiss preceded him pulling out. I sighed and bit my tongue. He rolled off the bed and stood, giving me the most amazing view of his ass as he walked to what I thought was a closet. The muscles were just as defined from his back to the divots just above his glutes.

Instead, the door opened to a tiny bathroom. He barely fit inside. I stifled a giggle when the thought one could probably pee, take a shower, and brush one's teeth all at the same time if that was a thing.

His front was even more impressive as he walked back over. Every line defining a wealth of muscles I couldn't explain all the way to the long, think one that hung between his legs. Had that really been inside me?

The bed dipped as he placed one knee and reached between my legs. He used a damp washcloth I hadn't noticed to clean me up. It should have been embarrassing, but there was no judgment on his face. However, I was reminded that we once again hadn't used a condom. Good thing I'd gotten on the pill.

We got dressed. I popped into his bathroom to make sure I didn't look too frightful. I did my own cleanup and finger-combed my hair. When I stepped out, he stood chest bare in jeans that hung low on his hips. Damn, my stuttering heart. He was more gorgeous than should be lawful.

I'd never once seen Ashton smirk, but there it was. He watched me watching him, and one side of his perfect mouth lifted.

"Now don't you go getting an ego on me," I said.

He laughed. "That will never happen. I'm not Sawyer." He caught himself and things got awkward for a second. "Besides, I like the way you look at me."

I didn't want things to get weird by the mention of his best friend's name. So I walked over and wrapped a hand around his waist and plastered my ear to the spot where his heart was.

He wrapped a hand around me. I enjoyed the feel of him and how my stomach took flight like a swath of butterflies. It was nothing like I felt when I'd been with Derek.

I took his hand. "Are we staying or going?"

He squeezed my hand before letting go. Then he pulled a shirt over his head.

"Let's go."

He held out his hand again. I took it, weaving our fingers together.

We both stopped in the hallway, glancing at Derek's closed door before moving swiftly down the stairs.

He'd been right. There were certainly more people in the house than when I'd gone upstairs. Music was also playing though at a tolerable level. When two guys came through the door carrying a large keg between them, I knew that would change.

Though that asshole and the guy who'd given me the invitation watched as we stepped into the living room, Ashton said nothing to either. I almost waved but feared the asshole would think I'd meant it for him. So I gave the nicer of the two a half-grin before we were out into the night.

Good thing I hadn't driven. We walked to Ashton's car with its distinctive stripe down the middle. He let me in before getting in himself. The boy certainly had manners.

The engine rumbled to life, the sound droning out any potential conversation. I wasn't sure what to expect when we arrived at a street on the other side of campus. Each side was lined with brick townhouses.

As he parallel parked, I wondered which one was his. I'd been lost in thought when my door opened, and he proffered his hand to me. I got out and he didn't let go.

I didn't want to be nervous, but I was. It was like meeting your boyfriend's parents. I had a feeling the judgment his friends placed on me would weigh heavy on our relationship, especially Sawyer's.

He led us to a brightly lit house about four doors down on the same side we parked. There was a large window in front on the lowest floor. I could see people moving inside. My stomach flipflopped, and I hid it behind a toothy grin when he glanced down at me.

The door was unlocked, and we stepped inside. There were several people there.

"Hey," Ashton said, his voice deep and gravely.

All eyes spotlighted on our joined hands, heating my cheeks to flame broil.

A girl I recognized as Celeste's nemesis stepped forward, hand out.

"I'm Shelly."

Before I could introduce myself, Ashton spoke next.

"This is Willow, my girlfriend."

Points for Shelly, there was only a moment of shock before she said, "Welcome, Willow."

I took her hand, and another girl stepped forward. "I'm Brie, Chance's girlfriend."

She looked familiar. We shook as well until a tall handsome boy came forward.

"I'm Chance."

Good God, was this where all the good-looking boys lived? Then it hit me. They were the couple that found me sprawled over Ashton at the pond months ago.

After all the hellos, things went silent. I glanced up at Ashton who was looking past the three that stood before us. I followed his gaze to Sawyer, who hadn't come forward. Just as the others started to look back, Sawyer hopped off the stool, famous grin plastered to his gorgeous face.

I glanced between Ashton and Sawyer, unable to interpret the silent communication going on between them.

Sawyer took my hand and brought my knuckles to his lips.

"Willow, a pretty name for a pretty girl."

His eyes held mine, and I couldn't make heads or tails over what he was thinking.

"Let go, you flirt," Shelly said, knocking a fist into his bicep.

He flinched, but I could tell he wasn't hurt, not physically at least. He let go and his gaze shifted back to Ashton.

Sawyer pointed at him. "Ash, you sly devil. You've been keeping her from me."

Shelly's eyebrow quirked, and I wondered if something was going on between them. She hadn't introduced herself as his girl-friend like Brie had for Chance.

"We were just about to eat," Shelly announced.

My brows shot up. It was late, like well past ten.

Shelly shrugged. "These boys are always hungry."

I nodded and finally everyone moved, and Ashton drew me from the foyer to the kitchen only feet away. I glanced to the right and spotted the living room with its large couch, chairs, and massive TV. A stairwell split the open area to the dining room beyond. Straight ahead there was a short hallway with a door to the back. A porch light on gave me a sneak peek through the window to green that lay beyond. Clearly, they watered the backyard.

Conversation started up, but I felt silent eyes on me. I glanced up and knew before I saw him that it was Sawyer. Chance was speaking to Ashton as were the other two girls, leaving my mind to scramble over what Ashton's best friend was thinking. If Ashton hadn't been holding my hand still, I might have found a shadow to hide in.

"Are you hungry?"

I shifted my gaze and found Brie standing next to me. Her face was open with a genuine offer.

"A little."

She laughed. "No worries. We have plenty. Eat as little or as much as you want."

"Can I help?"

I would have offered regardless, but I also wanted something to do besides worry about Sawyer.

"There's not a lot, but sure," she said, seeming to understand my need as her gaze flitted over to Sawyer as well.

Before I could follow her, Ashton drew on our clasped hands, pulling me over. He pressed a kiss to my temple before leaning and speaking softly into my ear.

"I'll be right back, okay. Unless you want me to stay."

I spotted Sawyer standing near the stairs and guessed they were going to talk. As much as I wanted him near so I didn't feel like a fish out of water, I decided that conversation needed to happen sooner than later. If Sawyer was going to do something to break our relationship before it began, it was better before my heart was any more invested in Ashton.

"I'll be fine," I said with a less enthusiastic smile than I was going for.

Shelly concurred, "She'll be fine."

Brie also chimed in, "We'll keep her safe."

It was an interesting choice of words, but Ashton nodded. He gave me one last look, which I returned with a reassuring smile I didn't feel. Then he disappeared up the stairs.

"Now that they're gone, you can tell us how you two met," Shelly asked.

Chance held up his hand. "Maybe I should go."

"No, stay. Besides, don't you remember when we stumbled across the two of them at the pond?"

Chance's eyes widened as it was clear he remembered.

"Wait? You never told me that," Shelly chided.

Brie shrugged, giving a stern side-eye to Shelly. "It wasn't my business like how they met isn't ours."

Shelly sighed and glanced at me. "She's right. You don't." She shrugged. "I'm just curious. Ash doesn't say much. You've obviously seen a side of him none of us have."

"Well, stop prying. Is the food ready?" Brie asked.

Shelly blew out another exasperated breath and then pulled a steaming pizza from the oven. It smelled delicious and looked homemade.

My stomach rumbled as much as my mouth watered.

"I'll resort to bribery. A slice for a story," Shelly teased.

"Leave her alone. Besides, I already offered her some."

Because there wasn't any malice or jealousy in Shelly's tone, I decided that there was nothing secret about the first time Ashton and I met. He'd only changed my tire. I didn't think he would mind. And I needed a distraction from what was going on upstairs.

"Okay, I'll bite. My tire was flat in the parking lot behind the quad," I began.

As I spoke, my mind was still upstairs with Ashton and Sawyer, wishing I could sprout wings and be a fly on the wall.

40

Ashton

WE'D BARELY WALKED into my room before he unleashed on me.

"Girlfriend? When the fuck did that happen?" he spit out the words like a lash.

My knuckles popped as I fisted my hands, breaking the sudden silence.

"I don't tell you everything."

I was surprised I could speak the way I'd ground my teeth together.

"Apparently," he said.

He crossed his arms like I was some spoiled child needing scolding.

"It's what you wanted."

I didn't know why I said that, because no matter his response, I decided that it was Willow not Sawyer whom I wanted. Maybe I just wanted him to hurt a little, considering how angry he seemed. His jealousy was over me not needing him the way I used to.

As we remained glaring at each other, the tension it created could be cut with a power saw.

"How well do you know her? How long? Does she know?"

The last of what he asked didn't need more words to comprehend. *My past.* His accusing questions stung and bothered me more than I cared to admit.

"I warned her," I admitted.

He nodded like that was acceptable.

"I wondered what happened to you when Julie showed up spitting mad."

I could only imagine. She'd played like she was okay with how we'd left things, but I'd known better.

"You're welcome," I said, noticing for the first time I'd used few words with Sawyer.

Was it practice for the future? Once graduation happened, I doubted our paths would cross more than once or twice a year if that.

"You're welcome?" he repeated. His face screwed up like a lemon had taken residence in his mouth. "She stormed in like Hurricane Julie muttering but not speaking to anyone." He meant him. "She grabbed her bag, which I hadn't known she'd left here, and then disappeared."

"You're welcome," I parroted.

"For what?" he spat.

"She won't be back."

His eyes widened, and he shook his head.

"I don't understand what's going on with you anymore."

I blew out a breath, remembering his lecture to me what felt like so long ago about my feelings and how misguided they were. It was time I reciprocated.

"Maybe that's for the best. It's not like we were going to end up in the same place," I said.

You would have thought lightning struck in front of him for the wide-eyed step he took back.

"So that's how it is?" he asked.

For the last year, our friendship had taken a beating. Though I'd moved back, things between us weren't completely resolved.

"You made it clear where you stood. Now let me make mine. I like her a lot. Don't be a fucking dick to her because someone else is playing with your favorite toy."

He stepped forward, remorse on his face.

"It's not like that."

I held his gaze in a chokehold, stopping him in his tracks.

"Isn't it? I've found someone and you're jealous."

I raised a brow, waiting for him to balk.

"I'm not jealous. I don't want this chick to take advantage," he retorted.

Everything we'd been through, I believed him.

"Thanks, but I can handle it."

He didn't give me a chance to breathe before he countered.

"Can you? Last we spoke you weren't even sure if you were gay."

I tried not to be pissed off knowing he didn't mean it as an insult.

"And you were right. I'm not."

"How do you know?" he challenged.

There was no point in hurling back an answer. I took my time deciding how much I wanted to say without telling him it wasn't his business.

"I know."

And that was all the truth he deserved from me. We may have been friends, once closer than brothers, but like everything else, nothing lasted forever.

Though a wound grew in his eyes, he only nodded.

There was nothing more to say. I'd left Willow far too long. She and everyone else weren't stupid about what was going on up here.

"Be nice to her," I warned.

I didn't have to add that I'd never asked him for anything before in my life, not even when I told him so long ago how I felt.

He tipped his head again and I left, hoping the rest of my night with Willow hadn't been spoiled.

41

Willow

MY FIRST NIGHT as Ashton's girlfriend ended shortly after he'd come downstairs. Though he'd given me a smile, it hadn't quite reached his eyes. I could tell he wanted to leave, but I'd been in the middle of eating a slice of pizza that was so good I'd told Shelly I wanted to marry her.

Sawyer had come down a few minutes later, and everyone tried to ignore the weird haze that clouded the room.

"I should take you home," Ashton whispered into my ear.

It hadn't been the words I'd hoped for. The ache between my legs was a real thing, but I still wanted more. He'd made me a whore. I finally understood what the damn fuss was about, and I found myself greedy with need.

Though I'd been fearless earlier, I clammed up in the face of the sorrow he couldn't quite hide.

"Okay," I said, trying for a grin myself and was sure I'd failed.

That daring part of myself hid, wondering if I would get the brush-off by the time we arrived at my place.

I waved goodbye, but the girls decided to circle in for a hug. You'd thought we'd been long-lost friends for all the promises they made to keep in touch. We'd already exchanged phone numbers. Though I didn't tell them that phones for me were like socks in a dryer. I never knew if I'd see it again, and I currently didn't have one.

Once again, Ashton had been a true gentleman, but conversation was lost in the roar of his engine. One thing that made it more apparent that things had changed was his lack of touch. He'd guided me out the house at the small of my back, but his hand hadn't sought mine.

We arrived at my apartment with little fanfare. When I reached for the door handle, wanting to be out before he said anything that would damage my heart, he stopped me.

It wasn't as if I loved him. It was too soon for that, wasn't it? But my feelings, whatever they should be called, were very much wrapped up in him. They had been since he first kissed me or before.

"I'm sorry about earlier with Sawyer."

I blinked at him, probably because I'd been expecting a far different statement.

"No, he's fine," I said.

He shook his head. "No, he wasn't. He was an ass and I told him as much."

"He's probably worried..."

I trailed off because what did Sawyer have to be worried about? Nothing from me, unless my presence made him realize something else. My stomach curdled like old milk.

"That's what he said."

His reply didn't miss a beat. He hadn't noticed my confusion because he'd aimed his gaze at the steering wheel before glancing over at me.

"But it isn't his choice. It's mine," he finished.

That took some of the sour out of my gut until I noticed his grip on the steering wheel.

"I don't want to come between the two of you."

It sucked to be altruistic. At the same time, I cared enough about him not to want to hurt him any more than his secretive past had.

His hand left the wheel in favor of taking mine.

"You're not. I want this."

His penetrating gaze was fierce in a way that demanded acceptance.

"I do too," I said.

He leaned down and kissed me. It started slow, just light pressure against my lips and a tingle down between my lower ones. Then I let his tongue slide in. His hand slipped up my arm and into my hair. I thrilled at his touch. For whatever reason, it gave me confidence I needed about where we stood.

I whimpered when he pulled back.

"I should go, unless you want us to give your neighbors a show," he said.

The question of asking him up to my room played briefly in my mind. The weariness still in his eyes answered the question for me. He needed time to get over whatever happened between him and Sawyer.

I leaned up and brushed my lips over his. Then I bit my lower one when the noticeable bulge in his pants boosted my confidence.

"About that show," he teased.

I giggled and leaned back. He stopped me again. "Let me get that for you."

He got out and rounded the car to open my door. My grin held a lot of teeth, and I had to cover my mouth. He took said hand and moved it down.

"Stop laughing. You see what you're doing to me."

I reached out and cupped him through his jeans, tossing out my vows not to ask him to stay.

"You could come in."

I giggled at my Freudian slip.

Next thing I knew, his hands were on my ass hoisting me up. The chirping of the car locking was his answer.

"Where to?"

I directed him, winding my legs firmly around his waist. We stumbled into my apartment and would have woken the dead with our laughter, knocking furniture and walls to get to my room. Celeste didn't come out. I assumed that meant she wasn't home. It was a good thing, because I didn't remain anywhere close to quiet this time around.

At some point later, he told me goodbye. He whispered he had practice, and I murmured something I couldn't remember, dozing back into dreamless sleep.

When I did wake, there was disappointment of him not being there. The hour was late, near noon. Most of my classes had unofficially ended. Papers, projects, and end of the semester testing were underway. The only class I worried about was my Entomology III class. I needed to go to the pond to perform my ad hoc labs.

Though I questioned myself on my major as much as my professor had, I still believed firmly there had to be more humane ways of studying insects than killing them. Maybe it made me a bad scientist. At the same time, innovations and inventions didn't happen without going against the grain and testing new theories.

I got up and showered. Before I could leave, Celeste clad in a fuzzy robe holding a *be silent until I finish my coffee* mug grilled me.

"Had company last night, did you?" she asked, her eyes holding mine.

I blushed like a schoolgirl with her first crush.

"You heard?"

She eyed me, lips curling into a knowing smirk.

"No, I missed that. I did, however, see the boy leaving."

She'd warned me against him so many times I waited in vain for her to add more commentary.

"Not going to say anything?" I asked.

"About Ashton Westborough, Sawyer's best friend?"

Her lips pursed in disapproval.

"You were wrong about him." I pointed my finger at the counter while saying so.

"Apparently, given the sex smell wafting from your room."

Talk about moth to a flame. My face needed a firehose to cool it off.

"Don't be ashamed. I'm happy for you. Am I to assume he's the one you gave your virginity to?"

I nodded. No reason to lie about that. Plus, I needed a confidant. Despite Shelly and Brie's insta-friendship, I didn't know them well enough to spill these secrets to.

"Good for you. I'm glad I was wrong about him."

There was something suspicious about her quick acquiescence.

I narrowed my eyes at her. "Did you talk to him?"

She put the coffee to her lips and drank before answering.

"Talk might not be the right word. I told him if he valued his balls he wouldn't hurt you." My jaw dropped. "Don't get mad. I've been waiting for years to say those sisterly words."

I was almost afraid to ask, but did anyway. "What did he say?"

"Not much of a talker, that one." I glared at her. "Fine, he said two words." She must have seen my move, ready to shake the answer out of her. "*I won't*. Then he just left."

I smiled more to myself than at her.

"Did you have the conversation with him?" That wiped the

grin from my face. "You know, about whether you're exclusive and I hope you're being safe."

She looked down at her still flat belly as if I needed a reminder about the birds and the bees.

"He's my boyfriend," I said and hoped she left the other question alone.

I didn't need a Mom-like lecture from her about the risks I put myself by not insisting on condoms. It hadn't been a conscious decision. I'd been too caught up in him to care, which was stupid.

"Boyfriend, huh?"

I nodded, and she graced me with a grin from ear to ear.

"Good for you."

She'd grilled me, but that didn't leave her off the hook.

"Did you tell him?"

She focused on me, after her stare having found the limits of space.

"I told him," she said.

I wasn't giving her an inch she hadn't given me.

"And?" I queried.

She shrugged. "Not much he can say or do until I decide."

"He can have an opinion," I urged.

"He's not really an opinionated guy."

I frowned. That sounded so much like bullshit until I thought of Ash. He hadn't been very talkative to me or anyone for that matter. He'd only opened up to me after a lot of prodding on my part.

I let it be and dropped my eyes to my hands. A minute or two later, she said something else that would leave its mark.

"Be careful, okay." I nodded, knowing that meant many things. "And don't think I didn't catch that you didn't answer the question about being safe. Don't end up like me, okay?"

Her eyes didn't sparkle with mischief. Like Ash, there was a certain sadness there that was new for her. I moved over and hugged her, silently given her support.

I bobbed my head and watched her go to her bedroom. I grabbed an apple and headed for the door, with my notes and other lab supplies tucked in my messenger bag.

Was I being stupid? Maybe. Only time could answer that question.

42

Ashton

Football practice sucked and not for the usual reasons. Because Coach thought the chance of a bowl game rode on our next game, practice ran late. That meant I missed spending time with Willow.

With the classes wrapping up, we'd both been too busy to see each other. She had tests to study for and I had papers to write.

"Westborough, get your head out of your ass and catch some goddamn balls."

I shifted my focus back onto the field.

"Yes, Coach."

"And Cargill, stop throwing the ball like you have a broken arm."

He and I eyed each other but said nothing. His father was riding him about his new position as quarterback. Cargill men were destined for greatness and all that jazz. With the way things were, he didn't talk to me about it much.

We got into formation as I counted seconds to minutes, waiting for the season to be over. It was never my future to play ball. I'd rather write the commentary than play the game in the pros. That didn't mean I didn't have skills. It was hard not to when Sawyer's dad had played father to me for all my games from elementary to high school. That made me think about the photos in that museum of a room in my father's house. He'd been to some of my games and could have been the father I needed him to be.

Sawyer counted off, and I moved automatically when the snap count was done. I ran for my life, hoping that if we executed this play perfectly, Coach would show us mercy and end practice.

The ball landed in my arms like a newborn baby, but the corner covering me was one step faster. I went down hard. My bell rang like a fire drill, jumbling my thoughts like scattered pages in the wind. I couldn't think beyond the pain.

When my vision coalesced into a single image, it was Sawyer's face above me.

"At least you caught the ball."

His signature humor took the sting out of my pride. Plus, I still held the ball.

The doctor performed the mandatory concussion test, which I passed. However, practice didn't end. We endured another hour until we were finally set free.

I stayed under the spray of hot water as I thought about Willow. It had been days since I'd seen her. Talking on the phone wasn't my thing. Texting her also was a fruitless task. I needed to see her like a junkie needed a hit.

"Are you going to the café?"

Sawyer stood with a towel around his waist, having finished his shower.

"Nah, go ahead."

He nodded and left. I didn't linger too much longer. After I got dressed, I texted Willow. She responded quickly, though I didn't much like her answer. She had a lab she had to finish tonight. It was due tomorrow.

Me: Tomorrow?

Willow: Tonight, but it will be late.

Me: Cool. Text me.

I might suffer the next morning during practice, but it was worth it. I was beginning to see why Kelley and Chance had become so addicted to their girls. I walked home, having ridden to practice with Chance and Sawyer. I grabbed a quick dinner I planned to eat in my room. I would study for a test I had on Friday.

Good intentions and all that. Her text woke me.

Willow: Another hour. Too late?

I had to blink a few times to wake enough to answer.

Me: No.

Willow: My place.

Me: An hour.

Feeling groggy, I set an alarm. I figured I might as well sleep a little longer. There wouldn't be any of that when I saw her.

I set the book that had landed on my chest aside and closed my eyes again.

My nightmare-free sleep was interrupted by something worse. Hands held me down after a dark sack was put over my head. I woke to utter darkness. Terror like I hadn't known in years locked all my muscles.

I fought off the little boy who feared a fate worse than death. But no hands moved past my shoulders and arms. A rag had been stuffed in my mouth and stopped any protest I might have had. My arms were zip-tied at my back, the plastic biting into my skin. There was obviously more than one person as my attempts to get away were fruitless.

Hands urged me up. That's when I used my legs. Steel was

pressed to my temple and a safety released. I stilled. Months ago I might have welcomed death with open arms. However, I couldn't risk whatever this was spilling over to my friends.

Compliant as a lamb headed to slaughter, I let them guide me to an uncertain fate. It wasn't like they could do anything to me that hadn't been done before. Then again, maybe I lacked imagination.

For once in my life, I prayed like hell Chance, Sawyer, Shelly, and Brie were okay as I was marched through the silent house. Too silent.

I was shoved in the back of what I assumed was a van. Whoever orchestrated this had to be a professional. No one had said one word.

Once we were underway, I lost my bearings after the first few turns. Disoriented from the dark mask and rolling this way and that on a cold steel floor, my internal map had lost its way. We drove a while before we finally came to a stop.

I was marched to my death for all I knew. The sad thing was, who would miss me? Sure, Chance, Kelley, and Sawyer would be sad for a minute. But they all had lives and would quickly move on. Willow... that thought made me stumble. Something in my chest tightened. I hadn't known her long enough for my death to make an impact. She'd cry, for sure, but like the others would soon move on.

The chair I was thrown into squeaked some under my weight. My arms were set free, only to be secured again to an oddly flat surface. I had a growing suspicion the chair wasn't an ordinary one.

Once that was done, my shirt was lifted and sticky probes with trailing wires were attached to my chest.

Dim light filled my world when the hood was finally removed from my head. Once the rag was removed, I found myself sucking in lungfuls of air like I'd been suffocated.

When the metal that had been aimed at me landed hard on a

desk before me, I took stock of what I could see. It wasn't much. The room was mostly hidden by shadows. The one man behind the computer was illumined by the screen he studiously watched. The other man was little more than a face though he stood.

Given his disembodied look, I assumed he wore all black.

"Mr. Ashton Westborough. May I call you Ash?"

The wad of spit I aimed his way was my reply. It had missed him by miles but had the desired effect. His pale face grew dark with a rage I'd felt myself, many times. My choice might have been stupid on my part as he picked up the gun he'd left on the table and walked slowly but purposefully my way, unafraid, considering my legs had been bound to the chair as well.

"Have you heard of the game Russian roulette?"

His question only lowered my estimation of him. I wasn't a member of some shadow organization where fear like this would be used. That thought died in my head and all the pieces fell into place.

He'd ejected the magazine from the gun and plucked out the solitary bullet, only to push it back in and slam it back home. The gun was whole again.

He aimed it at my head. "Not much of a game since this isn't a revolver. One shot and you're dead."

I didn't flinch, banking on my theory being right.

He wasn't phased by my non-reaction. Just moved behind the desk again.

"This is how it works. I ask questions and you'll be truthful if you want to live. See, the thing is, I need your honesty. You've seen my face and I need to trust you."

I nearly rolled my eyes, unimpressed by this show.

"Your name?" he asked.

The battle of wills began until a phone vibrated on the desk. The nameless man smiled and picked it up. Then he turned the screen toward me, freezing my blood.

"Willow, is it? Pretty girl, blonde curls and a fuckable body."

My chair jumped as I tried to get to my feet.

He laughed. "I bet you want to talk now. Name?"

If it had just been me, I would have held firm waiting for the game to reveal itself. But he described her, and I didn't have a picture assigned to her profile.

"Ashton Westborough."

My teeth might have been filed down to dust for as much as I'd ground my molars answering that question.

"That's the name your bitch of a mother gave you. What should have been your name?"

That question gave me pause. I wondered then if I was right about who I thought was behind this. They should know that answer unless this was just a baseline question for the polygraph I'd been set up to take.

"Billings," I grudgingly answered.

"Full name."

"Ashton Westborough Billings."

His head turned, leaving only his profile for inspection. The guy behind the computed nodded his way, and I heard his hands sliding across the other.

"Good. Remember, everything is in your hands. You're honest with me, all will be fine. Willow will sleep happy, though she sounds pissed you haven't shown up."

I wanted to scrub my face. How could I explain this without scaring her and making her believe me?

He asked me another series of yes or no questions, like quizzing me on where I went to high school, what my home address had been. Then he began another line of questioning.

Him: "Do you want to play football?"

Me: "No."

There was no harm in answering truthfully there.

Him: "Is your best friend named Sawyer Cargill?"

Me: "Yes."

I wasn't exactly shocked by his next question.

Him: "Are you in love with him?"

Me: "No."

Love meant many things, but he'd meant romantically. I held his gaze longer as he waited for me to change my answer.

Him: You do realize I expect the truth one hundred percent.

Me: "Yes."

Him: "Do you want to change your answer?"

Me: "No."

My heart remained steady, not skipping a beat or speeding up.

Him: "Were you molested as a child by a certain Supreme Court Justice?"

Time had to have slowed as I processed his question. Only Sawyer and I had known the answer to that question if you exclude the devil and the monster themselves. Sawyer wouldn't have told anyone in a million years. I would stake my life on that. My father had just found out. What would he have to gain by spilling that fact? Nothing. He was running for president. If anything, he needed fewer scandals if he had a prayer's chance of winning the primary next year. His wife... She was the wild card. She'd played like she felt for me, but in the end, I was the object of her husband's betrayal. She'd admitted as much and that she'd resented me.

"Why does that matter?" I asked, trying to buy time.

"Your answer or I could send pretty Willow a text to meet you outside. My men could take her."

I flexed my muscles against my binds in my best impression of Bruce Banner getting angry. But I wasn't a Marvel character with superhuman strength. The only thing I did was cause welts in my arms and legs.

Him: "Answer?"

Me: "Yes."

It was an admission that killed some part of me inside. I wanted nothing more than to forget the past. Once again, I was faced with it. Would it always be this way?

Him: "That wasn't hard, was that?"

I gave him nothing, hoping he would move on.

Him: "When did it start?"

I would have preferred him slitting my throat than answering and remembering the horror of my childhood. My eyes fell to where my phone sat illuminated only slightly by the single bulb above my head that dully gave off what was a poor excuse for light. I thought about Willow and didn't want to imagine what they might do to her. My fate shouldn't be hers.

Me: "Young."

Him: "How old?"

Me: "I don't know."

My shrug only pulled at my binds, sending pain shooting up my arms.

Him: "That young. When did it stop?"

A flash of Sawyer coming out of my closet like some avenging angel reminded me all the reason why I'd mixed up my love for him. Twisting it into a fantasy for something more.

I shrugged again as the entire scenario played out in my head.

Him: "I need an answer."

That had been a truth I didn't want to share. How pathetic I'd been to let it go on for so long.

He picked up my phone.

Me: "Twelve."

I'd vomited the word, and he grinned like a well-fed cat as he stole pieces of my soul, one truth at a time. He set the phone down again as he pulled at my marionet strings.

Him: "Did you like it?"

I wanted out of that room and raged that I wasn't strong enough to free myself and kill the sadistic bastard in front of me.

He laughed maniacally. Apparently, he was only riling me up as he moved on.

Him: "Have you slept with the lovely Willow?"

That was none of his fucking business, and I silently said as much with my burning stare.

Him: "I'll need an answer."

Me: "Yes."

Him: "How many times? I bet she was as good as she looks."

The laughter unfurled on his lips was enough to have me on my feet, stooped with a chair riding my back.

Him: "Down, boy."

His amusement only made me want to swing this chair and see what and how much I could break.

Him: "I said down."

This time the room temperature chilled with his words. We both looked at the gun at the same time. His hand curled around it and aimed it at my head.

Him: "You won't be much help to your pretty girlfriend if you're dead."

If he thought that would scare me, he was dead wrong. I gave him a cold stare.

Him: "I like you. You're not crying yet."

I gave him no reaction.

Him: "Cold bastard, aren't you?"

When I still said nothing, he went on.

Him: "Let me just lay it out there for you. You've guessed who we are?"

I had.

Me: "Vanderbilt."

Him: "Smart boy. Here is the deal. Your membership comes with many perks. Like say the word and we can make a certain judge's life hell."

I couldn't say I was unmoved. I'd spent many nights dreaming up ways for the man to die. But what would that make me? Another monster?

Him: "The only thing we ask in return is complete confidence. You say nothing ever and we're good."

Then he laid on the consequences of not keeping my mouth shut.

43

Willow

Had he just blown me off? I'd asked myself a thousand times as I stood looking out the window hoping I'd see his car any moment. I glanced down at my phone Mom had found and overnighted to me. My text to him was still the last. He hadn't responded. Would it be desperate for me to call? Maybe he'd fallen asleep? I didn't want to think he'd blown me off.

I considered all my options. I could call Shelly or Brie, but it was late.

What was that saying? The simplest reason is probably the right one.

I left the window and went to bed.

When morning came, there wasn't a message from Ashton explaining what happened. I tried not to be mad, but I was. I got ready and headed for my Entomology III class. I checked my attitude at the door and made my way to my professor's office.

All the way there, I searched faces for Ashton. I gave up when I walked into the science building.

I was so busy thinking about my boyfriend, I nearly ran into Derek.

"Hey," I said.

His scowl was his only response. I turned as he passed, wondering if I should go and try to make things right somehow, but the alarm on my phone said I had five minutes until my allotted time slot.

I knocked on the familiar door, and I was greeted with a "Come in."

"Close the door," my professor said.

She barely glanced up from the computer screen.

"Miss Young, I have your project."

I'd emailed it the night before, but also had a hard copy I'd printed off. "I've gone through it, and I must say I'm impressed. Though your techniques were unorthodox."

Yeah, because I'd been banned from the lab. I managed to keep my mouth shut.

"But your conclusions were correct."

She finally leaned back and steepled her fingers like a prayer. I wanted to pray that she would pass me. There was no room in my schedule to retake this class next semester and graduate.

Her fingers tapped as my heart raced.

"I'll be honest, I don't want to pass you. You're more suited for PETA than a scientist."

That pissed me off. I sat straighter in my chair.

"With all due respect, PETA's mission statement is a good one. That doesn't mean I necessarily agree with their methods." When she didn't say anything, I continued. "Innovations and inventions weren't attained by staying the path of the status quo. Isn't the basis of a scientist to try new methods? We don't have to kill to study. In fact, I'll venture that studying an insect that died in its natural habitat is more useful than a controlled environment."

Her praying hands stopped their tapping in favor of a light clap with a smile on her face.

"Very well. Between the Shakespeare paper and this lab, you've passed. The final grades will be posted in a few days. Good luck, Miss Young."

I hopped out of my chair, a grin plastered to my face. Had she really given in so easily? Though I had no idea if I'd only barely passed or how the grade might affect my final GPA. None of that mattered. At least I could graduate. I practically skipped out of her office and down the hall.

The air outside smelled a little sweeter until I spotted a couple hand in hand. My phone hadn't buzzed, and my heart sank. Where was Ashton?

The football practice field was halfway across campus from here, but I found myself marching in that direction. He may have been new at the boyfriend thing, but texting me was just simple courtesy. I couldn't imagine any excuse he'd have not to pick up his phone and say something. My steps faltered a second when I thought he might have broken his phone or lost it like I was prone to do. If that was true, I'd gladly eat my mad, every bite.

I'd just past the café when I spotted Sawyer with a group of guys. Ashton wasn't in sight and neither was Chance.

Sawyer would have walked right by me. His eyes met mine for a second, his joyous smile flattening until he responded to someone who spoke to him. A girl came out of nowhere and draped herself around him. I stopped even though I didn't want to watch. He said something, and the girl giggled like he was a professional comedian. She waved goodbye, but it was a clear invitation for him to follow.

"Can I talk to you for a moment?" I cut in.

His followers snickered and patted his back for being such a horn dog. I rolled my eyes.

"I'll catch you all in a minute."

The guys left sounding as if they were making bets. He waited for me to speak and I took a breath.

"Have you seen Ashton?"

Unfortunately, even I saw why his devilish smirk worked on most girls. Good thing I wasn't *most girls*. If Ashton wasn't my boyfriend, Sawyer would be the last boy I would be interested in.

"What? He dumped you already?"

I'd never wanted to punch someone until that moment.

"No. He was supposed to come by last night and he didn't show up."

If eyes could beg, mine did.

"Sounds like none of my business."

We could agree on that.

"It's not, really. But it also doesn't seem like something he'd do. Can you just let me know if you've seen him?"

His eyes narrowed, and his lips parted. Just when I thought he would answer, he said, "I'm not his keeper."

He made a move to walk away. I stepped in his path, because this was important. If my relationship had any shot at working, I needed peace between us.

"What is your problem with me?"

His laugh lacked any humor and almost sounded like a bark.

"Problem. I'll tell you my problem. Ashton doesn't need some girl clouding up his head. There's a lot of shit you don't know. And I don't want my boy messed up when you decide to walk away after you find out."

I lifted my chin, even more than the angle I had to look up to meet his eyes.

"You don't know me." I snapped out the words.

"Exactly. And neither does Ash."

I should have let it go, because a fight would not serve me in the long run. But I was tired of his arrogance.

"Really. Because I've known Ashton since the beginning of the school year."

A flash of surprise briefly graced his features.

"You must mean very little if he never mentioned you to me."

I curled my hands into wrecking balls.

"Or maybe he didn't tell you because he was afraid you'd react this way?"

I didn't know this for sure, but I didn't think I was far off the mark.

"Or maybe I'm right and that's why he hasn't called you?" The jab landed squarely on my chest and forced my lips shut. "Now I have to go."

My chest heaved with unbridled words I didn't get to say. Years of insecurity wormed their way into my head. They'd been unlocked by all he'd said. I didn't want to believe he was right, but he knew Ashton better than I did.

The reasonable conclusion was he hadn't called. He'd warned me he was fucked up and I'd still walked through that door with my heart available as a punching bag.

44

Ashton

A ROUGH HAND shook me awake. It was the first time in my life I sought darkness over the light, wanting nothing more than to ignore the summons to wake.

"Fuck, bro, leave me alone," I grunted, rolling over and hoping to slip back into sleep.

"Dude, you missed practice again."

It would take more than a crowbar to open my eyes. But Sawyer was a persistent son of a bitch. He shook me relentlessly until I was glowering at him.

"Where the hell were you? I covered for you. But Coach isn't buying it."

I scrubbed a hand over my aching head.

"What time is it?" I asked.

"Time for you to get the fuck up."

I glowered at him hovering over me. You'd think I was some derelict solider and he was my captain for the disapproving glare he was throwing my way.

"Your girlfriend is looking for you," he said.

That got my attention. I fought to a sitting position.

"You talked to her?"

He snorted. "More like she gave me the third degree. She caught me off guard, so I couldn't cover you."

I lifted my head, eyes narrowing. "What did you say to her?"

"What do you care? You stood her up from what she said."

I groaned, rubbing my eyes remembering the night before, and forced myself to my feet.

"Was she pissed?"

He barked a laugh. "What do you think?"

The contents of my stomach marched up my throat, and I barreled my way past him and into the bathroom. I was fairly sure anything I'd eaten in the past week was excavated from my gut.

I hadn't locked the door, so when I finally heaved myself up from my crouching position, Sawyer stood in the doorway.

"A little too much to drink last night." He shook his head. "I'm worried about you."

How many times had I heard that in recent months?

"You don't have to."

I closed the door on him and stared at myself in the mirror. Dark shadows circled my eyes. I rubbed my mouth before scooping up a handful of water to rinse it out.

Willow. What the hell would I tell her? I stripped and got into the shower, hanging my head in the warm spray, trying to get my thoughts together. I hated the idea of lying to her. But what choice did I have?

Sawyer wasn't waiting for me when I left the bathroom still shaky on my feet. I burst through my room door, eyes darting on every surface until I spotted what I was searching for. I snatched up my phone, but it was dead.

I plugged it in and sat on my bed waiting for it to power up enough for me to use it. Flashes of Willow's face plagued my mind. I closed my eyes against the onslaught. Would she forgive me, or was this just a sign that I'd been selfish to think I could be with her?

When my cell woke up from the dead, I sent a text.

An hour later, I waited in the field, watching tall grass lazily wave side to side in the breeze. I didn't hear her approach. She sat cross-legged next to me, but wouldn't meet my eyes.

"I'm sorry."

It was inadequate.

"What happened?" she asked.

Her quiet words carried on the breeze straight to my chest.

As much as I wanted to tell her the truth, the warning I'd been given made the lie worth it.

"I fell asleep."

That much was true.

"Your phone?"

Out of my reach. "Dead."

Eyes like fire burned into mine. "I want to believe you. It's not like I have the best relationship with my phone. But can I trust you?"

No, because I'm lying to you. If I told you the truth, you would run far away from me. I'd assumed the Vanderbilt Club harmless. The CIA agent who'd interrogated me proved me wrong.

As he'd pinned the tiny gold crown onto my shirt, he said, "We're king makers. Ask your father or Sawyer's. On different sides of the aisle, but with a common goal. One will be president. We rule this country on every level. That only happens when our secrets are kept safe. If you tell anyone of this, I'm afraid accidents... well, you get my point."

That was enough to keep me silent.

I'd taken too long to answer. Willow was in the process of getting to her feet. She was ready to run, and I couldn't tell her how she'd be a target if I gave her what she wanted. I snagged her hand.

"Give me a second chance," I offered, unable to tell her an all-out lie.

In her eyes, I could see a salvation I didn't deserve. She was innocence in a perfect package unmarred by life.

She looked down at where I held onto her hand. I got to my feet but couldn't let go. To be able to touch was an ability I wasn't willing to let go.

"Let me take you somewhere."

She didn't know about the dragon that lurked under my skin and didn't pull away. I led her around the pond to Chance's truck.

I answered her questioning gaze. "I borrowed it."

Like the gentleman I wished I was, I opened her door and helped her up into the cab. After I eyed the basket in the back, I got in on the other side and turned on my phone, using the preprogrammed directions.

"You don't have class, do you?" I asked a little late.

Class was over, but she could have a test she couldn't miss. Her head moved side to side, her wide eyes too trusting.

I backed out the empty lot and took her hand, unable to get enough of touching her soft skin.

Chance's truck was too old for satellite radio. I tuned to a station on FM that hummed between us. A breeze blew through the open windows, swirling loose hair around her head, creating a pretty picture.

By the time I pulled up to the lake, the sun was cresting the horizon. The glow bounced off the water in a picture worth a thousand words. I backed the truck up over a worn ruddy path, stopping shy of plunging it in.

"Stay here," I said, my voice raspy from disuse.

She nodded, and I got out, climbing into the flatbed. I pulled the folded blanket from where it had been stowed. I spread it out and then went to help Willow out of the cab.

"What's all this?" she asked, placing her hand in mine.

I helped her down, only to boost her up in the back.

She sat midway with her back to one side. I sat across from her as she waited expectantly for my response.

"My attempt at a first date," I answered.

Chance had been my source of information. He understood I didn't like crowds. If I had any chance of not fucking this up, something just for the two of us was the only option.

I dragged the basket over, and with my eyes on hers, opened it. I had to look away to grab the first thing, a thousand-dollar bottle of Perrier-Jouet champagne I'd pilfered from the kitchen. Sawyer had stocked up on expensive wine and liquor when he heard his dad was in town.

Two flute glasses were next to come out. I set them between us as she watched thoughtfully. I couldn't get a read on her mood. I had no idea if I was scoring a touchdown or fumbling the ball. I brought out fresh organic strawberries I'd also found in the fridge. Shelly had come to my rescue when choosing what to bring.

The whole setup reminded me I had a family, more than I thought. Friends that I'd had for years or formed in the last few had been there for me in my panic over what to do to make up my fuck-up with Willow.

The red ripe berries were already plated. I just had to remove the clear film that held them in place.

"Champagne?" I offered.

"Yes." As I uncorked the bottle, she said, "You went all out."

I shrugged. "I won't lie. I had help."

I poured us each a glass.

"That you thought about it is what matters."

I plucked a perfect berry from the plate and held it out to her. She surprised me when she leaned in and bit the fruit from my fingers. Juice burst on my hand, and as I watched her chew, I licked my fingertips clean.

"Oh, this is so sweet."

"Organic," I tossed out, not even sure why.

A grin blossomed on her face.

"Then I should tell you that bees, one of the most feared insects, had a hand in creating these wonderful fruits. They are in danger of extinction because of pesticides." It was a good thing I'd brought organic. "If they die out, mankind will too."

She spoke like a true activist. It should have weirded me out, but it didn't. Her passion only drove one of my own.

"I'm sorry, probably not date conversation," she said, ducking her head.

"No. It's good stuff the world needs to pay attention to."

That was true and something to think about. Maybe I could write an editorial piece and send it around to the national papers for publication.

"If I was good with words like a journalist..."

She drifted off. The fact that we were in sync spoke about my attraction to her.

"Maybe we could collaborate," I said.

Our hands had bridged the distance. Our fingertips brushed the tips of each other's.

Touching her was one of my favorite things to do. The simple act had never been a vice until her.

"Does this mean you've changed favorites?"

Her brow crinkled in confusion.

"Bees versus dragonflies?" I added.

The perfect little O her lips formed had me hard in an instant. I had to shift to release pressure as I watched a tiny amount of red juice at the corner of her mouth.

"No, still dragonflies," she said.

I thought about what she'd told me about how the male dragonfly protected his mate even though they wouldn't be mates for life.

She drank from her flute, but that spot of sweetness remained in place.

"Come here," I said.

I curled a finger in my direction. I'd only expected her to lean in. But she shoved the plate aside and carefully erased all the distance between us.

Watching her on her hands and knees only fogged my brain even more. As soon as she was close enough, I licked the corner of her mouth before going for a deep kiss.

Her lips parted, allowing me entrance, and I took full advantage. The mix of champagne and strawberries on her tongue had me drunk on her. We both reached for each other, she on her knees. My hands cupped her face as she locked her arms around my neck while climbing onto my lap.

All my dinner plans forgotten, we feasted on each other like it was our last meal.

Her parted thighs and sweet center rubbed against my hard shaft. I shifted us to lay her down and cover her body with mine.

Thank God for the privacy we had in the place because I didn't care and it didn't seem like she did either.

"I have dinner," I said.

"It can wait," she murmured, taking the cap from my head and tossing it aside.

I shoved up her shirt and watched her breasts spill from her bra as I pushed it out of the way.

As I sucked one tight bud in, she'd unhooked the front clasp I'd ignored.

"You're so fucking beautiful," I declared like the world should know.

I probably shouldn't have cursed but, damn, I felt like a fucking virgin every time I was with her.

In my haste to remove her shorts, my glass of champagne spilled over her belly and down between the juncture of her thighs. We looked at each other as she shivered from the cool liquid.

Time was not wasted as I dipped my head and licked from her slit to her nub. Her wetness mixed with the champagne was a tasty treat I would need to repeat. In fact, I grabbed the bottle and poured some into my mouth. Then I went in and let the liquid flow inside of her only to lap up every drop as she squirmed underneath me.

"What was that?" she asked, panting the entire time.

I lifted my head to meet her gaze. "That was me having dessert before dinner."

"I want dessert."

Her eyes trailed down the gap between us to land on my dick, which strained against my zipper waiting to be freed.

"I'm not done yet."

I went down again and ate her like she was the main course at a fancy restaurant. I sank my tongue so deep inside her pussy, her walls quivered around me.

Her nails raked over my scalp as she shoved me farther into her silky depths until she was calling out my name.

When she went limp, I thought we would return to our original scheduled program. But my girl got her second wind. She sat up and shoved me to my back. We had to scoot around to make it happen in the small space. But soon, she was hovering over me with a demand of her own.

"My turn."

45

Willow

THE STUPID BUTTON of his jeans wouldn't give as a breeze reminded me of my half-naked state. Finally, he felt pity on me and unbuttoned his fly as I drew my shorts back up and over my bare bottom.

There was nothing between him and his jeans except skin. "Wow," I murmured softly, not realizing I'd spoken out loud. His dick was a thing of art. Smooth skin over taut muscle in a long, thick package. The crown of which was plump and almost red straining in my hand.

I leaned down and took a lazy lick from base to tip before sucking the head into my mouth like a blow pop. A hint of something salty touched my tongue, and I sucked harder for more.

"Fuck," he muttered, gliding his hand to the back of my head.

Gently, he guided me at the pace he wanted.

The whole thing was so erotic, my panties were damp with need even after just having one orgasm.

I lifted my eyes to see his hooded as he bit on his lower lip. I could have come at that very moment. Using a tighter grip, I worked my hand up and down on the part of him I couldn't swallow. It was hard enough keeping my cheeks hollow and my teeth from grazing him.

When his hand fisted in my hair, slightly tugging me off, I knew what he wanted.

"I need inside you."

I nodded, already on the same page.

We frantically tugged our bottoms off. He was faster than me and sat watching. His stare sent tingles down my spine and to all the female parts of me. I crawled over to him when he beckoned, trying my best to look sexy.

This time when I crawled onto his lap, I sank down onto his shaft, loving every stretch.

I moaned before nibbling on his lip and rocking myself up and down. He dug his fingers into my hips as I drew closer, needing contact with that certain spot.

"You feel so fucking good," he said.

He groaned against my mouth, and an orgasm shot out of me so hard and fast I couldn't contain a scream. It echoed across the lake.

Then I found myself on my back, him driving inside. His thrust felt purposeful, and soon he was grunting my name as I felt the warmth jetting inside me.

"Jesus, Willow, what are you doing to me?"

I was too busy catching my breath to answer, but a similar question was on my tongue. He rolled us to our side and just stared at me.

"I should feed you," he said.

I grinned at him. "You did."

He smirked. "Does that mean you're full?"

With him still inside me, I saw the dirty side of everything he said and glanced down before meeting his glazed eyes.

"What are you offering?" I asked.

I couldn't believe I'd said that and lost that thought when he thrust his hips up, forcing his cock deeper.

It didn't end there. This time, he went deliciously slower until we were both breathless, panting from another explosive orgasm. After, he insisted on feeding me. I ate shrimp cocktail from his fingers and drank more bubbly champagne.

"Tell me something about you." A flash of panic crossed his beautiful features. "Like, what's your favorite color?" I tossed out, easing the lines that had formed across his brow.

He put another delectable shrimp into my mouth, and I chewed while he answered.

"Gold." I arched an eyebrow, searching for more. Instead, he tossed the question back at me. "You?"

My new favorite had to be the stormy blue-gray of his eyes, but I felt too self-conscious to answer that way.

"Blue, I guess."

"Dragonflies?"

I grinned like a schoolgirl. Was I that predictable, or did he know me better than even my stepsister? That was indeed the color of my favorite of the dragonflies.

"Yes."

The conversation went on as we asked each other about more of our favorites. Then when that lost steam, he asked, "Where is one place in the world you'd like to go?"

I sat for a moment and pondered that. I didn't have to think too long for an answer.

"Rome, and before you ask, it's because it's one place where there is evidence that the world existed over two thousand years ago."

He nodded.

"Have you been?" I asked, sure he had as he'd accepted my answer.

"I have, but I have a feeling if I go with you, it would be a new experience."

We talked and ate more as the sun completely set. He had a four-course meal for us that was restaurant worthy. As the night cooled, I ended it wrapped in his arms with another blanket around us.

I hadn't realized I dozed off until he jerked in my arms. Alarm rang in my head with the instant jolt of panic in his eyes as he nearly scrambled away from me.

"Are you okay?"

He heaved in a breath and nodded like he couldn't speak, spooked from whatever nightmare had woken him.

"We should go," he said.

I was still reeling at how desperate he'd looked to get away from me until recognition settled in his gaze.

"I—" I tried to say something, but he was already in motion.

His determination to leave stilled my tongue. My words got glued to my throat as I worked to make sense of what happened. Then we were on the road with nothing but the radio to interrupt our thoughts. I didn't want to be confused, but I was. What had happened? More importantly was, what had happened to him to put that kind of fear I'd seen in his eyes? It haunted me all the way to my place.

When he turned off the engine and walked me to my door, I had hope for the rest of our night.

"Will you stay?" I asked when he didn't follow me inside.

He framed the doorway with his forearm, leaning just outside.

"I can't. I have practice in the morning."

"That's fine," I rushed to say.

"I wouldn't want to wake you. You don't have to go to campus in the morning?"

As much as I wanted him to stay, I didn't lie and shook my head.

"Maybe we could meet for lunch or dinner?"

I nodded and slid my phone from my pocket to wave at him.

I'd made a point to keep track of it the last few days. I had a boyfriend now who might call me. It gave purpose to what used to be a useless device.

He bent his head inside to give me a kiss that left my knees weak. Then I watched his back as he disappeared down the stairs.

Celeste came out of her room as I was headed in.

"Looking bowlegged, little sister," she jabbed.

I gave her the finger and kept going. My thoughts were a jumbled mess, and I didn't have time to play her games. It took me a while to find sleep as my mind kept circling back to his waking panic.

The next few days were a dream. All the little things couples did that spiked jealousy in me before became my life. Ashton was back to normal. Whenever I was near, he was touching me, my hair, my face, my hand as he held it like he didn't want to let go. All those things made me push away asking about his fear from the other night.

I was home when Celeste came in. She glanced around.

"Where are you hiding him?"

I followed her glaze. "Hiding who?"

"Your boyfriend, silly."

"Oh, he's home. He has a test in the morning."

"And?"

"And he has to study."

She gave me that *are you kidding me* glare.

I tried not to think about how he'd always had an excuse as to why he wouldn't spend the night with me. I'd told myself repeatedly it was fine. I wouldn't worry about it until after the new semester when he wouldn't have a reason like major tests or football. Plus, things were going really well. Why rock the boat?

"How about you and your boyfriend?" I asked to switch the subject.

Her smile died a saddened death. "What boyfriend?"

She gave me her back and busied herself in the kitchen. As I formulated a follow-up question, she added, "I should tell you I'm not going home for Christmas."

That stopped me in my tracks. I'd been headed her way, so she couldn't avoid me.

"What did your dad say about that?" I asked.

She lifted her shoulders, and then they dropped like she had not a care in the world. "He thinks I have a holiday internship."

"A what? They have that sort of thing?"

She tilted her head to the side as I braced my hand on the counter.

"Probably, I just don't have one," she admitted.

"So, where are you going?"

"It's better if you don't know. That way you don't have to lie."

I braced my elbows on the counter and palmed my chin to hold up my head.

"Do you think that's safe? Someone should know where you are."

She thought about it as I studied her.

"Fine, I'll send you an email with the details, but promise you won't open it unless it's an emergency."

"Okay."

My response was half-confusion and half-promise.

"I'm telling you so you'll be prepared."

I thought of Ashton. He too would be alone for the holiday unless he was doing something with Sawyer. Maybe I could make plans with him. The idea of being home and getting the third degree from Dan wasn't appealing. I was a terrible liar, and I held the knowledge that Celeste wasn't going to an internship.

In my room, I sent Ashton a text asking him what his Christmas plans were.

46

Ashton

CHRISTMAS. The thought about the upcoming holiday hadn't been a welcome one until now. Although I'd gotten an invite from my father, I was probably going to spend it with Sawyer's brother Finn if Sawyer didn't go himself.

Now, I had another option. Maybe Willow would want to go with me to England. I wouldn't leave Finn on his own. That was a fate I wouldn't wish for anyone. Plus, Finn's quick wit was good company and kept me from dwelling on the sorry state of my life.

The locker room had mostly emptied. It was Friday, and practice had been light due to the game tomorrow. I took the chance to call her.

After she said hello, I asked, "How about going to England with me?"

"You can't be serious."

I imagined her nibbling on her lower lip. It was something she did when she was deep in thought.

"Why not?" I asked.

"One, because I can't afford a ticket."

"No worries there," I tossed out. "It's on me."

"I couldn't."

"You can."

I had more money than I could spend in one lifetime. A plane ticket or a charter jet was a blip compared to my trust fund.

Her silence meant that she was considering or trying to find another excuse.

"It's my treat. I'm going to see a friend who needs cheering up," I said.

That was mostly true. Finn pretended he was fine, and the nurses kept him busy in more ways than one. Behind his façade, I knew better. There were times when Finn let his guard down and let it slip how much he missed his family.

"Then I would only be a distraction," she said.

"Trust me, Finn would love you."

It was true. Growing up away from the rest of the Cargills hadn't made him any less sexual than the entire family. Despite his health aliments, Finn had probably gotten laid more than Sawyer had. He was the biggest flirt even over his older brother and would find it hilarious to tease my girl and me.

"If you think it's okay. I still don't like the idea of you spending all that money on me."

Money wasn't something I liked to talk about. I'd grown up privileged, and it hadn't made my life any better. Knowing everything had belonged to me was actually more uncomfortable than thinking it was Mother's. Still, I didn't want Willow to think it was a big deal for me to do this for her.

"You do know I'm rich, right?"

She sighed. "Yes, but the last thing I want you to think is I'm after your money."

That had never crossed my mind. "I don't and it's not an issue. You let me know when you can go, and I'll make the arrangements."

I thought it was a slam dunk until she said, "Let me talk to my mom and I'll call you back."

Although I said okay, I was confused why she had put the idea in my head if she wasn't sure she could do it.

"You all right?"

I glanced up to see Sawyer.

"I thought you were gone?"

He shook his head. "I had to see the trainer."

Several games ago, he'd taken a hit that had worried everyone but his dad. The bastard was more concerned about his business partners seeing Sawyer on the field than with his health.

"Everything good?" I asked.

"Yeah, I'm good." There was an awkward pause before he added, "Going to hit the shower. Are you going to the café?"

"Naw, I'm going home."

Sawyer nodded and looped off. I wondered briefly if we could ever be true best friends again.

When I pushed out the door, I spotted a tall, lanky, blond kid milling near the wall. The boy was big, nearly the same height as me. If not for the baby face I might have mistaken him for a student. After I shook off the notion that I recognized him from somewhere, I made my way in the direction of home.

"Hey, are you Ashton Westborough?"

I stopped and turned around. The kid jogged over to me. I narrowed my eyes, racking my brain to put a name with his face.

"That's me. Can I help you with something?"

The kid looked around like he didn't want to be overheard.

"You're like a legend." I was grateful when he didn't offer his hand, but still uncomfortable with his starry gaze aimed at me. "Your stats are like out of this world. They call you Ghost because you come out of nowhere to catch balls."

I'd never heard that before. Then again, I didn't search write-ups about myself. Besides, I wasn't that good. He was blowing my head up, or he thought he was.

"I'm not that good."

His eyes bugged out like he'd been zapped by a blue light.

"That's crazy. SportsCenter doesn't lie. They talk about you going to the pros."

I cut that idea short. "I'm not."

He sort of resembled a cartoon, the freakish way his eyes got larger.

"Why not?"

I had no idea why I was talking to the kid. I didn't know him, though I could swear we'd met before.

"Not my thing."

He nodded. "I totally get it. I only play because my dad wants me to. Thinks I have a future. But I'd rather write."

Had I stepped into the twilight zone? Or was he yanking my chain? He knew enough about me, maybe he'd read what my major was and wanted to say something that related. So I just nodded.

"Which brings me to why I'm here," he said.

There was something about the way he said it that had me searching my surroundings. He looked harmless, but these days you just didn't know.

My silence urged him to continue.

"I had to meet you, even though my parents told me not to."

Talk about sounding the alarm. My gaze dropped to his empty hands. Mentally, I checked him for bulging pockets. He acted like a fan, but maybe his obsession crossed over the crazier than hell line.

I took a slow step back, adding distance between us. I'd grown accustomed to the friendliness of Southern folks, but people shooting people for no apparent reason was just as bad all over the country.

"Why wouldn't they want you to?"

My hand remained loose at my side in case I had to act defensively. I still wasn't getting the vibe that I should fear for my life, but caution won over foolishness.

A sadness flatted his grim smile. "Because they weren't sure you knew."

My heart picked up the pace like I was running for the finish line.

"Know what?" I asked.

His next words were like a thief stealing all the air from my lungs.

"That you're my brother."

My first coherent thought was that of my son of a bitch father. He'd lied to me, pretending like I was his long-lost and only son. Yet, here stood evidence that wasn't true. I filed through all that the kid said. His parents. I'd been to my father's home. Outside of that museum-like room, there hadn't been signs that any other kids had ever lived there.

"Hey."

I looked up and saw Sawyer and instantly felt relief. I couldn't breathe let alone speak an intelligible sentence.

I tipped my head at Sawyer. He turned his focus to the kid.

"I'm Sawyer—"

"Cargill, I know. Holy shit, you're a legend too."

Sawyer was more comfortable with praise. He'd gotten it all his life, from his family to girls to fans like this kid.

"And you are?" he asked.

"Oh yeah. I'm August Farrow."

When his hand came up, Sawyer shook it and sidestepped a little in front of me. Sawyer had spent a lifetime saving me from awkward situations like this. He'd protected me from those that would have thought it weird I didn't want to touch them.

"What brings you here?" Sawyer said, easily shifting the introduction into a conversation that wouldn't require social gestures like handshakes.

"Football, school, well, both. I'm here on a college visit." He'd mentioned none of that to me, which only raised my hackles. "That and meeting my brother."

Sawyer's head swung in my direction.

What the hell was I supposed to say? I shrugged, unable to admit that I believed him. That recognition I'd noticed had been common features between us.

"Why don't we talk about this somewhere else?" Sawyer suggested.

The kid nodded, and we piled into Sawyer's car. Chance wasn't around, and I figured he'd already gone to the café. I sent him a text not to wait on us.

Though we arrived quickly, I had no recollection of the ride over. I'd been calculating why I had fallen for the bullshit that had been fed to me about my virtuous father. Had the Vanderbilt Club orchestrated the whole thing? Had they only been protecting the viability of a future president?

No one was home when we arrived, and I was grateful this secret wouldn't yet spill to the rest of our group. We landed in the living room. I pounced on the kid with a question that had been bugging me since his revelation. It was disguised to resemble a query.

"You said you live with your parents. Do they know you're here?" Sawyer asked.

He shocked me again with his side to side head action.

"Dude, that's pretty fucked up," Sawyer said, plucking out my thoughts exactly. "They're probably worried as hell about you."

The kid seemed unconcerned.

"My dad doesn't want me to go here. But I want to make up my own mind."

Sawyer held up his hand. "I get it, but you can't disappear without telling someone. Do you have a phone?" He nodded. "Use it."

August rolled his eyes and groaned like any teenager would when asked to do something they didn't like. Had I been like that? I couldn't remember. I'd been taught never to question my mother.

Though he'd balked, when Sawyer gave him that parental look, he caved and moved to the kitchen area to make the call.

"Brother?" Sawyer questioned in a whisper.

I couldn't deny that sense of family as the resemblance was there outside of our coloring, his light to my dark. It still bothered me that I hadn't known.

"He does look a lot like you now that I'm looking."

August stood in profile, and I could see it in the grim set of his jaw. I'd seen that reflected in my mirror. He turned then and held out his phone... to me.

When I made no move to get it, he came to me.

"My mom wants to talk to you."

I reluctantly took the phone and put it to my ear.

"Hello."

In the distance I heard my phone ringing. In fact, I saw it on the table when Sawyer reached for it, but the conversation I was about to have took my entire focus.

"Hi, I'm August's mother. I've been so worried. When Bea and Cooper couldn't tell me where he'd gone, I've been worried out of my mind."

"Bea and Cooper," I repeated like the words were foreign.

"Yes, his sister and brother."

There were more. I was sure my head would blow up with all the revelations.

"I'm so sorry he showed up," she said, sounding genuinely concerned.

"It's cool."

But it wasn't. The automatic response robotically came out of my mouth.

"We told him specifically not to reach out to you. I had no idea how much or little my sister might have told you."

"Sister?"

I hadn't realized I'd said it out loud until she responded.

"Yes, Victoria is my sister."

Mother had family. She'd claimed they were all dead.

"I assume by your silence, she never told you about me."

I shook my head and only said no a second later, remembering she couldn't see me.

"Oh, dear lord," she muttered in a prayer. "I figured that was the case, and I hate this is how you are finding out. As soon as my husband gets home, we'll drive up."

She hadn't asked where. Then again, August had known how to find me.

I noticed my *brother*, which was still a foreign concept, trying to get my attention. His head swung almost violently side to side as if he'd guessed what his mother said.

"We can drive him home," I suggested.

August nearly deflated with relief.

"We wouldn't want to put you out."

"It's fine." Though I had no idea where they lived.

I assumed if they were willing to come, it must not be too far.

47

Willow

MY TEXT HAD GONE UNANSWERED, so I'd called. The phone had already rung a couple of times, so when it picked up, I'd assumed I'd been thrown into voicemail.

Then I got a hello.

It wasn't Ashton.

"Can I speak to Ashton?"

There was a long pause, and for a moment I thought maybe we'd been disconnected.

"He's busy."

Though he hadn't been rude about it, he wasn't about to stay on the line.

"Sawyer, wait," I said, sure he would quickly hang up. "Can you tell him I called?"

"Yeah."

Then the line went dead.

"What put that sour look on your face?"

Celeste came over and planted herself next to me on the sofa.

I pushed my hair back, trying to form words without sounding like some petty girlfriend.

"Sawyer hates me."

Her face pinched in disbelief.

"Sawyer loves everybody. That's why everybody loves him."

Before Ashton and I had become a thing, I'd never seen Sawyer so much as frown. He'd always had a smile and a kind word for anyone he'd come across.

"He doesn't love me."

I held her gaze for a meaningful moment, letting her piece together what had changed.

"Oh," she said, finally getting it. "You can't blame him, though."

My jaw dropped. "Seriously! You're taking his side."

She didn't give me any ground.

"From what I've heard, they've known each other since they were in diapers and have been inseparable." This time she held my gaze, urging me to add up everything she hadn't said. "Like they did *everything* together."

I closed my eyes, wondering if I wasn't being fair as she continued.

"Think about when my dad and your mom got together."

I remembered that conversation with Mom all too well. I'd already lost a father, and when Mom told me she'd met someone she had fallen in love with, it had felt like I'd lost her too.

My fingertips ran over the lines that had formed above my brow.

"So, like yeah, he's probably pissed you're taking his place."

When she put it like that, I got it.

"What can I do?" I asked.

The smile she aimed at me fell flat.

"Not much really. Ash has to decide if you're worth it."

That was the problem, wasn't it? What if Sawyer realized he

had feelings for Ashton? Between us, whom would Ashton choose?

She patted my arm and got up, leaving me to stew.

It was late as I lay in bed dozing but unable to sleep. Ashton hadn't called back, and I'd debated a million times if I should call him again. Then, as if I'd conjured it, my phone rang, scaring the shit out of me. It fumbled in my shaking hands before I answered it. I hadn't noticed the caller with my juggling act, but assumed it was Ashton.

"Ash," I said, realizing too late that I'd used his nickname.

"Willow."

The voice was distinctively female and very motherly.

"Mom."

My heart galloped in my chest as there had to be something wrong. Why else would she call me after midnight?

"I need you to come home."

Panic held my lungs in a crushing embrace, but I managed three words.

"Are you okay?"

"Yes, honey."

I took in a ragged breath as some of the anxiety let me go.

"It's your father. He's been arrested."

I didn't bother correcting her. The alarm in her voice had me talking to her like she was the scared child.

"What happened?"

"I don't know. Little things at first," she began.

She hadn't given me a timeline, but that didn't seem important at the moment.

"What things?"

"Like I couldn't use our credit card, and when I tried to use an ATM to get cash instead, I couldn't. Dan had said everything was okay, that there was a misunderstanding at the bank. But then the FBI showed up at our door and took him away..."

Her voice had turned nearly hysterical.

"Did they say anything?" I asked.

"No." The word ended on a sob.

"Have you called a lawyer?"

"A lawyer. We can't even buy groceries. Christmas is going to be ruined," she cried.

Mom didn't do well in situations like this. When my father died, I'd felt more like the parent. I blew out a breath.

"Have you checked his office?" I suggested.

"Of course, but everything is locked tight. I need you to come home now."

I wanted to remind her that Dan had a daughter. However, with Celeste dealing with her own problems, I didn't want to stress her out more.

"Okay. I'll come home."

It was a good thing I had an open return ticket to use. I wasn't sure how she would have paid for my flight home otherwise.

I promised to contact the airline and see what flight I could get on. Then I called Ashton again. He didn't answer. I left him a message with a short version of events, including that I wouldn't be able to spend Christmas with him. My mother needed me. Despite all her faults, she had done her best as a mom.

As I packed my things, I didn't know if my message was necessary. The fact that Ashton hadn't contacted me again, not even a text, spoke volumes. Hadn't we talked about the importance of communication in a relationship? Though I hated thinking it, I was sure ours was over.

48

Ashton

SAWYER HAD OFFERED TO DRIVE, but I needed something to do. Besides, using my car meant I could avoid giving... my brother—the word still sounded weird to me—the third degree.

That didn't stop him and Sawyer from talking like they'd known each other for years. Sawyer avoided the topic of siblings. They stuck to sports. Though August had denied wanting to play football, he seemed more knowledgeable about the subject than some sports commentators.

Three hours later, we arrived in Dallas. The last time I'd been here was to visit Kelley, a former roommate who now played ball for the pros.

We wouldn't have time to stop for a visit, as we would need to turn back around in the early morning hours to be back on campus for our game. August's Mom had offered to put us up for the night.

The house we arrived at was almost as large as the one I'd grown up in. Every window seemed to burn with light, which should have been welcoming considering my aversion to the dark. Yet, there was a foreboding that clung in the air like molasses.

Sawyer had to call my name to get me out of my head and the car. August had already disappeared into the big house.

"You're not alone, brother," Sawyer said, slinging his arm over my shoulder as we walked into the house of revelation.

I came to an abrupt stop when I looked up from the floor to spot a woman who was almost a twin to Mother. She stopped in front of us with friendly eyes and open arms.

I caught Sawyer's quick shake of his head out of the corner of my eye.

She dropped her arms, only to draw them up as a gasp left her lungs.

"You look so much like her," she said, her hand muffling her words.

Being the wordsmith I wasn't, I said, "You too."

She nodded. "I'm Alice Farrow."

I nodded and introduced Sawyer and me.

The large foyer filled with two other kids around August's age as I was doing so. In fact, they had to be very close in age.

"Beatrice and Cooper, come say hello," Alice said.

Cooper said it without much enthusiasm. He'd probably been torn from something he'd much rather be doing. If only he knew I felt much the same.

I'd been focused on August's twin, if I guessed, and wasn't prepared for Beatrice. She'd caught me off guard and had come in for a hug.

Strangely, the agony I usually felt when I was touched wasn't as bad, probably because she'd pulled back before it could register.

"Hi, I'm your sister, Beatrice. Though I prefer Finley which is my middle name."

There was something kind and genuine about her. Over her

shoulder, I spotted another guy hanging back in the opening, half-hidden by shadows. His hard gaze softened when it landed on Beatrice and hardened when he looked at me.

"Shepard, come in. You're a part of this family too," Alice said.

It turned out, he was August's best friend, and due to circumstances they didn't elaborate on, he lived with them.

Loud voices stopped us all. I guessed it was August and his father. Both were missing.

"Guys, can you give us a minute?" Alice asked with a wave of her hand.

Cooper, Shepard, and Finley all nodded as one and disappeared up the grand staircase that curved around the backside of the foyer.

Sawyer and I followed Alice deeper into the house where the voices got louder as we neared.

"How many times have I told you, you aren't going to that school?"

The older man loomed just slightly taller than his son.

"It's my decision. Besides, Cooper and Bea are going."

"Jerry," Alice said.

Both guys turned to see us.

The older man pointed at August's chest. "We're not done with this conversation."

August didn't cower. He stalked from the room.

Jerry turned his steely glare at me. "You must be Ashton."

When his hand extended, Sawyer stepped in. "I'm his best friend, Sawyer." Sawyer was used to dominating fathers and didn't flinch away from Jerry's scrutiny.

The man's gazed narrowed on me.

Alice seemed to understand and said, "Please, sit. I'm sure you have questions."

Once we were settled, I said, "Did you know about me?"

She sat straighter. "Honey, no. If I did..." She ended the awkward pause with an unsurprising revelation. "My sister and I didn't exactly keep in touch. In fact, I hadn't spoken to her for years after she left home until..."

"What my wife is trying to say is when we failed at getting pregnant, we contacted Victoria. Alice wanted the kids to be of her blood too."

Alice jumped in, her hands holding on to Jerry's. "Since the problem was mine, I just thought it would be easier for the kids if they had a chance of looking like me or their father."

The idea Mother would help anyone but herself still caused me confusion.

"Mother agreed?"

"Not without a lot of bargaining and conditions," Alice admitted.

There was more, but my aunt, I guess that's what I should call her, didn't seem so eager to discuss.

"She gave birth?" I asked.

August was younger than I was.

"No. She made it hard for the three cycles to work. And when they didn't, she took her money and left."

None of this made sense other than Mother being greedy. This time I let silence prod her into saying more.

"My sister wanted money, and I wanted a legal document so she wouldn't come back later and try to change the rules before we started the process. As such, the three remaining fertilized embryos belonged to us. And with a final Hail Mary, I had them implanted in me, even though I'd been unable to carry a single child. But with the grace of God, all three survived."

I couldn't say I understood what was involved in *the process* or *their agreement* with Mother, but I understood the last of it.

"Does she know? Mother, that is."

"I don't think so. She hasn't come around," my aunt said.

"Be grateful for that," I admitted. "How long have they known?"

I waved gravelly toward the bay windows where lights spot-lighted the pool my siblings were playing in.

Jerry took over. "We never intended to keep the truth from them, but as time went on, it seemed less and less important for them to know."

"My name is listed as their mother on the birth certificate."

That was the most surprising thing they'd said, though I had no idea how that worked.

"When did you tell them?" I asked.

Jerry said, "They saw you on SportsCenter. One of their friends commented on how you and August could be brothers."

I could imagine the uncomfortable conversation that followed.

"We did a little research first because August was way too curious about you. He started following all your games," Jerry said.

"The trail eventually led to Victoria and you were her son. Something she failed to disclose when we reached out to her about helping us make a family. Now, Beatrice wants to meet her."

Triplets. I had siblings, and my first instinct was to protect them.

I got to my feet. "You can't ever let that happen."

Alice looked startled by my outburst.

"My sister has always been money-hungry and a liar, but you've met August. My kids are nothing but persistent."

I didn't sugarcoat it.

"If she finds out, she'll only use it against you," I said, fists held tight at my sides.

"I've kept tabs on her. She's doing well. You should know that," Alice said.

The fact that she had meant she was just as wary about her estranged sister.

"The house, everything belongs to me. She has nothing. Trust me when I say she'll blackmail you or threaten to take the kids. You can't let her know about them ever."

Alice had gone pale at the vehemence of my tone.

"She wouldn't. Would she?" I nodded, like their life depended on it. In a quieter voice, she asked, "What did she do to you?"

My stomach contents went into reverse. Before I hurled, I said what I had to in order for her to understand. "She sold me for money."

Alice gasped, and I headed straight for the French doors that led out. Sawyer jumped in and filled in some of the gaps I left out. I was grateful for him and his presence. I couldn't have done this without him.

The air hit me like a heat balm. Still, I was grateful to feel. It was a reminder I wasn't the robot Mother programmed me to be.

Once I was sure I wouldn't throw up, I headed to the only place shrouded in shadow. My brothers and sister hadn't yet seen me, and I didn't want to explain anything to them at that moment.

But the darkness wasn't empty. Shepard sat in a lounge chair with a guitar in his hands and his eyes on the fun being had in the pool.

There was something in his expression I understood.

"You're in love with her," I said.

Questioning him was a respite from my tormented past.

When he didn't answer, I followed up with, "Does she know?"

Heated eyes met mine. He didn't want to talk about it.

"What makes you think I love her?" he asked.

Because I was well acquainted with that look of longing.

"It's obvious. You should tell her."

"And risk being kicked out. I have a good thing here. If her father knew, I'd be on the streets. You heard him. Besides, August would never forgive me."

It had come full circle for me. I understood why my very words had been hurled at me so many times.

"I'm surprised no one has figured it out. The way you watch her—" I began.

"I'm just looking out for her. If I can't have her, I can make sure only the right guy does."

Sawyer came out and surveyed the pool. Then he did what I expected. He took a running leap, shouted cannonball, and jumped fully clothed into the water.

It was times like this I envied him and the easy way he could talk to people. He made friends easily, and everyone loved him.

That thought had me looking at my phone and seeing that I had missed texts and calls from Willow. One call had come before we'd driven to Texas. Remembering back, Sawyer had answered my phone. What had he said to her this time?

49

Willow

BY THE TIME I arrived home, Mom was beside herself with worry and fear.

"Relax," I said, with a hand on her shoulder to stop her from entering his domain.

Dan sounded as surly as a bear waking from hibernation behind the closed door of his office.

For the few hours I'd been home, he'd been in there the entire time.

"He won't tell me anything," she said, biting her nails to the quick. "But I overheard them talking."

"What?" I asked, the fear in her eyes scared me.

"He's being charged with money laundering under RICO rules."

I didn't know what RICO was, but I did the other.

"Something about his involvement with a motorcycle gang, but that's crazy."

She clawed at invisible pearls and the neckline of her shirt that had taken the beating.

The door swung open, and Dan lumbered out. When his eyes landed on me, he muttered, "Great, another mouth to feed."

Mom wasn't used to his dismissal of me and gaped as he shoved by us.

"I can't believe he said that."

She might not have, but I was used to Dan seeing me as someone he had to deal with because of Mom.

"I need to talk to him," she said, ready to follow.

I shook my head. "I think you need to give him time."

She spun her head back to face me. "Time. We have little of it. We have no money, and the only food we'll have to eat is in this house."

I blew out a quick breath. "I have money."

Mom's features softened as her hair swung with the side to side movement of her head. "No, honey, I couldn't ask you to do that. We'll figure something out."

Truth was, with Mom not working, the money I had came from Dan.

"It's fine. You can pay me back," I said, smoothing out the frown lines in her forehead.

She nodded. "We don't have to go today. I really need to find out what's going on."

I let her go and decided it was time to call Celeste. As much as I didn't want to worry her, she needed to know what was going on. I scurried to my childhood bedroom, not wanting to be overheard.

The phone rang, and I muttered, "Come on, Celeste. Pick up."

But after another two rings, I was sent to voicemail. I left her a quick message, asking her to call.

I didn't let go of the phone. Ashton popped in my head. I remembered the first time I met him and the mask he'd worn with haunted eyes. Was I being too hard on him?

He'd warned me he was fucked up, and all the evidence I'd witnessed before we got together proved that. Something bad had happened in his life that had profoundly affected him. Who was I to put pressure on him to be perfect when he'd told me he wasn't? He'd never hurt me, not intentionally. In fact, since the moment we'd met, he'd gone out of his way to protect me.

If I wanted things to work, I had to give him the benefit of the doubt and trust he had a very good reason for not calling.

The phone vibrated in my hand as a text came through. My heart sank a little when I saw it wasn't from Ashton.

Celeste sent a text responding to my voicemail. I'd asked if she was okay, and her short message said she was. The only other thing she added was **I know about Dad.**

She and her father were close. He must have called her. Since she hadn't said more, maybe things weren't as bad as Mom thought. Still, I sent her a message back asking her where she was. I didn't get a reply. I worried, but there wasn't much I could do if she didn't tell me. I thought about the email she promised to send with her whereabouts, which she hadn't done yet.

When I left my room later, I heard raised voices behind Mom and Dan's bedroom door. I scooted past, letting my growling stomach lead me to the kitchen to see how bad things were.

The pantry was full and the fridge was bare. Though we weren't in dire straights like Mom suggested, things like milk and eggs would be missed if we didn't go to the store soon.

My skills weren't master chef level, but I knew enough to get by. I put on a pot of spaghetti and opened a jar of Ragu, which were well within my skill set. I also toasted bread, adding some garlic butter I hoped would lure Mom and Dan out of their room.

I was stirring the sauce when vibrations sent my phone skittering across the quartz countertop.

The screen read *Ashton*, which sent my heart making an attempt to free itself from my chest.

"Hello."

His deep voice rasped over the airways. "Hey."

Although a barrage of accusatory questions lined up at the opening of my mouth, I managed to hold them back.

"Is everything okay?" I asked instead.

"Yeah."

His one-word answer was far from acceptable, yet I couldn't seem to press him more.

"I'm sorry I haven't called sooner. Something came up," he said.

I could have laughed given the overwhelming understatement that was. When he didn't explain, I asked, "Will you tell me what?"

I gave myself points for not yelling. Having heard the screaming between Mom and Dan, I saw the fruitlessness in that. Neither could hear the other because they were both too mad to. I'd taken a different approach.

"Yes, but not over the phone," he said.

It was a good answer, but an ominous one.

The boiling water began to percolate over the sides.

"Oh," I said, cradling the phone between my shoulder and ear while I reached over to turn down the heat.

He took my response as aimed at him. "It's not that I don't want to tell you. It's complicated."

"Okay." I exhaled and breathed in a lungful of heated air from the stove. "I guess you'll tell me when I see you next. With everything going on, I won't be able to go to London with you."

That meant it wouldn't be until after spring semester started that I could see him.

"Are your parents okay?"

I gave him a basic rundown, leaving out the nature of my stepdad's charges.

"Things aren't great, but we'll survive." I laughed then. "Christmas should be interesting."

My bank account wasn't bursting. The spending money Dan had given me for school wasn't a lot, and I'd never asked for more. As much as Mom wanted him to be, he wasn't my dad and never acted like it.

"Will you give me your address? I want to send you something?"

That made me pause and my pulse raced.

"You don't have to. Besides, the way things are, I can't give you anything. We'll be lucky to have Christmas dinner." I sucked in a breath. I hadn't meant to say that. "It will be fine, though."

"Have you ever heard that saying it's better to give than to receive?"

He sounded a little sad, which made me feel like a scrooge.

"This is true. But really, I don't expect you to get me anything. I'll just feel bad," she said.

"Okay." His reply put weird vibes between us.

"I should go before I burn dinner. I'll talk to you next year."

Next year. Had I really just said that? Then again, he wasn't willing to tell me what was going on over the phone. I didn't want to tell him how bad things were at home. Still, I didn't like the way that sounded.

"I meant *see* you next year," I amended.

"Yeah. Okay."

I hung up, not wanting him to do it first.

I stared at the food, no longer hungry.

Mom entered and smiled at me. The food had done the trick to draw them out. "Smells good."

My stomach had soured, but I mustered up a half-grin as Dan walked in. Dinner went about as well as my conversation with Ashton. Back in my room, I kept replaying it in my head. He hadn't sounded fine. I debated calling him back and trying to coax out whatever was brothering him. But then, Mom came in crying, and I ended up consoling her the rest of the night.

As Christmas neared, Mom and I had to face the reality of our budget. Dan wasn't any help. His reply to Mom's every question was he was working on it. He spent most of his time behind closed doors with his lawyer working on whatever. Defense? I didn't know. He didn't go to his office building nor explain anything to Mom.

It wasn't my relationship, so I could say nothing. Mom had chosen this life where she was taken care of. When I thought back to my dad, it had been similar. She hadn't known what to do when he'd gotten sick. That was not how I wanted to live my life, but I couldn't judge her for those choices.

"What is Christmas without a tree?" Mom said.

"We've talked about this. We don't have the money."

"But your Christmas will be ruined."

I held her shoulders and stared in her eyes. "It will be fine, Mom. I don't need things. Really."

She'd broken out into hiccupping sobs that were ignored by Dan when he walked his lawyer to the front door.

The looks that were traded between them should have freaked me out. It didn't. I glanced around the oversized house. There was nothing in it that felt like home, and I told Mom as much.

I had been sending texts to Ashton every night. Little messages like *goodnight*, *thinking of you*, and I might have sent one out of frustration about Christmas not needing a tree. He'd send me back messages like *sleep tight*, *is it next year yet*, and *do you want a tree*.

The thing that worried me was the ominous call I'd gotten from Celeste.

"You should go back to school," she'd said.

"Why? Mom needs me."

"This business with Dad isn't good. You don't need to hang around after Christmas."

I hadn't liked her tone. She was being too cryptic.

"What do you know?"

"Just trust me."

She wouldn't explain and didn't respond to any more texts. I didn't know what to make of it. Maybe Dan had told her he'd be arrested soon?

The conversation had me on edge. When a knock came at the door late Christmas Eve, I felt like the stupid girl in a horror movie innocently opening the door knowing it was probably a dumb move.

Ashton stood in the doorway with a huge pine tree propped next to him.

"You're here."

I might have sounded a tad too breathy. Then again, the sight of him had stolen all the air from my lungs.

"You wanted a tree."

I could have thrown myself into his arms, but I held back.

"You didn't have to."

His eyes held mine. "I wanted to."

I sprang a leak from the corner of my eye.

"Can I come in?" he asked.

"Oh yeah."

I stepped back, my cheeks heating. He lifted the large pine as if it were a feather.

"Where should I put it?"

In the past we'd gotten two trees. One for the formal living room that could be seen from the street through the large picture window. Another in the family room off the kitchen. That was the one we gathered around on Christmas Day.

I led him to the back of the house. Though it was a longer journey, he didn't seem hampered by the heftiness.

Mom had all the decorations and tools needed for this very thing lined up near the unused hearth. It was as if she'd known we would have one. I quickly pulled out what was needed to have the tree standing upright. Once that was done, I did leap into his arms.

His kiss only reminded me more of the holiday with the minty taste on his tongue.

"Thank you," I whispered. When we parted, his hands remained snug on my hips.

The sound of a clearing voice had us separating. I unlocked my legs, which I'd wound around his waist. He set me on my feet, my face in flames.

"Mom, this is Ashton, my boyfriend."

Her eyes widened.

"Mrs. Young. Nice to meet you."

He extended his hand, and I found myself holding my breath. Outside of me, I'd never seen him intentionally touch anyone. I thought it was one of his quirks. But there he was shaking her hand.

"It's Mrs. Roberts, actually, but it's very nice to meet you. Are you from the area?"

Young was my father's surname, not Dan's. I looked to her as I hadn't exactly told her about him yet.

"No, I drove here," he said.

That surprised me.

"Well, that was very nice of you to..." Mom waved at the tree.

"It's not a problem. Seeing Willow smile is worth it."

Mom winked at me as I tried to hold myself from launching at him again. It was little things like this that had made me fall in love with him. I nibbled at my lip, trying not to cry.

He'd taken my hand after letting go of Mom's and squeezed it now, making nothing else seem to matter.

"We should decorate," Mom announced.

"I should probably get the groceries out of the car," he said.

Mom looked at me and I shrugged. He'd thought of everything.

"Let's do it then," Mom said.

We followed her out of the house, hand in hand.

"Thank you for saving Christmas," I whispered.

The only thing that could have stolen some of my joy from this moment came in the form of his next words.

"It's my first."

50

Past

"MOTHER, WILL WE HAVE A CHRISTMAS?"

My teacher had told us all about it. We'd cut out paper and glued our picture in the middle. She said we could hang it from the tree. I held mine out as a present to Mother.

She snatched it from my hand.

"Don't be silly, Ashton," she said.

I shouldn't backtalk, but I spoke out of turn anyway. Maybe if she understood.

"But she said Santa wouldn't come if we didn't have a tree."

Mother frowned at me, and I knew she was mad. I stiffened, afraid she would slap me. Instead, she began to rip the green paper into pieces. She hadn't even looked at it.

"Listen to me. There is no Santa. You won't be getting any presents. Therefore, we don't need a tree."

Then she tossed my hard work into the trash.

I tried not to cry. I knew what would happen if I did.

"Don't you cry," she warned.

Tears burst from my eyes anyway.

She yanked me by the ear and marched me to the door. I couldn't get away. It hurt too bad.

"You know what happens to bad little boys."

"Please," I begged.

"Too late. You know the rules."

"Please," I begged again.

The door to the scary basement opened and she pointed.

"Cry all you want down there."

I took a step. If I didn't, she'd drag me down and turn off the lights. The door closed behind me.

When the lights went out, I sat on the stair and put my arms around my legs. I laid my head down on my knees. If I went to sleep, when I woke up, she would let me out.

Maybe...

51

Ashton

FOR THE FIRST TIME EVER, I'd felt part of something. Putting orna-
ments on a tree might have been insignificant to most who celebrated Christmas, but not for me.

Sawyer would have happily had me share every Christmas
with him, but Mother wouldn't have it. Even after everything,
Mother took pleasure in denying me to go with their family to
Aspen as they did every Christmas. Since I was a minor, they
couldn't take me. Sawyer would always give me a present, but it
wasn't the same.

Once I turned eighteen, I saved money to go spend the
holiday with Finn. He, being like me, hadn't wanted the reminder
that we were unwanted. So we never mentioned the holiday or
celebrated while I was there.

In the here and now, Christmas music played in the background as we worked.

"So, Ashton, your family isn't going to miss you for the
holiday?"

It wasn't an outrageous question. Automatically, I glanced at Willow.

"No, ma'am. My mother is out of town."

That was the truth, though I didn't know where she was exactly.

"Your father?"

As much as I wanted not to talk about this, I answered anyway.

"I didn't live with him growing up."

That was the truth. The rest I kept to myself.

She nodded. "Well, we are very happy to have you." She clarified her meaning. "What hotel are you staying at?"

"Mom," Willow said, giving her pleading wide eyes.

"I hadn't thought that far," I admitted.

"You can stay here," Willow offered.

Before her mother could say otherwise, I said, "It's fine. I'm sure I can find a hotel."

"No." Willow glared at her mother. "He drove all this way. He can stay here."

Her mother glanced to the ceiling. I didn't get it at first.

"Sure." She shook her head. "I'm sure it's fine. It's a big house."

Willow's stepfather hadn't made an appearance.

"I don't want to be any trouble," I said.

Mother and daughter spoke in meaningful silence I wasn't privy to.

"If you go, I go with you," Willow announced.

Her mother's smiled was forced. "He can stay, but in a different room."

"Mom, I'm almost twenty-two."

"It's still my house. My rules," her mom said.

"It's fine," I said, squeezing Willow's hand.

It was probably better that way. I wouldn't want to defile her daughter under her roof.

After a bottle of wine with a dinner whipped up in no time, Willow's mother regaled us of tales of Willow on Christmas Day. Later, I'd been shown to my room. It had been pointed out that I was on the opposite end of the hall from my girl. Her mother had winked when she remarked that her room was halfway between the two. Willow kissed me at the door as if to prove something to her mom. I kissed her back, but quick and sent her on her way. I hadn't been taught to be a rule breaker.

Sleep came in spurts. It was a good thing the room had a TV, which I'd kept on all night. I woke up a final time with Willow in bed with me, looking like an angel with her golden hair haloing her head.

"Should you be in here?" I asked.

She crawled over and straddled me. It was a damn good thing a comforter separated us or I'd been inside her.

Her lips were like honey. My hands slid down her back to her ass. I pulled her tight as I could to me and she ground her hips.

"Jesus."

She laughed. "It is his birthday and all," reminding us both what day it was.

I groaned when her mother's voice could be heard on the other side of the door.

"Time for breakfast."

Willow giggled when I let my hands fall away.

"Are you regretting bringing us food?"

"You're going to need food," I said, reaching for her.

She dodged and was off the bed before I could get to her. I would so have to apologize to the guys. I understood why they couldn't keep their hands off their girls.

Willow was so close, I could reach her before she could get out the door. I could have her against the wall and deep inside her before she could blink.

"Willow," her mom called, reminding us she was there.

I blew out a breath. "You better go."

"Are you coming?"

I groaned. "Not soon enough."

She laughed. "You're bad."

"And you have to go and be a good girl."

Her flirty smile had me reaching under the covers to fist my cock.

After a quick, cold shower, I followed the smell of food to the kitchen. The house was large, but homey like Sawyer's had been. A vast difference to the stark minimalist house I'd grown up in.

There were pictures on the walls of Willow and her stepsister as girls into women. In every one, Willow looked happy.

"Good morning," her mother greeted.

A large man looked over from the screen where CNBC was on.

"Ashton, this is my husband, Dan. Dan, this is Willow's boyfriend, Ashton."

He didn't make a move to greet me with a handshake.

"Nice to meet you, sir," I said instead.

He grunted a reply.

"He brought the tree and groceries, honey. Don't you want to thank him?" her mom prodded.

The glare he threw her way was enough for me to intervene.

"It's not a big deal," I said.

Willow was frowning at her stepdad as her mother had wilted under the big man's stare.

"Is this for me?" I asked, pointing to a plate, and both women turned their focus on me.

"Yes." Her mother immediately asked me if I wanted juice or milk.

We ate in companionable silence. When I was done, her mother spoke while giving furtive glances at her husband.

"Willow, I'm sorry I don't have any presents. I was out, but—"

My girl jumped in and patted her mom's hand. "I told you it's okay."

I slid one of the two envelopes I brought downstairs in her mom's direction.

"I wanted to thank you for having me."

I'd never given Mother a present after that first one I'd made her in kindergarten. Willow's mom pulled the envelope to her chest like she cherished it. Her reaction was the one I'd hoped for all those years ago.

"You really shouldn't have," she said.

"Please, open it," I said.

She pulled the card trimmed in gold foil from the envelope and gaped.

"This is too much." She tapped her husband's shoulder. He was focused on the TV and hadn't spoken at all while we'd eaten. "Ashton gave us a trip to Pebble Beach Resort for three days."

"There is a spa package for you and a golf one for you, sir," I said.

Dan's face shifted into a level of respect. "Your father is a member."

"Yes, sir. I didn't know what I could give you all and he suggested it. If you don't like golfing—"

I'd called my father because I had no clue, and bringing a bottle of wine felt insufficient.

"I love to golf. If you're sure, I wouldn't want to put you out."

He stared at me as if he could gauge my level of wealth with my next answer.

"Willow mentioned things have been stressful. I thought you and your wife would enjoy a quick getaway."

Her mom jumped in. "We can drive there," she offered with hope all over her face.

He nodded at me. "Thanks."

I held out the other envelope to Willow. Her eyes lit up and she took it. After she opened it, she covered her mouth.

"Italy," she gasped.

It was the one place she wanted to go.

"Yes. If your mother is okay, I thought I could take you there tomorrow."

Willow was old enough to make a decision, but again, respect.

"Rome," she breathed. "You remembered."

Little did she know that I hadn't forgotten anything she'd told me.

"Mom?" Willow asked.

She didn't even look at her husband. "Yes. I think you should go."

Willow hopped up and down clapping.

"You should pack. We leave first thing in the morning," I told her.

Willow's mom cooked Christmas dinner while my girl packed. When Dan left, I'd slipped an American Express gift card to her mom.

"For food."

I should have expected the hug, but I'd only known one mom. Sawyer's grew up with my boundaries and never pushed the limits. I stood rigid waiting for the feeling of glass shards to prick my skin. When it didn't happen, I marveled in the moment and hugged her back.

Her tears wet my shirt, and she thanked me profusely.

"We'll pay you back as soon as this mess is cleared up."

I understood that feeling. I'd grown up not wanting to take advantage of Sawyer's parents' kindness for fear it would end.

"No problem," I said.

I hadn't given it with expectation to get it back.

"You're a good man, Ashton. Your mother must be proud."

I only smiled. No need to spoil Christmas with that truth.

The next day, as we sat on the private plane, Willow finally questioned me about my whereabouts days before.

52

Willow

NEVER IN MY life did I imagine flying in a private plane. I'd ridden business class to and from school and first class for some family vacations, but never a private jet.

Ashton had driven us to a small airport in San Diego and left his car there.

I'd been so amazed at the bright interior with buttery leather upholstery and rich wood grain tables in between the seats that faced each other.

"There's a bedroom in the back if you want to sleep," Ashton said, straight-faced.

His finger was aimed at a closed door behind us as his eyes smoldered on me, sparking my pilot light on.

"Sleep?" I teased.

He shrugged. "You'll need some eventually."

When he reached for me, I danced out of his hands.

"We should talk first."

His lips pursed like he'd been expecting it. I sat, sinking into the seat. He chose one across from me.

Before he could answer, the stewardess came in and informed us we'd be ready for takeoff soon.

As the jet propelled forward, the force of it holding me in my seat, Ashton began to talk.

"I grew up very differently than you. Parts of my life would probably disgust you."

"I doubt that," I said.

There was nothing about the man in front of me that I didn't love even when I thought it was foolish to do so. So what if his life was different than mine?

"My mother and I aren't close." I'd guessed that much. "In fact, calling her a mother is a stretch." That saddened me. "Not too long ago, I found out she had a sister. Something she'd never shared with me."

I couldn't imagine a parent holding that secret, unless that family member was poison.

"Is she not a nice person?"

"My mother?" he laughed, and it sounded bitter. "No, she's not."

I hadn't meant her, but I let him speak.

"My aunt, on the other hand, is."

That had to be a good thing, right?

I watched as he leaned back and shifted his hands under his legs.

"My aunt and uncle have three kids. They're triplets, actually."

"Wow," I said.

I'd met twins before, but never triplets.

"Yeah, two boys and a girl. They're seniors in high school."

His reaction suggested this was as new information to him as it was to me.

"And you just found out you had cousins?"

"Not exactly." I could tell for whatever reason he was embarrassed to mention this. "My aunt couldn't have kids. They used my mom's eggs. So, technically they're my siblings."

"So, you're just finding out they're your brothers and sister." He nodded. "That was really great of your mom to help them, right?"

His mother couldn't be that bad if she'd done that.

"I didn't know I had an aunt, and they didn't know about me. Mother negotiated with them for how much they would pay her to do them that favor. During these conversations, she didn't mention she had a son. In fact, the way my aunt explained it, she made it seem like she never wanted kids, which was true in a way."

I fish-mouthed a few seconds, not understanding why she'd lied to him and her sister. Why was she keeping them from the other?

"Was the money to pay for the medical expenses?"

Another round of humorless laughter came from him.

"No. They covered that. My mother loves nothing and no one outside of money."

I leaned forward, reaching for his wrists, pulling them free so I could clasp his hands.

"I'm sorry."

"There's nothing for you to be sorry for." He drew away and rubbed his hands like he was cold. "August, my brother, showed up the other day on campus. I didn't call because he hit me with all of this. Plus, he'd come without his parents' permission. I had to drive him back home."

I knew there was a reasonable explanation. But the words were out before I could stop them.

"You took Sawyer along."

He nodded. "He was there when August found me after practice. I was shocked as you can imagine."

No time like the present, right? I took in a deep breath and continued down the path we'd found ourselves on.

"Did he tell you I called?"

His eyes shifted away before coming back to focus on me.

"Not at first. I got on him about that."

"He doesn't like me."

It was a statement, not a question.

"It's not like that. He's protective," he said.

I didn't quite agree.

"He's jealous."

Ashton frowned. "Not in the way you're thinking."

"Are you sure?"

Part of me didn't want to know the answer.

"Yes, he's just not used to sharing me. You have to understand, he's the only family I've ever had. Until Kelley and Chance moved in with us, I've only had him to rely on."

"But he's never been jealous of them," I said, drawing the obvious conclusion.

Softy, he said, "No."

"What does that tell you?"

He unbuckled his seat and shifted forward.

"You're a threat," he admitted.

I unbuckled mine. "Why?"

I'd spoken barely above a whisper.

"Because I would much rather spend time with you than him."

That was all I needed to hear. We crashed into each other. His mouth devoured me as I ran my nails over his scalp, tipping his hat off his head. Then he scooped me up, leaving me airborne in more ways than one. I was too lost in him to notice where we were going. I just wanted us both skin to skin.

Sometime between me hitting the bed and him sliding into me we accomplished that task.

I clawed at him, the need for total possession dominating my mind.

He couldn't keep his hands off me. He was rough at times, but that might have been during his eagerness to get me naked.

He drove in so deep, he hit the end of me. It was a new sensation, and I didn't have time to process before his mouth sucked in a nipple, sending me over the cliff's edge.

His desire hadn't ebbed, and he used his fingers to bring me back to a fever pitch.

I'd be lucky to walk when we landed, but I loved every second. There was so much need in his eyes I felt love he hadn't admitted to yet. Or maybe that was just wishful thinking on my part.

I drifted off like he'd predicted but woke up to mewling noises coming from him. The spot next to me was cold. I pulled on my shirt and left the room. He thrashed in his seat, murmuring something I couldn't hear.

When I put my hands on him, his eyes popped open.

This wasn't the first time this had happened. I thought about wanting to ask, but he'd revealed so much I figured he would tell me in his own time.

"Bad dream," I said.

He scrubbed a hand down his face and nodded.

"Want something to drink?"

I searched for the stewardess, who had disappeared, but was pulled onto Ashton's lap. He nuzzled my head.

"I'm good now," he murmured.

I gave him comfort by being there. We stayed like that and his breaths evened out. He'd drifted back to sleep. Not wanting to disturb him, I let myself fall back into dreamland too until we were prodded and asked if we wanted a meal.

When we arrived in Rome, I had to admit, I was amazed but a little underwhelmed.

"Don't worry, it gets better once we get into the city," he said.

I nodded, taking in the midcentury buildings marred by graffiti. He was right. When we drove by the Colosseum, I got tongue-tied.

"Amazing, huh?" he asked.

All I could do was nod. It wasn't exactly beautiful, the coloring not bright white but a grayish brown like mud dotted with holes. Even in the state it was in, I could see majesty in the finer details still there.

"I promise we'll see it up close."

I still couldn't speak. As we drove, the buildings got more impressive. It was so different than anything in America. There was history in everything I saw.

Finally, our driver pulled up to an innocuous hotel.

"Hotel Golden," I said, reading the sign.

"It's not a five-star hotel, but I like it. It's family-owned. The matriarch still cooks the breakfast for the guests."

"Sounds wonderful."

In fact, I was thrilled we weren't at a fancy place, which would only remind me how rich he was. The room we were shown at the end of a hall had a traditional feel, certainly not modern but clean. It was the service, however, that had warranted a return visit. From the moment we walked in the door, we were treated like family. I totally got why he would come back here.

It was early enough that we ate breakfast. Wanting to stay up to beat jetlag, we opted for a self-guided walking tour. We took pictures at the Spanish Steps. At the bottom there were designer shops. He tried to buy me something.

"How about this?" I said, pointing at a small tote bag with the word *Rome* on it from a souvenir shop. The jean material was also screened with the words *Rome with love* or rather the love was a heart. Underneath the words was a picture of the Colosseum. It was perfect.

His brow raised.

I shrugged and started to walk away.

"If you want this, you'll have it."

The whopping price tag was five euros.

"Do you want to rent a vespa?"

The idea thrilled me, and I nodded. He drove, and I rode behind him, arms curled around his middle. I enjoyed the sights, but mostly him and being that close.

Before we made our way back to the hotel, we stopped at the Trevi Fountain. The larger-than-life sculptures with all the details were more impressive than I'd expected. Add to that, I marveled at how long ago it had taken to construct. Things like it just weren't made to last anymore.

Dinner was amazing. I had the best pizza of my life at a restaurant two blocks from the hotel. By the time we ended up back in the room, I could barely keep my eyes open. He couldn't either.

I was awakened by the sheer terror coming from him. He hadn't turned out the lights, so I didn't have to grope around for one. Though it crossed my mind that a light had been on in the room he'd used at my house when I'd woken him.

"Ashton, wake up."

He curled more into himself, begging for the ghost that haunted him to leave him alone. Tears pricked my eyes. I wasn't sure if I should rouse him, something I'd heard before, but I couldn't watch him lost in that nightmare a second longer.

"Ashton, please."

His wide eyes searched the room as if he got his bearings.

I used the back of my hand to wipe at the stubborn tears that spilled from my eyes.

"Did I scare you?" he asked.

I shook my head.

"You know you can talk about it. I promise I would never betray your confidence." When he didn't look convinced, I added, "I love you."

He didn't respond, not that I expected him to. Hoped maybe.

"You don't have to say it," I said, so he didn't feel obligated.

He shifted positions, scooting up so he was sitting with his back to the headboard. I mirrored him.

"It's not that I don't want to say it. I honestly don't know what love is. But I want to." He reached up and took the finger I'd used to wipe another stray tear away. He put it to his lips.

"You know how to love," I said, wanting to remain positive despite the deep sadness ever present in his eyes.

"Sawyer," he said. I nodded. "Sawyer saved me. My home life wasn't normal. I didn't know that until Sawyer showed me what normal was, and when he saved me, he became my hero. I guess without any idea what love should feel like, I thought..."

I wiped a single tear from his cheek.

"What happened to you?" I asked with quiet words, taking his hands in mine.

I felt like we would both need each other if he answered me. His eyes had found his lap, and I braced myself for what he might say.

"You might as well know. I tend to have nightmares most nights." His gaze lifted and shimmered with so much emotion I cried for the boy who hid in the depths of his mind.

"I was molested."

The sob tore from my mouth as I wrapped my arms around him.

I whispered, "Your mom?"

His head bumped mine as he shook it.

"No, but she profited from it."

I squeezed him harder, wishing somehow I could take that reality away from him. It took a few moments, but soon, he gripped me like his life depended on it.

An eternity wouldn't have been long enough for sobs to rock through us.

I pulled back at some point and peppered kisses on his lips.

"I'm so sorry," I said.

"For the longest time, I hated touch. The only time Mother touched me was to hurt."

Everything made sense.

"You don't have to explain. I get it."

"I want to feel it, experience it," he said.

"What?"

"Love. I want you to show me."

I took his hand in mine and pressed it to my chest above my heart.

"Every time I see you, my heart flutters."

I moved the tip of his fingers to my lips.

"Your kisses send tingles through me, and I look forward to being with you."

I took his hand lower.

"When you touch me, my body spins out of control. I might have been a virgin when I met you, but I've messed around before. No one has made me wet like this."

His fingers found that spot.

"You are the first person I think of in the morning and the last at night."

"That's love?" he asked.

I shrugged. "There are some things I can't explain. But yes."

"My thoughts are never far from you. Football has become a chore because I'd rather spend time with you. I told Sawyer if he was really my friend he would apologize and accept you because you were here to stay."

"Really?"

He nodded.

Then he moved, inserting himself between my legs, the head of his cock not far from that pulsing part of me.

"And my new favorite place—"

"Rome?" I guessed.

His head shook. "You."

Then he pulled my panties down my legs before burying his face in my center.

I'd forgotten our conversation when I came with abandon until he slipped inside me.

"I'm pretty sure based on what you described, I'm in love with you too."

There was nothing fast with his movements. It was a slow, gradual hike to the summit of what could only be described as making love.

We crested the wave together, crashing together. Before I slipped into sleep, I felt him press a gentle kiss to my eyes and whisper.

"I love you, Willow. You're my Wendy."

I would dream of Peter Pan that night knowing that he wasn't a lost boy anymore. We'd found each other. I wouldn't ever let him go.

"I love you too," I said before darkness claimed me.

EPILOGUE

Graduation had come and gone. All of our families tucked back into the places they'd come from. I hadn't heard from Mother, though I hadn't expected to. She'd either given up or hadn't found a way to get in touch with me. But I doubted our paths would cross again until one of us was dead and maybe not even then. My father, however, was making the effort. He'd been there.

"Hey." I glanced up as Sawyer put down the box he'd carried out of his room. "Mom called and said you sold the house."

I nodded. "I would have never gone back there even after she'd moved out."

Mother had tried and failed with a legal injunction to stop me.

"I guess I can't blame you. It will be weird, not having you here or there." He blew out a breath and laughed. "It's really happening. We're moving away for good."

Kelley and Chance exited with boxes in their hands. Kelley had come back last semester and worked his ass off to graduate with us.

We all looked at each other. The pair set their boxes down.

"This is it," Chance said.

"Don't get all sappy on me, brother," Kelley said with amusement.

"We've got the dude ranch," Sawyer said, straight-faced until I broke the silence with a laugh. "Don't you start. You and your haunted hotel suggestion." Sawyer glared at me before turning a pouting frown to Chance. "Why couldn't we go to Vegas with the girls?"

I put a fist to my mouth to cover a snicker.

"I promised Brie."

"That fucking sucks, bro. A dude ranch in Colorado? What kind of bachelor party is that?"

"We can get one with nature."

Sawyer glared at me. "Take your nature ass there. Willow is a bad influence." But he said her name with affection. She'd grown on him as I'd known she would. He still pretended he wasn't sure who put a smile on my face, but we both knew the truth.

"I'm going to Vegas," he announced.

"We're going to Colorado," Kelley said. "This is Chance's time, not yours."

"What the fuck ever. If I get married, it's Vegas. You can bet on that," he said.

"Pussy whipped," Kelley coughed. "If Shelly told you to go on a spa retreat, you'd be there."

Sawyer wasn't deterred. "Hell yeah, happy endings and all that."

"Don't be a dick, Sawyer. It will be fun. Something none of us has done before," Chance said.

Sawyer rolled his eyes, but good-naturedly.

Then things got quiet as we eyed the boxes.

Kelley cleared his throat. "That's the last of it."

Chance agreed.

Then Mason, Kelley's son, came barreling up the stairs.

"Uncle Ash, Uncle Ash." He wrapped his little body around my leg. "I'm going to miss you."

I bent down and gave him a hug. "Me too, squirt."

"Mason." The call came from Lenora, Kelly's girl or Lenny, his nickname for her. "Come get a snack."

He squeezed me tighter before letting go.

"Mason, go on now," Kelley said.

He'd taken on fatherhood like a seasoned professional.

I scrubbed a hand over my godson's head, and he waved to the rest.

Kelley pointed at me. "If I didn't know for sure you were in New York when Lenny got pregnant, I'd think you were his father."

Everyone laughed. Mason and I had bonded.

"I guess I should go pack this in the car. Lenny's got us on a schedule," Kelley said.

"I should head out too. We have a long drive," Chance added.

"Do you need help packing?" I asked.

Chance was moving out of his dad's small ramshackle house into a bigger one closer to Oklahoma City where he'd been drafted to play with their new expansion NFL team.

"Not much to move," he said. "But we have to register Ian at his new school in a few days."

Chance had taken on his little brother when their mother had deserted him too. He wasn't much older than Mason.

We all nodded. Then it was bro hugs all around.

"Don't cry on me, bro," Kelley teased Chance.

Truth was, I felt the sting in my eyes. Chance wasn't the only one of us emotional. I remembered when I gave him the necklace to give to Brie. He'd cried and that was between us. He tried to pay me back from the bonus he'd earned signing his NFL contract. I'd declined.

Chance pointed at all of us in turn. "Don't be fucking strangers. You guys are my only family."

"Mine too," I agreed.

Kelley nodded.

"The best of my family," Sawyer said.

"Let's make a pact to see each other at least once a year. Like this day next year," Chance suggested.

We all bumped fists in agreement. It would be a surreal adjustment not seeing them every day.

Kelley picked up his box and slung an arm around Chance after he got his as they headed downstairs.

"I'm really going to miss this place," Sawyer said.

"At least it's going to be put to good use."

Sawyer had talked his dad into not selling. August, Bea, and Cooper were moving in to start their next semester. Somehow, August had stood firm about attending school here in the fall.

"And Finn," I said.

Sawyer nodded. "Who the fuck knew?"

I had. Finn had the full use of an arm and was working on the other. The experimental stem cell treatment was working.

"A professor, that little fuck."

His brother was smarter than all of us combined and had graduated with a degree before we had. He'd applied and gotten a position here at Layton he would start later this year.

"And you'll be in Tennessee," I joked.

He and Shelly were going to law school there.

"Ain't that some shit. My brother moves back, and I'll be halfway across the country."

"I'm sure Shelly will keep you busy."

My lips twitched as I tried not to laugh.

"Very fucking funny." Then he turned serious. "I'm going to miss you, brother."

We hugged like only brothers would.

"I'm going to miss you too," I said, fighting hard not to shed any tears.

He clapped my back. "You could always come to Tennessee. You can write anywhere, and there has to be plenty of strange bugs Willow can study there."

His offer was tempting, but we'd made plans. I shook my head as we parted.

"Africa," he said somberly.

"And South America."

"When do you come back?"

I shrugged. "Who knows."

"My boy is all grown up."

He slung an arm around me, only to dig his knuckles in the top of my head. I pushed him off, laughing. Things had almost gotten back to normal.

"She's good for you," he said.

"I love her."

I knew that for sure. There had been chances for me to peruse other people before her. She'd been the one who pulled me in without question of other motivations. She'd taught me what love was. I would always love Sawyer. He was my brother. But I wanted her to be my forever.

"So wife her and have little babies and shit."

Some of my smile faded. "Marry, yes. I see that one day. But babies." I shook my head. "I'm no one's father."

Sawyer's brow lifted. "Whatever the fuck, man. Mason likes you more than us."

"Mason's different."

He shook his head. "I thought that therapist was helping. If anything, you have the best shot of being a future father of the year. You just have to do the opposite of what your mother did."

Now that I was in charge of my life, I'd sought out a private psychologist and had found someone I was comfortable with. I didn't want nightmares ruling my life and scaring the shit out of Willow. Things had gotten better, but I was far from cured.

"I'll leave that award to you guys," I said.

Things got silent again. We'd said everything that could be said.

"What do you think about your dad going public?"

My father had held a press conference and claimed me as his son. I didn't think it was the best idea. Mother would see it as an opportunity to profit from the revelation. But he'd done it anyway.

I shrugged.

"And the crown?"

Sawyer hadn't asked about the pin on my lapel I'd worn at graduation. I assumed it was because membership into the Vanderbilt Club wasn't discussed. Then again, he hadn't worn one.

"It wasn't a choice," I admitted.

I hadn't known that the initiation wasn't them choosing to accept us like you do into a fraternity, but rather by making it through all the steps, I'd accepted to join. I still wasn't sure why they wanted me.

"You didn't?" I asked.

He shook his head. "I have my reasons. But something tells me, they aren't going to give up."

Their tactics were uncompromising. "Good luck with that," I said.

I still hadn't told anyone about that night they'd stolen me from my bed. I glanced around, wondering if we were under surveillance.

"You need any help?"

I shook my head. "There's only a few left."

He nodded. "Don't be a fucking stranger."

Though he'd used the same words as Chance, there was a different meaning. "And none of that once a year bullshit. I expect to see your ass on my birthday and every damn holiday and if I just fucking need my brother."

He wrapped an arm around my neck and bumped his forehead against mine. There was a bond I thought had been broken, but I was wrong. We were family and families fight, but there was no getting rid of them.

"You're my best friend. My fucking brother. And this isn't goodbye," he said.

I clung to him for a second longer, grateful for him. Without him, I would have never survived this life. I pulled back and knuckled moisture from the corner of my eye.

"You can never get rid of me," I said.

He nodded and got his box. He said nothing more as he departed, staying true to his no goodbye rule.

I left my box and walked into my room one last time.

Sawyer was right. Even though my four years in school hadn't been perfect, I would miss this place.

I stared out the windows, watching my friends finish packing cars. No, not my friends, my family, the people in the world I knew I could count on.

A soft hand rested on my shoulder.

I turned around and found my girl. Her hand slid up my shirt, revealing the tattoo I'd gotten. Her fingers traced over the words I'd inked onto my chest. Each line held its significance to my life.

All that glitters is not gold.

Hell is empty and all the devils are here.

It is not in the stars to hold our destiny but in ourselves.

Love is blind and all I can see is Willow.

I took her wrist and kissed the sensitive skin there. Then I drew her close, sweeping her off her feet for a second and kissing her soundly. Though words came easier than they had before, I thought that last line said it all.

"What was that for?" she asked a little breathlessly.

"I'm craving dragonflies."

Dominating and possessing that tight little body of hers was the first thing on my mind when I saw her there. I thought about what Sawyer said about wife-ing her and put that on my list of things to do.

Her smile brightened my world as her brow arched. "Are you now?"

I nodded, glancing at the bed, sheets long gone, but I didn't care.

She took my hand, and I thought she'd lead me that way.

"I guess this is a good time to tell you."

I waited because her grin faded around the edges. I held my breath, waiting for bad news when her smile no longer reached her eyes.

"We're pregnant."

I didn't need to be punched to be knocked out. I opened my mouth but closed it. I was still learning how to be in a relationship.

"It wasn't planned," she threw out, sensing my shock.

"This is your decision too," she added.

I thought about it and how rough my life had been. But there had been good in the bad—Sawyer, Willow, just to name a few. I wasn't conceived out of love and hadn't thought myself capable of it outside of my best friend.

But here I was surrounded by family. I wouldn't be alone.

"We're having a baby," I said slowly. She nodded. "What about South America, your fellowship, and Africa?"

"I've had my shots, and people get pregnant there too. I'll be fine. It's not like we're going right away. I'm going to see Celeste before we go."

Her stepsister had a lot going on. It looked like her father was going to cut a deal with the government to stay out of jail. I wasn't sure I wanted Willow to go to California. The guy, Taylor, Celeste was with wasn't exactly a model citizen. But it wasn't my place to tell Willow what to do.

"Don't tell Sawyer. Shelly got him a Safari trip to Kenya. We're invited along," she added.

I blinked, so much information, I circled back to the most important.

"We're having a baby," I repeated.

The smile that had once been bloomed on her gorgeous face grew there again. "Yes, we are."

"Then we have to tell everyone."

I felt like a male dragonfly, clasping her hand solidly in mine, feeling overly protective. I would make sure she was safe and that our child was safe too.

We went downstairs where we found Kelley, Lenora, Brie, Shelly, and Sawyer standing near the door. Ian and Mason were running around Isabella who was waddling toward Kelley on her little feet.

"Guys," I said, gaining their attention.

Everyone turned.

"We're having a baby."

We were surrounded by our friends, congratulations, and well-wishes.

I hadn't known love like this before, and she had shown me how possible it was.

I kissed my girl in the midst of it all and whispered into her ear, "You're not off the hook. I'm still craving dragonflies."

THANK YOU

I'd like to thank you for taking the time out of your busy life to read my novel. Above all, I hope you loved it. If you did, I would love it if you could spare just a few more minutes to leave a review on your favorite e-tailer. If you do, could you be so kind and **not leave any spoilers** about the story? Thanks so much!

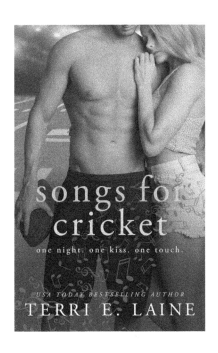

WANT TO KNOW MORE ABOUT
August, Finley, Shepard & Cooper
SONGS FOR CRICKET
is Finley and Shepard's story
coming February 2019

Find out more about
Kelley & Lenora in Chasing Butterflies
Chance & Brie in Catching Fireflies
Sawyer & Shelly in Changing Hearts
www.terrielaine.com
for buy links.

ACKNOWLEDGMENTS

First and always, thank you to all my readers. You guys make this worth it. I appreciate you for your continued support. If not for you, I couldn't do this. Your mean the world to me. A BIG Thank You!

To my beta readers, you guys Rock & Roll. Your feedback is much appreciated. To Diane, Samantha, Ashley, and Kelly, Thank you and much love!

To Michele, thank you for always coming through with my last minute request. It was so great meeting you in New York.

To Scott, I bought this picture years before it was the in thing to buy pictures from fashion photographers and I still love it.

A HUGE THANK YOU to Paige. Thanks for working me in. I appreciate you so much. Thanks to D for putting the shine on.

ABOUT THE AUTHOR

Terri E. Laine, USA Today bestselling author, left a lucrative career as a CPA to pursue her love for writing. Outside of her roles as a wife and mother of three, she's always been a dreamer and as such became an avid reader at a young age.

Many years later, she got a crazy idea to write a novel and set out to try to publish it. With over a dozen titles published under various pen names, the rest is history. Her journey has been a blessing, and a dream realized. She looks forward to many more memories to come.

STALK ME AT

Facebook: terrielainebooks
Facebook Page: TerriELaineAuthor
Twitter: @TerriLaineBooks
Instagram @terrielaineauthor
Goodreads: terri e laine
Newsletter Signup: http://eepurl.com/bDJ9kb

I have several upcoming releases, make sure to sign up for my newsletter or check my website for details.
www.terrielaine.com

ALSO BY TERRI E. LAINE

Because of Him

Captivated by Him

Chasing Butterflies

Catching Fireflies

Changing Hearts

Craving Dragonflies

Ride or Die

Sex, Alcohol, and My Neighbor (in Beer Googles Anthology)

Honey (in Vault Anthology)

Sugar

other books co-authored

by Terri E. Laine

Cruel and Beautiful

A Mess of A Man

A Beautiful Sin

One Wrong Choice

Sidelined

Fastball

Hooked

Worth Every Risk